“Utterly captivating and highly insightf
a story line while building suspense an
It marks the emergence of a tremendously wise and talented novelist.”

—ANDREW SOLOMON, Pulitzer Prize finalist
and National Book Award winner

“A beautifully written, emotionally resonant novel that left a lasting impression.”

—*READERS’ FAVORITE*, FIVE STARS

“As original and complex as the finest perfumes . . . compelling.”

—MARY KAY ZURAVLEFF, author of Oprah’s Spring
Reading List selection, *American Ending*

“Captivating. Blending the allure of a love story with a dark secret and a heartrending choice.”

—LOUISA TREGER, author of *The Times*
Historical Fiction Book of the Year *Madwoman*

“Current, sophisticated, and sexy. Lacey had me with the first scent of bergamot in this high-octane romp through the beautiful Alpes Maritimes.”

—GRETCHEN CHERINGTON, author of *The Butcher, The Embezzler,*
and the Fall Guy, Winner Maine 2024 Book Award Nonfiction

“A well-crafted tale of self-discovery with a compelling protagonist.”

—*KIRKUS REVIEWS*

"Strong characters and a deep knowledge of France's perfume culture make this a delightful escape read."

—SUJATA MASSEY, author of *The Widows of Malabar Hill* one of TIME Magazine's *100 Best Mystery and Thriller Books of All Time*

"A deftly plotted suspense, a sexy love story, a fascinating guide to the secret business of perfume. An ending that will keep me thinking for a very long time."

—SHERI T. JOSEPH, author of *Edge of the Known World* Winner 2024 Best New Fiction, American Fiction Awards.

"So sassy, so relevant, and yet a classic. Hooked from page one."

—JULIA HOBSBAWM OBE, author of *The Simplicity Principle*

"Brilliantly written, compelling, and profoundly sensual. A tour de force!"

—CAROLE BUMPUS, author of *Adventures on Land & Sea: Searching for Culinary Pleasures in Provence and along the Côte d'Azur*

"Pithy but elegant writing, suspense, sophisticated characters and an international flavor. I couldn't put it down."

—JUDE BERMAN, author of *The Die*, 2024 International Book Awards Winner in Visionary Fiction

"It held me in its grip. I was entranced by the mastery of Lacey's storytelling, the sensory splendors of the South of France, and a cast of unforgettable characters."

—ELIZABETH HARLAN, author of *Becoming Carly Klein*

"A skillful, fun and sexy page-turner! *The Perfumer's Secret*, an enchanting debut, artfully layers buried secrets, moral dilemmas, and matters of the heart, with the complexities of truth. A sensational and fast-paced read."

–Zelly Ruskin, 2024 American Fiction Award winning author of *Not Yours to Keep*

"Sweeps the reader away into the hills above the French Riviera, infuses the story with delicious scents . . . gorgeous settings and complex characters, woven into a multi-layered plot."

–Linda Moore, author of *Five Days in Bogotá*
2024 International Book Award winner in Literary Fiction

"A love of France's centuries-old craft of making perfume shines bright throughout Lacey's fast-paced debut. Sure to delight fans of women's fiction."

–Sue Mell, author of *Provenance*,
winner of the Madville Publishing Blue Moon Novel Award

"A fascinating journey. Fast paced, worldly and exotic."

–Susan Wands, author *Magician and Fool and High Priestess and Empress,* winner 2024 Visionary Fiction, American Book Awards

"A charming, perfectly-paced mystery full of relatable characters, and enough trouble to keep me engaged late into the night."

–J. A. Wright, author of *Eat and Get Gas,* Sarton Women's Book Award Winner, optioned for film and TV

"A sensual journey through the South of France . . . will leave readers longing for lavender fields and for a bottle of Lindissima for themselves. I loved it!"

–Lori Duff, author of *Devil's Defense*,
Winner, Georgia Bar Journal Fiction Competition 2023
and President, National Society of Newspaper Columnists

"An electrifying and thought-provoking read."

–Grishma Shah, author of *Anagram Destiny*

"A great book club read, a skilled writer, a strong protagonist and a thoughtful story."

–Ellen Barker, author of *East of Troost*,
Still Needs Work and *The Breaks*

The Perfumer's Secret

A NOVEL

Neroli Lacey

She Writes Press

Published 2025

Printed in the United States of America

Print ISBN: 978-1-64742-764-1
E-ISBN: 978-1-64742-765-8
Library of Congress Control Number: 2024918959

For information, address:
She Writes Press
1569 Solano Ave #546
Berkeley, CA 94707

Interior design and typeset by Katherine Lloyd, The DESK

She Writes Press is a division of SparkPoint Studio, LLC.

For Roger,
the love of my life.

"Ask no questions, and you'll be told no lies."

–Joe Gargery, *Great Expectations* by Charles Dickens.

"Fair is foul and foul is fair."

–*Macbeth* by William Shakespeare.

"The truth is rarely pure and never simple."

–*The Importance of Being Earnest* by Oscar Wilde.

"He was a sincere man who believed in everything he said, even if it was a lie, which makes him not so different from most."

–*The Sympathizer* by Viet Thanh Nguyen.

"A Frenchman is self-assured because he considers himself personally, in mind and body, irresistibly enchanting for men as well as women."

–*War and Peace* by Leo Tolstoy.

". . . summer life on the Continent, where men in smart lightweight suits and designer sunglasses glide around calmly in smart air-conditioned cars, maybe stopping for a *citron pressé* in a shady pavement café in an ancient square, totally cool about the sun . . . at the weekend, they can go and lie quietly on the yacht."

–*Bridget Jones's Diary* by Helen Fielding.

Chapter One

ALEXANDRA "ZANDY" WATSON

Thursday, April 29, New York

"Can I pitch?"

"Yep."

I stand facing Stewart, and he shunts his chair back. As he swings his feet up onto the desk, I get a whiff of his aftershave and starched cotton shirt. "I'm booking twenty-four months out," he says.

"*Your Climate, Your Change.*" I speak slowly to enunciate my words.

"Three minutes, max. I'm starting my watch."

I focus on his bushy eyebrows and black *Mad Men* glasses. "The story is how each of us can save our planet."

"Nice."

Adrenaline burns through me. His corner office is quiet, with tons of light and space. I thrust the sleeves of my oversized white shirt above my elbows. "I've got 2.4 minutes of Greta Thunberg, up close, speaking to camera." He's going to bloody love this.

He rests his head back in interlaced hands. His lips part and his face is relaxed. "How'd you get that?"

I tell him about the conference in Queens. "I opened the stall door, stepped towards the bank of sinks and she was six inches to my right, gray and tiny with those mousey braids."

"Okay."

"I had lighting and acoustics right there in the bathroom. I stood her against the white tiled wall, yanked out my camera, and rolled."

"Impressive."

My body is alight as though I'm standing in a forest fire.

"You've got the treatment?"

"Of course. It's in the bag." I hop from foot to foot. "She was all soundbites, like 'thirty football pitches of tropical forest are cut down every minute.'" He can't refuse.

He nods. "I'll take a look sometime."

My mouth parches. "Sometime? What about your kids? Don't you want a planet for them to live on?"

"Thank you, Zandy."

"It's a catastrophe and we're pretending it's not happening."

"Zandy, I don't have a slot."

I stand dead still. "You'll make one."

He raises an eyebrow at me. "I've got you your first crack at Director/Producer."

"Yeah, I was thinking that." I whoosh out a liter of air. I've been associate producer for three years, but it's the director who makes the story decisions.

"I'm sending you to the South of France."

"Sorry?"

"Settle down, Zandy."

"Something about the D-Day anniversary?"

"A ninety minute profile of a French perfume house."

I laugh. "Like supermodels on Russian yachts?"

"Zandy, listen up. They've got their three hundredth anniversary in September. That's our hook."

"You're joking . . . right?"

"Perfume sells. It's glamor. JLo sold $300 million in the first year. There's Britney, Rihanna . . ."

The room seems to spin. I squeeze the pebble in my pocket from that day at Fire Island. "Who's going to run *Real Jobs*?" It's smooth and round between my thumb and forefinger. I can almost smell the sea air.

The feet come off the desk. "Hand over to Cummings. He's waiting for you in the conference room." He sits up.

This can't be happening.

"It's a family business, a story of craftsmanship. The advertising folks upstairs are thrilled."

I clock his navy suit and the leather-soled Oxfords. "Advertising. Isn't that a bit scary?"

He ignores my taunt.

IDA awards paper Stewart's office walls. He made *Bush-Gore 2000*, *The Human Genome*, and *Immigration.*

"Could be Sunday night prime time."

In boxing, we relax our breathing even during intense fighting, but right now I can't. "How about you send Samantha? She's a better fit."

"Zandy, *I'm* commissioning editor."

"Kalsang?"

He shakes his head. "I'm telling you respectfully, Zandy, shut up and get on with your job. Unless you don't want a job."

I've been climbing the ladder for eight years, making my way towards *Climate*. "I do . . . want my job."

"So quit the back talk, okay?"

"Celebrity scents and artificial ingredients. How can I look myself in the mirror?"

His eyes contract into narrow beads. "This isn't about saving the world."

Of course it is. "Righto."

I need to do something to stop this, but I'm coming up blank. I run my finger along the edge of the picture frame on his desk. It houses a black and white photo of his son, Al. A special kid, whom I've looked after on and off for years. "How's Al?"

"He got a job in a record store on the West Side alphabetizing inventory. He loves that stuff."

"That's so great." I need a new tack to get back to *Climate*.

"Yes, it is."

I pick one up one of the colored stress balls, sitting in a metal basket on the edge of his desk. The rubbery stuff is smooth in my palm. I will myself not to squeeze it, to accept what's going on here.

"I need you to get off your high horse. You're a filmmaker."

I hear the words, and they bounce off me. This is *Bee-Keeping* again, only worse. "I'm thirty. It's time I made something meaningful."

"You should be able to make meaning out of baked beans. It's never the subject–it's the way you handle it."

He doesn't understand. "Shouldn't we be pressing the network to make films that matter?"

"There's a nugget of gold in every story. Zandy, your uncovering-the-truth thing, always taking the moral high ground. You're becoming a problem."

I squeeze the ball hard. It's dense and squishy. Must be a polymer. Bad for the planet.

"I understand, I promise." *Climate* is a "no." All those evenings and weekends. All that work. Those precious minutes with Greta. My chest is tight.

"The money is in ratings. This is a beautiful story, full of romance and history." He's flinging his arms around. "Give marketing something great to work with."

"Now we make advertorials?"

"Sweep us off to a better world."

I pick up a second ball. I've got one in each hand like a juggler. I squeeze them both hard.

"Remember those scent strips in magazines? Viewers should be able to smell these perfumes right in their living rooms."

It's growing, that tightness. Is this a heart attack?

"Director/Producer is a great step up for you," he says.

He's serious. Breathe, Zandy, breathe. D/P is a promotion. D/P is good. I lob a red stress ball into the hoop hanging on his wall. I miss.

"I want you in Nice on Monday."

He passed on Greta. "In four days?" What about climate justice? He must know it's going to pulverize the poor, and he wants me in the bloody South of France for the summer. Is this my moment to leave CNM and go indie? I lob the yellow ball. I miss again.

He pulls a sheet of paper off his desk and scrunches it. "Let me show you." He tosses it and lands a hoop in one. "You need to think about the weight."

That's what I'm trying to tell him. Think about the weight. "Stewart, we've got to wake up. By 2050 we'll have one billion climate refugees moving across the globe."

"I like you, Zandy . . ."

Eew. What do I say to that? "Thank you, Stewart. I like you too."

"You're committed and creative, but that's not enough. You think this is beneath you, but France isn't a choice. It's an order."

Do I repeat that I can't take this job, or do I give him time to come around? I lob a third time and miss again. Repeating myself isn't working. But I *cannot* make a puff piece about perfume and put it into the world. That would put me on a par with my sleazy father. I will not be my father. I rock back and forth on my combat boots. Showing the truth isn't some pie in the sky thing for me. My life depends on it.

"Okay, thanks, Stewart." For right now, I'll say yes. Later I'll figure something out. I have to.

"Mess this up, and you're in trouble." He stares at me with a weird, blank expression, then looks me up and down, as though I've got ketchup on my oversized, pleatfronted twill pants.

I play with the brass buckle of my old leather belt, which is cinched tight at the waist. "Is there something else, Stewart?"

"Grasse isn't a desert war zone. Get some decent clothes–you're not Kristin Scott Thomas, and this isn't *The English Patient*."

Chapter Two

Outside in the open plan, I bat away the paper plane that whizzes over my shoulder as I plod leaden-legged towards Cummings in the conference room.

I trip over electric cable coiled on the floor at the water cooler. I pick up someone's boom mike and put it on a desk. And the noise—everyone is on phones and the room thrums like a call center.

I need to figure out a response to this France situation. But I don't have enough mental RAM right now. I'm in shutdown mode.

"Give me something fresh," Mike yells down the long table. "Not that dumb image."

I open the door to the conference room and begin this handover. By 6:00 p.m., the mindnumbing task of explaining everything to Cummings has calmed me. My head and my body have reconnected, and I have a decision. Stewart liked my pitch. *Climate* is great. I'm taking it indie.

Everything hard in life calls for a leap of faith, including going indie. Crisis is danger plus opportunity. This is opportunity. I'll be free. No one will tell me to go to bloody France. I won't have to brook Cummings eyeing me up. I've made it on my own since I was eighteen. I can do this. Luke can do it, so I can too. Luke, my boyfriend and superpower. Luke will help me crank out the details.

Problem: Luke's working tonight, and he's on deadline.

Solution: Go to gym. Lamar, my trainer, will help me figure

out how to delay Stewart until I can get to Luke. Also, boxing will clear my head and get my energy up.

But when I get to the gym over in Queens, I'm jangly again, like I've had an electric shock. My body has been saving this for me all day, and now it wants to deal.

I jump rope in the warmup area, thrusting doubles in the tangy sweat of hard work. *Patta patta patta,* my cable whirs.

At the far end, two teens in gray sweats and torn white T-shirts hurl punches at each other. My trainer, Lamar, approaches. He's five feet, ten inches and compact, wearing a royal blue track suit with white detailing and *Queens Boxing Gym* emblazoned across the back. His shaved head gleams with shades of black and reds. His brown eyes droop with sadness.

He points downwards.

I drop to pushups, thrusting oxygen into my cells.

I stand and tell him about France and the Stewart disaster.

He nods. "Burpees."

Alright, burpees. He's earned his presence with one hundred daily pushups, squats, and burpees. I want to be like Lamar.

"Going to France on Monday is ridiculous," I tell him. "I'm either going to leave CNM and make *Climate* on my own . . . or I'll persuade Stewart to send someone else to France."

"Persuade him? He's your boss, ain't he?"

"Yes, but I need him to understand."

He pulls the puffy headgear from the cubby and hands it to me.

I glide it over my head.

"Sounds like you're the one who don't understand." He hands me a pair of heavy, soggy, sweaty gloves.

I slide them on. "I just need time."

"And he needs you to go to France."

Lamar slips on his padded mitts. We jog onto the red floor which marks off the boxing area of the low-ceilinged room.

We bounce in place facing each other. "You got your business plan?" he asks.

"No." I hurl myself at the pads he holds in front of his torso.

He twists, slipping my punch. "So, you ain't ready."

I've been telling him my climate documentary is early stage. I wish I hadn't. "Gimme a break, Lamar."

I'll waitress in the evenings and on weekends. I'm not afraid of hard work. I'll buy myself a little black dress and some lipstick. I'll get a front of house job as greeter and earn double bucks for that. I'll have all day to work up the business side of things. And I'll take my iPad to work and nail the details during the downtime.

I power into a left hook.

He blocks me.

When the bell rings, giving me a minute of rest, I bend to catch my breath. Sweat courses down the back of my neck into my shoulder blades.

The bell sounds again. We're back at it for three minutes.

"You're twelve months out, you said."

"You're making me mad."

"Mad ain't good. You stay cool, calm, in control of your moves."

I pull my shoulders down my spine and tighten my core. "Don't be afraid to fight, you tell me. Treat it like a challenge."

"Discipline and patience, girl. That's how you win in life and in boxing. Took me twenty years to get here. We plan and train, plan and train. Don't be coming to Lamar for BS talk."

Right hook. I miss.

"Sloppy. Move your feet."

He walks off the red floor.

I follow.

"Greta changes everything." I call out to his back.

He swivels and points to the kids at the far end, who are slumped into an exhausted hug. "My boys act impulsively to save face." He returns his pads to the cubby. "Know where that gets them? Shot in the face."

Outside the grimy window, sirens wail. "Your mama shooting up tonight?" asks Lamar.

"No."

"You got a bed tonight that someone ain't pissed in?"

"Yes."

"You put your fights in along the way, then you take on the champion. You want to train with me?"

"Of course."

"You want to mentor my boys?"

"Yes."

"Show me you're steady, Zandy. Bite the bullet and go to France." He points at the red EXIT sign over the door. "Now, stop wasting my time and get outta here."

He walks towards the far corner. "Boys," he calls out, "listen up."

I hurl my gloved fist at the fig-shaped speed bag hanging from the ceiling. *Thappita-thappita.* My brain tingles as I hammer out the little that's left in me.

In the changing room, I strip off, dropping my tank and shorts, bra and underwear into a puddle on the floor. I stand at the grimy basin, looking myself in the mirror, sopped in sweat.

Should I listen to Lamar? I soap my body with my hands. He knows Queens, the kids, the gangs, and the guns. Lamar trains street kids how to box their way out of poverty. No one knows boxing like him. But he doesn't understand the importance, the miracle, the perfect hook that is 2.4 minutes of Greta Thunberg talking straight to camera.

Only, Lamar is my go-to man. Some people have families to go to, but this is where I work out the kinks in my life. Lamar is why I've got TRUTH MATTERS painted in caps on my bedroom wall.

Is Lamar right? I cup cool water in my palms and rinse my body. Damn you, Lamar, for making me doubt myself. I cannot shillyshally. Our planet is out of time.

I grab my hand towel and dry off. Lamar doesn't get that filmmaking is an agent of change. The right films can save our planet and I've got Greta. Here's my chance to show the truth and make a doc that matters. I finish drying my feet, passing the towel in between each toe.

I yank on my underwear, Oxford bags, and shirt. From my messenger bag, I pull out the sandwiches I bought at the Stop & Shop on my way here and stack them on the bench. Six beef and tomato in Saran Wrap–terrible for our climate, but these kids need dinner tonight.

I ram my workout gear into my bag. I've had enough of the rancid stink, the peeling paint, and all the cement in this place. I grab my leather airman's jacket and slam the heavy EXIT door behind me.

Chapter Three

MONSIEUR DOMINIQUE SEVERIN

Friday, April 30, 1:00 p.m., Vence, France

Annabella is lying face down on the bed, her naked back showing above the sheet, which barely covers her rump.

Sitting beside her, I lean over to inhale the scent of lavender and hay in her thick flaxen hair. "*Bellissima.*" I run my finger down to the small of her back.

She is long-limbed but curvy where most blondes are straight up and down. She's Brigitte Bardot, my Annabella Santo Bellagio. Even her name is curvy.

She grinds her hips in circles.

"Not now, *amore*," I say. "I need to leave . . ."

She flips over. In a flash, she's out of bed and sitting astride me–naked. Her hair is held back in clips, half up, half down. Everything about her is pale and pearly. Her teeth, the whites of her nails, the whites of her eyes. Fingers deftly unbutton my shirt. She slides a warm hand over my chest, caresses my nipple.

I cup my left hand around her buttock. My heart rate picks up and blood thunders through me. I want her . . .

No! I tell myself. Control. I dig the nail of my right index finger into the flesh of my thumb–hard. I pant out a sharp breath and remove her hand from inside my shirt.

"What's wrong, *tesoro*?"

I place my hands on her shoulders. "I have urgent business to discuss with Camille."

Annabella stiffens.

"I'm sorry, *amore*."

My sister Camille, who is director of marketing for our family perfume business, Severin Frères, has got some hare-brained idea about a documentary and she won't drop it.

"No." A hand dives into my trouser pocket. She whips out my car keys. "No office." She leans her face in close to mine. Her breath tickles my skin. "You are my prisoner." She gyrates her hips against my crotch and tilts her head backwards, showing me her smooth arched neck.

Half lifting her body, I press her off me.

She steps back, glowering. "I come from Venezia to spend the weekend with you and this is how you treat me?"

She stands, snatches the white sheet off the bed and winds it around herself. It hangs in expert folds, making her a Greek goddess. "*Basta cosi*, enough."

I stand facing her, reaching out to stroke that delicious crinkle on her nose. "Please, *bellissima*. If I could explain it, you'd understand. But I can't because it's all confidential." I plant a kiss on her forehead. "I have to go."

"Dominique, *questa è l'ultima volta*. This is the last time."

"I know, *amore*. You have my car keys," I say, forcing restraint through my teeth.

She hurls the keys at the wall.

They clatter to the floor.

I bend to pick them up. "I have no choice. It's urgent."

"We always have a choice," she says. "It's time you made yours."

We've been dating for nine months now. I raise my forefinger to my lips. "*Bellissima*, not now."

Hands akimbo, she says, "*Assolutamente* now. You propose, or we are off–for good."

"You know I can't," I say. "The business . . ." All these women who treat me like I'm a piece of fish to catch. They don't know me, only what I stand for. And they have no idea what a disaster I'm in financially.

She turns away. "Always 'the business.'" She retrieves her bra and blouse from the back of the armchair.

"I'm not trying to hurt you. I have responsibilities to my employees. I'm not ready for marriage, *amo*."

She grasps the necklace with the diamond droplet I gave her, tears it off her neck, and flings it across the room.

My stomach tenses. I wish it didn't have to be like this.

"Get out!" she says. "I hope you'll be very happy together, you and your business."

I stand, my back to the door, my fists tight. "I'm not going to marry you now."

"Don't call me again."

"If that's your choice . . ." I love Annabella. I love her body. I want to keep this going with her, but I need to put an end to this documentary idea once and for all.

As I close the door behind me, my stomach is aquiver. I take the elevator down and cross the foyer of the hotel. The high ceilings, the elegant, spacious proportions, the wooden paneling, the patterned carpet, and the discreet staff hovering silently are nothing. All sensation rests in my stomach.

Outside, the valet opens my car door for me.

On autopilot, I nod to him. "Good afternoon, Étienne. Good to see you."

Severin Frères has been in business since 1721. We're in trouble now, and it's my duty to get it back onto a stable footing.

The business will not go down on my watch. That would be the ultimate shame. Plus, I've got two thousand families whose livelihoods depend on us.

I rev the engine and pull out of the hotel.

The craggy rock face cut away from the mountain overhangs the winding road back to Grasse. "*Merde, merde merde*," I shout at it. Annabella thinks me a cad, but this is my duty and it's important. Full of jitters, I accelerate out of the bends.

Ten minutes later, I pull off the road into the medieval village of Tourrettes sur Loup. I want to calm myself so I can handle this lunch from a place of strength. Camille can be a bulldog and Maman will also be there. I park in the square and sit encased in the cockpit of my little '87 Alfa Romeo. In here, I feel safe.

On the sandy rectangular courts mere feet away from me, groups of men are playing boules. I crack the window, so I can feel the breeze and hear the thud of the ball on sand.

I check my phone. Somehow I've missed a number of calls from Jean Bernaud. I will be gentle but firm, I tell myself as I speed-dial our banker of thirty years. I run my thumb around the varnished wood of the steering wheel, tracing its smoothness. "I'm glad you called," I say to him. "I want to extend our line of credit."

Silence at the other end.

My stomach hardens. I expect a bit of a talking to . . .

"I was coming to see you on Monday," he says. "I've got bad news, Monsieur Dominique."

I will myself to stay calm.

"The bank is withdrawing your line of credit and raising your loan rate to LIBOR plus two."

I grasp the steering wheel with two hands. "Plus two?" Numbers dance across my field of vision. Twos and threes. What is he saying? LIBOR, the bank rate. I see spreadsheets and columns. Pages and pages of numbers and down at the bottom, figures in red. "This is impossible. What are you saying, Jean?"

"The business has changed."

"We've been loyal customers of Credit Agricole since 1894."

"It's not relationships anymore, it's ratios."

I'm stunned. I swallow away the lump in my throat.

"You've tried everything?"

"I'm being replaced. They're sending in a new chap," he says.

My insides fall away. I see this new man, the stiff white cuffs sticking out of his charcoal grey suit jacket. A bristly, waxed mustache, skin smooth and gleaming. Buttoned up, implacable.

"I've done everything I can." His voice breaks.

"I know you will have fought for us." I gather myself. "Don't feel bad." My cheeks burn. How can it have come to this?

"I'm so sorry," says Jean. "I told them in Montrouge they're making a mistake. But they've turned into bean counters. God knows Grasse needs Severin Frères. All the jobs. You'll think of something, Monsieur Dominique . . . I have faith in you. Everyone here has faith in you."

The back of my throat is burning. "Enjoy your weekend. My regards to Marie."

I end the call. My chest blazes beneath my breastbone. From the boules court, cheers rise up. A cluster of old boys slap each other on the back. I envy them. They need skill for their game, but unlike me, they know what their next move is. Is Camille right in saying that an independent perfume house isn't viable in the twenty-first century? The fact is that every luxury brand in the world is part of a conglomerate these days. But selling out would be too shameful.

I drop my head and stare at the emblem in the middle of the steering wheel. On the left side, a red cross on a white field. It speaks of a strength and clarity I don't have right now. On the right side, a blue snake writhes, a human in its mouth. I am that man, caught in the gullet of the snake.

I must find a way forward. This is my duty. I need a new strategy. I open the glove compartment and retrieve the duster. I run it over the dashboard, wiping the surface of the dials, reaching into all the nooks where dust settles. I shake it out of the window. I return the duster to the glove compartment and shut it tight.

I pick lint off my light wool trousers until the burning in my throat subsides. I shall put the Annabella business aside. I'm going into this meeting calm and strong. I will not tell Camille about the bank rate, not for the moment, or she'll use it as a lever against me. The business of the day is to shoot down that wretched documentary. I rev the engine and pull out of Tourrettes.

Twenty minutes later I walk into the dining room of our family home. I approach Maman, who is seated at the head of the oval table gazing out of the window. "Thank you for making lunch, Maman." I bend to kiss her cheek.

"When is Camille coming home?" she asks.

"I'm right here." Camille is seated a few feet away in a tightly belted, bamboo-print dress that manages to be both elegant and ironic.

I walk to the sideboard and ladle the steaming *bouillabaisse* into three bowls.

I serve Maman first. She shakes her tumbler. The ice cubes tinkle. She takes a slurp of whisky and says, "For years we sponsored the yacht race in Saint-Tropez. It was *fabuleux*."

"You overspent, and now we're in trouble." She had flair when she first took over–some of Grandpapa's brilliance and swagger.

"It was the times," she says.

Who knows what goes on inside you, Maman, elegant today

in your lilac Chanel suit, but hollowed out. I wish things could have turned out differently for you. "You have to watch the cash, Maman. That was the problem," I say. One of the problems. And now we're in this sinkhole.

I take my seat opposite Camille. She looks at me intently. Her thick black eyebrows stately and powerful, set against that porcelain skin. "I agreed to the documentary. I've signed the contract."

"Excuse me?"

"CNM Documentary Channel is going to make a movie about Severin."

My stomach clenches. "You signed the contract? No, Camille. Certainly not."

She slaps the table. "It's ninety minutes of primetime TV."

"I said 'no' and I mean it."

"It's a total coup. The director is arriving on Monday."

Under the table I grind my right shoe into the rug.

She leans towards me. "It could drive up revenues by 40 percent."

"We wouldn't have the slightest control. What if they dig up matters we don't want publicized?"

"Like what?"

I swivel my eyes towards Maman. Icy dread slithers down my gullet. Maman was CEO until I took over seven years ago. She disgraced us in so many ways–fell off the stage at our annual meeting and was carried out by her driver. "What if this journalist goes round knocking on doors?"

"It's old hat."

"What's in the papers?" says Maman.

"The problems we had a few years ago." Maman damned near destroyed the company. I shoot Camille a strong look. "I'm not going through that kind of exposure again. Not for anything." I push my bowl away. I can't eat the soup.

"We've got nothing to hide," she says.

"*Au contraire*. Maman walked to the *pâtisserie* in her nightgown last week at four in the afternoon," I say.

"Are you talking about me?" says Maman, stick-insect thin, not eating, only drinking.

"We need to protect the business, Camille."

"There's one in every family. Why should we be different?" she says.

My sister can be undisciplined. She went wild at that art school in her early twenties. Left France, lived on a Thames houseboat, and went to crazy parties with club drugs. Although you wouldn't know it today.

"Camille, no movie. It's too risky. We need to protect this . . . work of art we've inherited."

Maman shoves her tumbler towards Camille for a refill. If only she could stop drinking.

Camille shakes her head. "That's enough, Maman. You want to see your granddaughter this afternoon, don't you?"

I look at Camille. "If this journalist doesn't dig into the past, what about exposing the challenges we face today? I can just see it, 'Financial Distress for Severin.' You want that on primetime TV?"

"It's not that kind of story. It's going to be super romantic."

Could she stop flinging her hands around like some conductor? "Look around, Camille." The yellow silk curtains are ripped, and the eighteenth-century mahogany table has a split in the center. "We should have overhauled this place ten years ago. I don't want anyone coming here. It's a disgrace." That's damp I smell. From under the carpet? Damp wool and wood.

"No one's coming to film the P & L. They're salivating about cobblestone streets and the terracotta roofs of Grasse."

I've lost control of this. "Journalists are paid to rake up muck."

"*Allez*. Their customers are advertisers. They want heaven in a perfect microclimate between the glistening Mediterranean and snowcapped Alps. It's going to be 'fabled *terroir* of jasmine, rose, and violets, home to the world's greatest *parfumeurs*.'" She nibbles a wedge of garlic toast. "I'll talk up the South of France as the backdrop, the superyachts at anchor in the bay. Who couldn't be seduced by all of this? They're American!"

"What's the fighting about?" says Maman.

"We're discussing business, Maman." I turn back towards Camille.

"Have you thought about formulas, proprietary information . . . ?"

"Of course. It's in the contract. I've discussed the whole story with their commissioning editor, Stewart Stevens, a decent guy."

How am I going to persuade her out of this?

"Can you smell damp?" she asks.

I purse my lips and nod.

I run my finger around the edge of my grandmother's soup plate, the rose Limoges. "You could destroy the brand that we've built for three hundred years, because some chap looking for a promotion decides to drag us through the mud."

"We've got to get in front of our public," says Camille. "I need this exposure. My budget is laughable." Camille pulls on the chunks of her amethyst necklace–three rows around the neck, Duchess of Windsor style. "We're making a documentary, using the anniversary as our hook."

I've failed to make her see reason. I don't know what I should have said or done. This is dangerous.

"If you want to save this business, you'll have to take the risk. We're sunk, Dom. We need money." She tucks a wisp of hair into the coil of her French pleat with a precision that shows her disdain.

"No, Camille." I realign my spoon and fork, redirecting an unwelcome spurt of irritation.

She and I have always been different. Camille spent her teens careening around town on mopeds, while I took the train to Paris with Grand-mère. Camille smoked joints with the boys, while we studied antiquities, Islamic art, and sculpture at the Louvre–silverware, cabinet making, porcelain, and tapestry. She taught me the culture and heritage of La Belle France.

Camille looks at me, a piece of garlic toast poised in one hand. "Even the animal kingdom adapts to new circumstances." The high cheekbones and sculpted features are regal even though inside she's all Sturm und Drang.

"We're going bankrupt," she says.

Langoustines hover in my bowl of *bouillabaisse*. Their bulbous eyes taunt, and their long antennae poke at me. I can't eat this.

She's finished her soup, so I clear the plates and stack them on the sideboard. I cut the *tarte aux citrons* and place it onto the dessert plates. I serve Maman, who fingers her packet of cigarettes. She hasn't eaten a thing. "Have some dessert."

I serve Camille, then myself, and take my seat. I take a forkful of *tarte*. It glides down my throat, the butter and egg yolks creating the perfect bridge between citrus rind and sugar. "I do appreciate all your hard work."

"How can I do my job when you're so secretive? If you won't let me market, we're selling to SBVD. The offer is still on the table. We have to take it."

My stomach tightens. "I'm not here to hash that out again. What about responsibility to our ancestors? Doesn't that mean anything to you? They'd outsource to Uzbekistan . . ."

"SVBD is the world leader in luxury. We'd be joining a talented tribe on a perpetual quest for excellence."

On the wall to my right hang the portraits of ten generations of Severin *parfumeurs*. "If we sold, what would I say to our forebears? 'I'm not strong enough to sustain what you worked so hard to create?' What kind of man would I be?"

In those dark days when Maman was battering our good name, I vowed I would repair the company and hand it down with pride. "SBVD would fire all the families who have devoted themselves to us for centuries. We'd be scattering our inheritance to the Earth's four corners. Think of what Grandpapa would have wanted." There's his portrait, closest to me. The great man, dominating . . .

"I need the money," says Camille. "And I'm sick of arguing about this. I do own 50 percent of the company."

"I've got the voting rights. It would be chaos if we both made the decisions," I say. "Don't you dream of passing Severin down to our children?"

"What children?" Camille is the single mother of adorable two-year-old Amélie.

"As soon as I've got the business back on a stable footing, I'll build a family."

"Whatever." Camille flings down her napkin. Her rings flash with topaz, peridot, and garnet. "We do the documentary, or I leave." She pushes her chair back and stands. "I'm not letting this go," she says.

Can she mean it? I thrust my plate away.

"D'you want me to leave?" she asks.

"Camille, you can't."

"It's my financial future."

"Camille, I need you. You can pluck from the air what our customers want now–to belong, to feel worth–and you can translate that into design and marketing. Grand-mère would be so proud of your work."

"Grand-mère is in her grave, and you're sinking my inheritance," says Camille.

"Don't be angry . . . we must be friends, *chouchou*."

"Gucci will take me back," she says.

I rotate Grandpapa's watch around my wrist. The leather strap battered and warm against my skin. Any minute we'll be in trouble with the bank too. "Camille, not now. Think of the family."

"Yes. I'm thinking of Amélie. She deserves the chances you and I had."

I will my chest to stop heaving. This is like sections of rock loosening themselves from the mountainside after prolonged rainfall. The destruction begins with rolling and toppling, soon huge boulders are bouncing downwards, building into a rock avalanche that tears down the mountain, destroying everything in its path.

She stands. "I resign."

I leap to my feet. "No, Camille."

Her eyes narrow. "I'm sick of arguing. You never see reason. We're in total collapse . . . Maman, it's time." Camille strides towards Maman and takes her by the hand. "We'll go and find Amélie."

Looking at me, she says, "You had your choice. You made it." She sweeps out of the room, supporting Maman in the crook of her arm.

Which is worse, losing Camille or exposing ourselves to media scrutiny? How can I possibly answer that? I make my way out through the swing door to the kitchen where I clasp the marble table, willing myself to receive its cool, unwavering strength. Part of me wants to run after her and beg her to change her mind. But I know my sister. That won't work.

My throat prickles. What in God's name will I do without Camille? The couture houses are trampling all over our market—Hermès, Dior—the big guns.

The kitchen is a disaster zone. Maman has left fish heads, saucepans of stock, and open containers over every counter. I can't leave it like this. I scrape off the chopping boards and dispose of the detritus in the bin.

I plunge the boards and knives into soapy, boiling water and scrub them clean. I twist lids onto jars and return the mayonnaise to the refrigerator.

We desperately need to reposition ourselves. Stumbling on without a marketing director would be a fool's choice.

I clear the plates from the dining room and carry them out on a tray. Back in the kitchen, I stack the crockery and cutlery in the deep porcelain sink. The drain at the bottom is corroded, which is just what my gut feels like.

I can still smell the fish and saffron in here. I douse everything again in boiling water.

Without Camille, I'll need to hire an agency to find us someone good. The new person will want more money than we've been paying her. And the agency will want 40 percent of the first year's salary. In the interim, I'll have to take over Camille's responsibilities. I feel sick to my stomach. Where's the money to come from?

I'm going to the office to pull up the cash flow sheets and plug in the new interest rate to see how long we've got. I'll take one more look at the balance sheet, see if there are any options there to raise money to pay for a new marketing director.

The gravel crunches underfoot as I pad across the driveway to my car. I allow myself to relish the heavenly scent of jasmine and the silence, punctuated by the chirp and twitter of goldfinch. The warm breeze caresses my skin as I survey the sweep of olive groves that fall away on either side of the garden. From the distance, children's voices call out. A perfect late April day.

I'd like to take a walk in the mountains. Instead, I slump into my car seat, turn over the ignition, and head to the office. Ten minutes later, I'm pounding up the stairs to the second floor. I'm panting as I make my way down the long white corridor. At the far end, I see the outline of Alain, our office janitor, in his blue overalls. He's pushing a sample cart over to the labs in the eastern section of the building.

I want to run down the corridor and hop on that cart like I used to as a boy–have him push me around, lose myself again in that physicality and innocence. Those days are long gone now. I lay my palm on the wall to steady myself.

I whistle coming up behind him.

He swivels towards me.

I wrap his bony shoulders in a hug. His overalls smell of mud and lemongrass.

"Want to catch the game next Saturday?" I ask.

The glimmer in his eyes light up his nutbrown face. "We'll crush 'em."

"Bring your grandson. It's time he came into the business."

He slaps me on the back.

"I'll pick you up at 6 p.m.," I say.

"*Merci*, Monsieur Dominique."

I retrace my steps and open the door to my office, which I've barely changed since it was Maman's. The midcentury wood furniture and eau de Nil upholstery with accents of orange exude a feeling of peace, like a Rothko painting.

But this afternoon, my legs wobble as I make my way across the thick cream carpet to my desk. My office is a sanctuary for me, a place to think, especially during the quiet of the weekend, but now it feels heavy and airless, dead with the weight of responsibility.

The cash flow and balance sheets are on my laptop, just there on my desk. I could pull them up now and plug in the new numbers. But the tightness in my throat tells me I'm facing a roadblock as steep as the mountains that soar behind my beloved Grasse. If I don't find some way out, we'll be closing our doors by September. Then Alain will be out of a job–and so too countless other families who have served us for generations.

I turn my chair around so that it faces the enormous picture window behind my desk. The outside forms part of the room, whatever the light, whatever the weather.

Numb, I sit and stare out of that window, looking deep into the dense green foliage. Out there, wild boar roam. Mountain streams wend their way through emerald glades. Ancient gnarled oaks stand firm against the calamities of weather.

I don't need the spreadsheets; I've run the numbers in my head. I need to make a decision. My eyes dart from side to side as I look for shapes and clues out there in the foliage. As night falls, encasing me in its darkness, I pull out my phone and consult Sun Tzu and his *Art of War*. He says, "In the midst of chaos, there is also opportunity."

I see no opportunity, only danger. I stand and pace the perimeter of the room, searching for inspiration, for a sign.

I look at my engraving of a tablet commemorating Tapputi of Mesopotamia. In 1200 BC she became the world's first *parfumeur*.

I pick up a nineteenth-century green slipware bowl ascribed not to an individual but to the whole village of Onta, Japan. A beautiful pot, made in the traditional way by families going back generations. An object of such simplicity, it signifies not just beauty but truth. It gives homage to artisanship in all its expressions. It links work and worship, and embodies a vision for a more whole world.

The act of making a pot seems clear and orderly. But the potters also had challenges. Wars, plagues, diseases, and hunger made their appearances. And still they made pots through the centuries. They survived. As must we.

I twist Grandpapa's watch around and around my wrist.

I reach across the desk, grasp my phone, and speed dial Camille. She can be emotional, unpredictable, and dramatic, but she's a creative genius. Just as important, Camille is family, a bulwark against our mother and our troubled past. I need her.

The documentary is a huge gamble. I'm not a gambling man. I've seen where that goes. But I'm CEO and I must lead. "I agree," I say, the phone clasped to my ear.

"What . . . ?"

"You asked me to trust you."

"Dom . . ." She pauses.

Amélie chirps away in the background.

Stop doubting, I tell myself, looking out into the forest and the night. Doubt is the enemy of the leader. "We'll make the documentary, and you'll stay on."

"Marvelous."

"I have two conditions. First, we will reinvent Evening Star and use this documentary to promote it."

"Ideal," she says.

"Camille, I will save this business if it's the last thing I do."

"Of course we will. What's the other condition?"

"I will handle the documentary myself, down to every last detail."

Chapter Four

ZANDY

Friday, April 30, 8:30 p.m., New York

I stand in line at the hostess desk at Thai Me, starving. When it's my turn, I order for two. Luke is on deadline, and normally I wouldn't disturb him. He might mind, but he'll understand. The glass noodle salad and pad thai are a salve to smooth my way. This is an emergency. Luke will tell me how to rent the equipment I'll need and the crew. "Also clearing rights . . . international rights," I dictate into the Todoist app on my phone. They're so complicated these days.

The lady hands me my order. I reach into the takeout bag and remove the food, leaving the plastic silverware wrapped in cellophane and the wodge of napkins behind.

"No plastic, please." I hand them all back. I keep a recycled bag inside my messenger bag for just this. I remove it and slide the four containers in.

Luke forgets to eat when he's working hard, so I'm also helping him. I head over there carrying my offering. I let myself in. "And post-production, how, where, with whom?" I dictate into my phone.

I'll help Luke with his edits–pull an all-nighter, whatever it takes.

La Traviata is blaring as I climb the stairs to his unit. One thing I love about Luke, he's generous with his advice. He doesn't do the "I'm so grand, and you're so lowly jig that bigtime directors love to do. I stand a moment in the hallway mouthing along, "*Folleggiare di gioia in gioia.*"

I round the bookshelf and enter his cavernous loft space.

Samantha walks towards me.

My mouth parches.

Samantha, from my office . . . wearing only a teeny red thong, her pendulous breasts swaying like coconuts.

My chest grips tight. Samantha. Naked. What the . . . ?

Samantha gasps, dances up and down on the spot, coconuts flying about. She screeches, "Luke!" and flees to the bathroom.

Luke emerges, naked to the waist, the top button of his jeans open.

"Zandy?" Luke runs his right hand around his jaw, looking straight at me.

I try to open my breathing, to slow it down. Instead, I hyperventilate. I'm rooted to the spot. My brain is trying to unscramble what's clear as day–they've been having sex.

The handle of the bag is cutting into my wrist. I drop it onto the uneven wooden floor. "What the hell?"

Luke comes towards me.

Bound in a towel, Samantha returns and bends to scoop up her clothes strewn across the floor.

I'd like to flee into the night air and scream until the cacophony in my head fades out. But I'm not playing the woman scorned. I take the few steps to the oversized sofa and plonk myself down on it. Adrenaline gushes through me. I access it and switch into strength. I gesture to Samantha. "Are you joining us?"

She scurries back to the bathroom.

"I've got Thai takeout," I call out. I've got zero appetite now.

Samantha reappears, the tightly housed coconuts thrusting through a yellow mohair sweater. "Zandy, this isn't my fault."

"Luke and I are going to talk."

He nods at her, taking a seat beside me. "I'll call you, babe." The German accent lingers in spite of his living in New York for twenty years.

"Babe?" I say to him.

She picks up her bag and rushes out. The door bangs behind her.

He reaches his hand out towards me.

I squirm away. "You lied to me." My voice warbles with emotion. "You said you were working tonight. Why did you lie to me?" The adrenaline has seeped away.

"I am working. I'm editing tonight. And I didn't lie about Samantha . . . I just didn't tell you."

At Fire Island, we'd skimmed stones. We'd snuggled under a blanket and he'd said, "It's important for each of us to keep our freedom."

I'd licked the curve of his neck, savoring the briny taste of sea, sun, and breeze. "Absolutely," I'd said because freedom was his persona, and I wanted everything that Luke was.

"You said freedom, and I said honesty." I've always said that. My breath is raspy.

It's not the sex I mind; it's the deception. From the coffee table, I pick up his *berimbau*, the percussion instrument used in Brazilian *capoeira*. Staring at him, I run my finger pads around its smooth, silky surface.

"You should have told me you were sleeping with Samantha."

"I'm not going to rub your nose in it."

I shake my head. "What is it you actually want?"

He pulls up a knee and turns so that he faces me. He strokes my cheek with the knuckle of his forefinger.

I yank his hand away.

"I want to . . . sample the pleasures at life's banquet," he says.

"Sleeping around?"

"No." The veins on his temples pulse. "I do enjoy your mind. I love your ferocity on set and in bed. I also enjoy Samantha."

Nausea rises in me. I return the polished gourd to the table and slide it away from me. I no longer trust its elegance, or him–he's too smooth by half. "This is a power trip for you?"

"No. You love new cultures. I also like to . . . discover new landscapes."

My ferocity on set and Samantha's breasts. "Women are Barbie dolls? You piece together this set of legs, with those breasts, mix-and-match?"

"Men are jerks sometimes."

"You don't get off that easily. You've never flinched from the truth in your work."

"And you're so totally perfect?" He grabs a blue Henley off the back of the sofa and pulls it on. "I help you learn about film. Am I right?"

Heat flames up the back of my neck. He's right, but I'm not going to admit it. I see the same muscled Luke with the designer stubble, but now he seems hard and bleak, black and white in a world of color. He doesn't look real, more like a Calvin Klein underwear advertisement.

"Samantha doesn't mean I don't care about you."

"I said honesty." Thirteen months and I thought I had a handle on who he was.

"Always so intense. Remember we looked at Vermeer? Places of dark illuminated by light. You need more light."

"Without truth . . . we haven't got anything."

"I don't know, Zandy. Is there a single truth? There isn't just one way to shoot a scene. There are several angles, multiple interpretations. For me there are many beautiful women to enjoy. You're one of them, but you aren't the whole world."

"Clever words . . ."

"I need to be free," he says.

"Forever running from your past, you mean." He was married in his twenties to a camerawoman who died in a train accident. Five years later, he made the stellar *Memory, Story, Love*.

"We're all walking histories. You too, Zandy."

I kick the table leg. "I thought you wanted to keep things light?"

"Why have you cut off from your family?" he asks.

"Go to hell," I say.

"Let's not make this into a *Schwarzwälder Kirschtorte*."

Long silence.

"Can we start the evening again?" he says.

I wish we could. That box of heaviness on my chest says I don't have the experience to go indie, and I need his help.

On the wall behind him hang oversized, brightly colored, framed posters publicizing *The Abattoir, Berlin,* and *After Porn*, all the amazing films he's made. He's a truthful, open, sensitive, brave, authentic moviemaker. *Rolling Stones Backstage* was searingly honest. OMG, his skill, confidence, and experience–I've been ravenous for it. But he isn't the guy I thought he was. I conflated the man with the moviemaker. I shake my head.

I swivel away from him, gawking out of the window at the brickwork and neat black window frames of the warehouse opposite–quite the reverse of the maelstrom I feel inside.

I've been in a dream these thirteen months. I'd gone to the screening of his movie, *LA Sex Workers*. I was wowed. He tells the truth of their lives with touching compassion for their struggle.

I was standing alone at drinks afterwards, wondering how to approach him, when some guy fell and pushed me over. In the process, I chucked the kombucha I was drinking right over Luke's shirt. A human pileup with a sticky aftermath.

"You did that on purpose, right?" Luke laughed, pulling me to my feet.

"Of course," I joshed. "It was the only way to get your attention."

We bantered for a while, then he slid away to talk to industry people, laughing as he pointed at the wet mess of his shirt. I was leaving when he appeared out of nowhere. "Where are we going?" Luke helped me on with my coat. He was forty-three and sexy as hell, with salt-and-pepper hair that he wore long to the shoulder.

We went to the Delmano bar, all dark and cozy. We talked favorite movies until late. He flicked back his hair in a teasing way as we flirted.

For thirteen months, we've been doing movies and sex. A lot of movies. A lot of sex. And as needed, takeout dinner from around the world. But we don't have what I thought we had between us, and he's half the man I thought he was.

I pick at tufts of the stuffing poking through a hole in the sofa cover and roll the scratchy batting across my palm. Do I hang in here because I need his knowledge and reassurance to produce *Climate*? No. I don't deal in coverups and lies. The truth matters. Greatly.

I take the pebble from my pocket, the one he gave me at Fire Island, and place it down on the table. "We're over." I stand.

He tugs at my hand and pulls me back onto the sofa. "C'mon, honeybee, don't do this. You're all verve. I love that about you . . ."

"It's okay, Luke. I don't want this."

He reaches towards my ear and curls a lock of my hair around his fingers.

"Please don't do that." Twenty minutes ago he was fondling Samantha.

"I'm on your side, Zandy."

"Not in the way I need you to be."

I walk to the center of the room. Peering into the take-out

bag, I see that brown sauce has oozed all over the place. The rice noodles look limp.

"Thanks for the memory," I say, my back to him. Inside, I'm jelly, but I need to be strong.

He doesn't come after me.

In his dark-blue hallway, his floor-to-ceiling shelves are stuffed with CDs and books. There's the DVD set I gave him: *Herzog; The Collection, A Limited Edition.* Part of me wants to slide it into my bag, but I control myself and don't.

Outside, it's dark. A chilly wind has whipped up, swirling debris and dust along the empty streets. I hold onto the lamppost to steady myself.

A text arrives.

`Luke: drop the key off?`

I quiver.

`Me: sure.`

A skip piled high with an old mattress, planks of wood, and a baby stroller stands in front of me. I fish in my bag, yank the key off my carabiner, and drop it right in there.

I both regret it and need the jolt of strength it gives me. In the ring, when you get knocked down, you stand right back up. Only now I'm not sure how to.

I walk across Brooklyn in the cool night air. An hour later, arriving home, I've regrouped. If Luke isn't going to help me get funding for *Climate,* Jenna will. Also, she can look over my personal budget and make sure my income and expenses are watertight; that I'm not missing anything. She's good at this stuff, and she's interested in saving our planet. Also, I could sublet my room during periods when I'm on the road.

I'll write my plan and email Stewart by noon on Sunday, tell him I'm leaving CNM.

I walk in the door to the weedy smell of pot. The coffee table is a mess of mugs and magazines. An assortment of lamps cast pools of yellow light around the room, and on the wooden dining table by the window, my three flatmates are playing Rummikub.

"Join us, Zandy," says Carter, a redheaded photographer with *People* magazine.

I approach the table. Its surface is cluttered with cream-colored Rummikub tiles. "I just broke up with Luke."

"Oh, sweetie. What you need now is a long drink and a board game. Join us," Jenna pleads with her warm brown eyes.

I spy a jug of Negroni–gin, vermouth, and Campari. Slices of orange float on top.

For a second here, I consider drowning the sorrows of the day in a cocktail, but I'm a wuss at drinking, and I've got a ton of work to do.

"Hey, Jenna, can you help me out, hon?" She's an analyst with Morgan Stanley, and she's really good with figures.

"Sure." Jenna twirls her lowball glass between her thumb and forefinger. "In the morning?"

"It's urgent," I say.

"I'm two games up, and I'm about to crush this one too." Her hand is poised above her rack.

"I need help now," I tell her.

She takes a tortilla chip from the packet and dips it into the plastic tub of salsa in the middle of the table. "Zandy, I've had three of these." She cocks an elbow towards her Negroni. Her words slur, and she looks like she might topple off her chair as she studies the combinations on the table.

"Drown your sorrows with us," says Delaney, who writes social media for a Hollywood actress. She picks up her lowball, plants wine-dark lipstick on its rim, and takes a slug. "Relax now. You'll do a better job tomorrow." She giggles.

"I'm rubbish at games and I've got big stuff going on. Stuff I need to get done."

Jenna lifts the glass jug full of amber-colored cocktail. Ice cubes glimmer in the reflected light. "The Negroni will sort that out." She refills everyone's glass.

"Thanks, guys. Maybe tomorrow." I head across the room and flip on the light switches in our galley kitchen to find that all the bulbs have blown. I turn on my phone flashlight and check the bowl into which we each put thirty dollars per month for repairs. It's empty, save for an old Tootsie Roll wrapper.

I reach for a brown rice and black bean burrito in the ice box, pull off the cellophane, and heat it in the microwave. Then I head down the corridor, dinner in hand. I'd like a good cry now, but there's no chance of that. I'm too wired.

I open my door. My room has a low double bed with wooden crates on each side bearing blue Ikea lamps. I place my burrito on the table and drop my bag on the floor.

Paddington Bear sits at my chair. I pick him up and place him squarely on the desk facing me. I was ten when we moved to the US from the UK, and Paddington came in my duffel. We're a team. He's small, robust, and entirely dependable. I straighten his red felt hat and stroke his nose.

"It was a tough day in the trenches. How 'bout you?"

Paddington is stoical, which I appreciate as I sit at my desk, take a bite of the burrito, and fire up my laptop.

From behind me comes a rasping, grating sound, like someone is sawing wood. I tense, half stand, and peer over the far side of my bed. A six-foot male is asleep, fully clothed and face down in my room.

Max. "Oh, dear." Delaney's boyfriend, Max is a freelance

screenwriter down on his luck. Now he's fallen asleep in my bedroom. On the floor beside him, I see an ashtray with the end of a joint in it. It was *his* skunk I smelled when I came in.

I walk around the bed and squat beside him.

He rolls over, shielding his face as he opens his eyes.

"Hey, Max . . ." I get him standing and walk him down the corridor to Delaney's room. "Hey, pal. You'll figure this out," I say as I lay him on her bed.

Back in my room, my phone is vibrating on my desk. The name "Stewart Stevens" flashes across the screen.

It's Friday night. Really? Just answer it, Zandy. "Hi . . ."

"You read the perfume notes in Google docs, right?" he says.

"I'm just sitting down now."

"They booked you the Hotel Virginie beginning Monday."

Monday. My chest tightens. "Great." I rip open the pack of Juicy Fruit on my desk and slide a stick out of its silver sheath.

"How's Al?" I ask.

"He's good. I know what's going through your mind, Zandy."

It's a problem, knowing your boss for eight years. "It's fine, Stewart. I'm on it."

"You'll do great. Can't wait to see what you make of it," he says. "And you'll have a D/P credit to your name."

I go limp. This isn't a suggestion, it's an order–three months in France making a perfume advertorial.

I chomp on the gum stick. I need to stop eating this stuff. It's bad for the planet.

"Call me with your storyboard ideas. Like, Thursday?"

The flavors release and pool into my saliva. Perfume vs. the truth that our planet is dying if we don't stop our madness now? I shake my head.

"Deliver on perfume, and we'll talk about *Climate* in the fall. And *bon voyage*."

"Yup. *Merci,* Stewart."

He ends the call.

Do I go to France? I chomp and chomp on my gum. Or do I leave my job and take *Climate* freelance? I'd need a twenty-five-page proposal laying out a compelling case for *Climate*, with statistics. Plus a trailer to go out and raise the $250K funding I'll need. I'm many miles from that tonight.

There's so much to think about and do beyond actual filmmaking; there's running a business as well as crafting the story. Going indie is harder than ever. I could do it, but securing distribution and promotion are key. Without distribution, will anyone actually see this doc? To save the world, this movie needs to be seen.

Gripping the gum between my front teeth, I pull it out of my mouth until all its fibers are stretched to their limit, like I am.

Also, I'm not going to be a Max, sweetheart that he is. Starving artist is one thing. But eating my flatmates' food and bumming off their rent checks is not me.

I slow down my breath. In . . . two . . . three . . . four . . . Out . . . two . . . three . . .four . . .

My throat is now wadded so thick, I can barely swallow. I haven't got Luke, and my people in the living room think the answer to life is Rummikub. I've got a better shot of showing the world *Climate* inhouse than out on my own, trying to learn sales and distribution while filming.

Work matters. Staying in the game matters. Getting stronger matters. Per my trainer, Lamar, "Day in, day out, you do the hundred burpees, whether you want to or not."

I'm going to grit my teeth and get through it. I'll keep my eye on the prize–as soon as I'm back from France, I'll make *Climate*. I'll live to fight another day.

I email the UN Special Envoy on Climate Ambition saying: "Regret I need to defer our *Climate* interview until further notice."

I head onto Travelocity. There's one seat left and it's overnight–Air France from JFK to Nice, 8:05 p.m. on Sunday.

I book it, then I grab my duffel from the top of the cupboard and pack. Paddington will go in last, so he doesn't get squished.

Chapter Five

It's hot when I land in Nice, France–very hot. My plan is in and out fast. Make the damned perfume thing, then get back to *Climate*. I'll get to my hotel and start work right away.

I peer around the arrivals hall across a throng of men in dark glasses, cigs hanging out of their mouths. They hold white signs bearing names. Sunlight bounces off the marble floors, making it hard to see. Someone from this perfume house is meant to pick me up.

I scan the space. Ah, there . . . in the distance by the sliding doors. A sign: ALEXANDRA WATSON CNM DOCUMENTARIES.

I wave and make my way over through the scent of dark coffee and something sweet like melon. I pass suntanned women poured into tight white jeans, with a slash of red lipstick and small hairy dogs in their arms. Not what I had in mind when I chose to be a documentary maker. I saw myself careening across the desert in an open jeep, sand in my hair . . . giving a good nod to Lawrence of Arabia. This is going to take some getting used to.

The driver removes his aviator sunglasses and proffers a hand. Large chocolate-brown eyes and a mass of thick, good hair.

"Dominique Severin, CEO of Severin Frères."

The boss? "Oh. Zandy Watson."

"Welcome to France, Mamselle Watson."

I shake his hand. "It's Zandy. Thank you, Mr. Severin."

"Call me Dominique–please."

Suntanned bare feet in loafers, crisp white shirt, cool linen jacket. Put together, but relaxed. Inviting. Not my thing, but nice.

He takes my duffel. We leave the arrivals hall with his left hand hovering close to the small of my back. I would be put out, but I'm distracted by a tall model-type in ripped jeans who sweeps past in a swarm of flashing bulbs.

He guides me towards the parking garage where he pops the trunk of his racing green Alfa Romeo. Jeez, this thing must guzzle gas. We're in the South of France; I guess no one here cares about climate change. James Bond slips in my duffel, opens the passenger door, and gestures for me to slide in.

He touches a button on the dash and the roof whirrs open. I don't trust attractive men. Especially when they drive sports cars.

The sweet, salty tang of the sea hangs in the warm air as we pull out of the garage and exit the airport. "Good of you to pick me up."

"My pleasure," he says.

Ahead of us a car full of rapper types–music blaring so loud we can feel the vibration.

"You'll drop me at my hotel?"

"First, we have a drink," he says.

"I need to shower and get to work."

"You will allow me to welcome you to France?"

It's hot. I want to get out of these wool pants.

A powder blue Bentley idles to our left. The driver who sports a mop of white hair hangs his bronzed elbow out of the window, inviting his diamond rings to glint in the sunlight. Jeez Louise. I've got three months of this? "I'm on a tight deadline."

"Just twenty minutes," he insists. "To show you the view. You will be ravished."

"Just a quick one, then." At the hotel, I'll set up my whiteboard and brainstorm perfume story ideas. And I'd like to see how France is handling climate change.

After the highway, a double carriageway, where the traffic eases. We climb up a winding road. He's got his foot down. We're doing 80 km/h. Elegant dark-green cypress trees point their tippy tops up towards the distant, forest-clad mountains that tower above the coast. Orange and lemon trees skirt the road. Bushes of rosemary throw off their pungency.

Wooded mounds carpet the distance. My shoulders relax. I'm floating inside a Renaissance painting. This is knockout–these hills are alive with the sound of music. We'll take wide, sweeping shots before panning in on the terracotta roofs of Grasse.

He takes a corner way too fast. I grip my seat and turn my head towards him, raising my eyebrows.

No reaction. He's calm in a way that exudes confidence. There's warmth and a hint of sadness in those big chocolate-brown eyes. He's taking things in, arranging them in his mind.

"We call these the Baou." He points to gigantic rock mounds that overhang the terrain. "Renoir, Dufy, and Chagall all painted them."

There's a strength in his face. The large crooked nose speaks of character. The olive skin gives him definition. He stands out in the world.

We pull into a hotel above Vence. Gravel drive, manicured gardens, the kind of place where everyone is draped in luxury brands. Is he trying to impress me? I don't need to be wooed with the five-star treatment. I want to scribble ideas on Postit notes, dream up shoots, scenes, cutaways.

"Trust me," he says. "The view is incomparable."

A gray suit opens my door. "Welcome, Madame. Welcome back, Monsieur Dominique."

"Bonjour, Étienne," he says.

We pass lines of uniformed staff, then glide through an arbor.

I brush my hand against its wall, deep green with white jasmine blooms, the scent so sweet, light, playful, I just about fall over. We pass through the hotel foyer and emerge onto a terrace. We are guided towards a small table floating out of the side of the mountain.

Whoa–the view drops away as far as the eye can see–rolling hills, then the sweep of the coastline, and wiggly forks of land jutting into the sea.

"Italy to the east." Dominique points with his hand. "The Esterel mountains in the west. Beyond that, Saint-Tropez."

I'd like to sink down and gawp. Or fling myself into this land.

"Behind us, lie the Alpes Maritimes–the foothills of the Alps that come all the way down to meet the sea."

Momentous crags reaching up to the heavens.

We take our seats. The waiter hovers behind his ear. "Veuve Clicquot," he says. "Two flutes."

I shake my head. "Espresso and water please."

"Allow me." He smiles. "Espresso, water, and champagne for the lady."

Whoa. He likes the driver's seat.

Again to the waiter, "If you would be so kind, some jasmine for our table."

The waiter bows. The champagne is presented. "Welcome to France." Dominique smiles and raises his flute towards me.

Is that Beyoncé at the corner table, the Queen herself? Perspiration bubbles at the back of my neck. This, I celebrate. I reach for my glass. "Just for today. I've got work to do. So, tell me something about you."

"What would you like to know?"

"Outside work . . . what do you do to relax?"

He colors. "I'm a private person, actually."

Smooth, calm, private. I was clumsy.

"We're very enthusiastic about the documentary," he says.

"Me too."

They bring a platter of hors d'oeuvres.

I shake my head. "I'm gluten free."

"In France?" He laughs.

Everyone in their right mind is gluten free.

The waiter returns with olives, anchovies, Marcona almonds.

"So, you're British?"

"Sort of. Born in London, moved to the US when I was ten."

"What took you to America?"

"My dad's work."

"Really? What kind of work did he do?"

None of his damned business. "Can we not talk about that?"

He looks intently at me, like he knows it's a sensitive spot, which is the last thing I want him to know. I look at the stone flagging of the terrace.

We were better off before we moved. Dad had a market stall. Mum did the books for my dad, kept a firm hand on all of us while he grew his business. Then Dad got a shop, then a string of shops that he sold and made a truckload of money from. He hit the big time. That's when the trouble began. He got ideas about making a bazillion dollars, and he got weird. We moved to New Jersey. He wanted to belong in a world where we didn't belong. Money corrupts. The more you have, the worse it is.

"You must allow me to show you the pleasures of French dining."

I must work.

Silence.

"We'll tell you everything. We're very excited about this. Very excited to work with you. Entirely at your disposal."

"Dominique, a story is a journey . . . an offroad adventure," I say.

His face tenses. "Grasse lies in the foothills of the Alpes Maritimes. I'd be delighted to take you hiking. We have breathtaking views." He pauses. "You dance?"

I laugh. "I run, I box, I *definitely* do not dance." I crunch on an almond. "You're up for this movie?" I tease. The champagne has bubbled its way through my veins. There's no way back now.

"We are thrilled and honored."

"Journalists have a terrible reputation, you know."

"All publicity is good publicity." He smiles.

"You don't think I'm going to uncover dark secrets about the house of Severin?"

"I think . . . you will fall in love . . . with Severin, with perfume, with France." The broad smile reveals beautiful, even teeth.

Finally, a sense of humor. I laugh.

I look out to the Mediterranean, glinting across the whole horizon. What's come over me? I shouldn't like this. I should be doing something real and important–*Climate*. No more champagne. "Feeling a bit woozy here." I smile. "Jet lag and champagne. Quite a mixture." I check my watch. It's 6:00 a.m. in NYC. I've been up all night, crammed in a middle seat between the pudgy, sweet Indian lady who wanted to feed me samosas, and a giant who slept for eight hours with his mouth open.

"I need to get to my hotel," I say.

"We go. I promised this would be quick."

I gulp my espresso.

"I've taken the liberty of renting you a flat."

"CNM has booked the Hotel Virginie in Grasse." I down the glass of water.

He shakes his head. "*Non, non.* You'll love the flat, in a beautiful medieval village close to the office. It's out of the traffic loop, very *charmant.* I know you'll like it," he says.

No way. "At the hotel I can be independent, and so can you. You'll drive me to my hotel?"

He purses his lips. "Of course."

My head is spinning. I've got to get back on my own turf. "*Fantastique.*" I smile.

Back in the sports car, navigating a bendy road towards Grasse,

I watch him from the corner of my eye. I hadn't imagined someone my age. Not running a business like this. Not James Bond in aviator sunglasses. We navigate a string of mini-roundabouts to arrive at the Hotel Virginie, which is not in Grasse but in a hightech park called Sophia Antipolis.

The foyer, pleasantly airconditioned, doubles as a bar and vibrates to the deafening beat of Justin Timberlake's "Can't Stop the Feeling."

My heart sinks.

"This is good?" His face is impassive.

"It's a zoo." Do I just stay here to show him he can't control me? It's important I establish my editorial independence . . . show him that he's the subject, I'm the storyteller.

But a coachload of beefy men in Hawaiian shirts are goofing around, slapping each other on the back and yelling at the tops of their voices–I can't work here.

"We go to the flat?"

"It's your flat," I say. "I don't want any complications."

"I can bill CNM, no problem."

"Promise?"

"*Absolument.*"

"Okay." I agree because I'm woozy with jet lag and champagne.

He drives me over and sees me inside.

"I send a car. We meet at 9:00 a.m. tomorrow at our office?" He shakes my hand before leaving.

I unzip my duffel and fish out my somewhat wonky, ever-faithful Paddington, companion-in-arms of twenty years. He must have been claustrophobic in there all that time. I settle him atop the sea-blue dresser.

I roll out my yoga mat in front of him. Exercising with alcohol inside me is *no bueno*, but I need this. I perform a modified routine: burpees, pushups, and squats, three sets of ten each.

Afterwards, I feel more grounded. I find the bathroom, strip down, and stand under a cold shower. Finally, I'm cool, clean, and myself for the first time today. I wrap myself in a bath towel and pad about.

The tile is cool underfoot. Everything is sparse, elemental, sensual in the sherbet colors of Provence. Each object speaks its purpose in the plain talk of a Van Gogh. The bed has a pistachio-green linen cover, which is calming, even if I don't want to be here. Totally don't want to be here.

I drape my leather bomber jacket and pleated wool pants on hangers in the wooden cupboard. It smells of cedar. Yum. Next to them, the three white shirts. I'll wash a shirt and a set of underwear every night and hang them to dry in the bathroom. I place my three sets of underwear on the open shelves, together with two sets of workout gear. I set my trail running shoes underneath.

I like a uniform. It helps me feel professional and focused. And we need to stop buying so many clothes; the fashion industry is responsible for more annual carbon emissions than all international flights and maritime shipping combined.

I think about Dominique Severin with his neat white jeans. Probably has some family retainer doting on him, pressing his clothes. The vibe is "I'm in control." And the Alfa Romeo–talk about cliché! Plus, all men are untrustworthy. Even the hip ones that look like Luke.

I sit on the bed, flip open my laptop, and fire up a new Word doc. I name it "Brainstorm." I begin with a bullet list:

- shape
- storyline
- random ideas

- things I like
- things I don't like
- commercial brands
- couture brands (Dior, etc.)
- signature brands (JLo)
- artisan brands
- people
- story
- heart

Those are my headings. So far I have nothing to fill in. I close the document and open Outlook. I email Greta, telling her the footage is great. "I'm working on scheduling, and I'll be back in touch as soon as possible," I write.

Not true. I'm drinking champagne and driving around in a sports car. How's that for the planet? I google "France and climate change."

I read about the 2019 heat wave that saw record temperatures of 45.9 C (114.6 F). Data showed that the trend of rising temperatures and flooding was set to continue. I'm excited to see that a Paris court had convicted the French state for "failure to address climate crisis," as reported in *The Guardian* on February 3, 2021. A "historic ruling," according to Greenpeace France. Yay! At least some Frenchies are paying attention.

Fatigue wraps me in its heavy blanket. My eyelids droop shut. Open, shut . . . open, shut. My world has been spinning for five days. Now it's stopped. There's nothing but silence and a raw, jiggery sensation in my chest. I shut my laptop and push it aside as I sink backwards. I clamber under the thin duvet and pull it over me, laying my head on the pillow.

I've never liked nights alone in a new place, even though I've been on the road a lot, all over the US. Making docs like

BeeKeeping, I'd call Luke from Motel 6 rooms for chat, encouragement, and phone sex.

I want to call Luke . . . but I don't want Luke . . . and nor do I want this empty hole where he used to be.

I reach for my laptop and email this Dominique guy, tell him I won't be there tomorrow morning. I need a couple of days to meet my crew, figure out equipment, brainstorm locations, and do a recce tour. I need to show him that I'm Director of this doc.

He's not the boss. I am.

Chapter Six

DOMINIQUE

Tuesday, May 4, 7:00 a.m.

Jacqueline Lacroix, our Nose, approaches the Café La Régence, heels clattering on the paving tiles. She's wearing a sleeveless sheath dress with a silk cardigan draped over her shoulders.

She bends to kiss me on both cheeks.

Ah, jasmine. The chief creator of our scents is wearing our Evening Star. It's been our bestseller since 1950, but our revenues have collapsed because younger women aren't buying it.

She takes a seat beside me at the round table.

"Shelve everything you're working on," I say. "I need you to reinvent Evening Star."

She places her handbag on an adjacent seat. "You're not serious?"

"The plan is to use the movie to drive up sales–hard." A cat slinks under our table.

Our waiter, Pierre, turns her glass right side up. He serves water and coffee.

"What do you mean reinvent?" says Jacqueline. "What scope are we talking about?"

"Our image isn't young enough. We need something for the twenty-five to thirty-five-year-old category."

She takes a sip of water, then coffee, imprinting the white rim of the china cup with scarlet lipstick.

Pierre places a basket of croissants wrapped in a white napkin at the center of the table. They've been out of the oven less than an hour.

"You don't dismantle an icon," says Jacqueline.

"You reimagine it."

"Tinkering with the formula is risky." She quirks an eyebrow at me. "What's going on? Risk isn't you." She breaks off a piece of croissant with her fingers and spreads a ream of butter on it. She's all woman. One that eats. Not an American wraith who nibbles on lettuce.

"You prefer to go under?" Does she judge me, as I know Grandpapa does from his grave? "We need something big. We need it fast." The shame of it.

She's thirty years older than me, a mother figure whom I needed when mine was falling apart, and she's a bridge to that old world of Severin.

"My father would turn in his grave." Her father, Antoine Lacroix, was the most revered Nose of the twentieth century. He created Evening Star for my late Grandpapa.

"We remain close to our roots and traditions. You add a note, subtract another. I want a masterpiece for the contemporary woman. No more Duchess of Windsor at her dressing table. Imagine Evening Star for the twenty-first century."

"A rebranding?"

"Burberry reinvented themselves–fusty Burberry! Severin Frères can too," I say.

She raises her eyebrows. "Evening Star took seven years, Voyage, three. Eclat! was . . . You know this can't be rushed," she says.

"Pull in anyone . . . the whole team . . . set up a war room."

"I need time to feel it in my imagination. Then I need to work in the lab."

"This documentary is our last chance to save the business."

"But you want the moon, *mon cher*. The time isn't enough."

"You can do it . . . and I need it to be perfect."

She presses a napkin to the corners of her mouth, leaving her mark of crimson on it. "A September launch gives me mere days to create. I can't hurry integrity. I won't. It's everything we stand for."

I clench my leg muscles.

She runs her finger across a heartshaped locket hanging from a gold chain around her neck. "This isn't a good time for me."

It houses a photo of Linda. Her daughter whom she lost to leukemia, aged thirty. Gosh, I've got goosebumps on my arms. Last weekend was the anniversary of Linda's death.

She bows her head. "You can't ask me now, Dominique."

I clench my fists. "I have to . . ." Even if it pains me.

Her eyes have the look of a wounded animal.

"I'm so sorry. I should have remembered."

"And you look like a truck landed on you," says Jacqueline. "He arrived in an oversized T-shirt with a beer belly?"

"It's a woman. She arrived yesterday . . ."

"What's she like?"

"She's kitted out in 1940s airman clothes . . . looks like she's walked off the set of a World War II movie."

"Eccentric?"

"Haughty. Why are you smiling?"

"She's a filly!"

"She asks if I think she might uncover dark secrets about Severin."

"She was teasing?" asks Jacqueline.

"God only knows. D'you remember when we had that awful creep from *Nice-Matin* hanging out at the corner day and night? I can still smell the onions on his breath as he rapped on the door, offering to buy me an ice cream."

"Difficult days," says Jacqueline. "You were so young."

We shuttered up the house and hid from the disgrace. Those ghastly articles about Maman.

"My dear, that's all in the past. Thank goodness you wrested control."

"I couldn't have done it without you." I rely on her. I trust her.

"I'm intrigued as to what story she'll make about us," says Jacqueline.

"She'll make exactly what we tell her to."

Jacqueline smiles and pats me on the shoulder.

"We'll be running this like the Élysée Press Office."

"I'll take her out . . ." says Jacqueline.

"*Pas du tout. Non.*" Where were we? It's the anniversary of Linda's death. Jaqueline is refusing on every possible count. Do I just order her to do this work?

Time is running out.

"Excuse me a moment." I get up and enter the cool darkness of the bar where a few old boys are perched on bar stools, nursing their pastis and watching soccer on the TV.

I squeeze myself into the WC, overpowered by the odor of drains. There's barely enough height or width in here to stand. I can't press Jacqueline now. She's in too fragile a state.

But I'm the boss, damn it. I employ my Nose to do my bidding. I soap and rinse my hands and shake off the water.

Returning outside, I see her outline through the darkness of the bar, this curvy woman who has been like a mother to me. God knows I can't afford another go-round like Friday, when Camille handed in her notice.

I must give her a little time to think. At the table, I summon Pierre and hand him my credit card. I'll ask her again over a glass of wine. I know her better self would want this of me. I sign the chit. I'll give her time, but I'll have my way.

Chapter Seven

ZANDY

On Wednesday, I pitch up at the glassfronted offices of Severin Frères at 9:00 a.m., rested and refreshed. Dominique Severin greets me in the huge white foyer, all business in a navy suit with brown suede Gucci loafers. A touch intimidating how handsome he is–in spite of being short.

I'm ready to set up my interviews and get cracking with this doc. In and out fast. The place is wonderfully bright. We take the sleek steel elevator upstairs, flanked by a neat young woman in a tight skirt suit who introduces herself as the PR director.

"Please, do sit down." She gestures towards the huge conference table in the board room.

She hands me her card: Ruth Carro, PR Director, Severin Frères & Cie. "I'm entirely at your disposal."

Dominique sits next to me, turning his chair to half face me–character and interest in that face with the prominent Roman nose.

Ruth slides a glossy PR packet towards me and smiles.

I push the folder a few inches to my right. "How about I give you a list of people I'd like to talk with? You'll help me set up interviews, Ruth?"

"Do you know, Madame, we trace our origin all the way back

to the artisanal roots of perfume in the 1500s?" She's across the conference table, clicker in hand, projecting a power point onto a dropdown screen at the far end of the room. "Our leather tanners were using foul-smelling ingredients to soften their leather . . ." She clicks to her next slide.

I'm going to need more than official PR. "I'd like to speak to journalists who have a feel for the issues in the region."

"Really?" asks Dominique.

"And your competitors."

"Why so? This documentary is about Severin," says Dominique. He nods at her.

She continues. "Catherine de Medici disliked the smell of tanned glove leather on her hands. She saw the potential of the area's mild weather and fine soil to grow jasmine and roses. And Grasse started making perfume to make scented gloves."

They don't seem to understand how I work.

"The glove makers split from the tanners," she says, "so when perfume became *à la mode* in the eighteenth century, they were poised for success."

"Ruth, I start broad. I interview as many people as I can. People who have different experiences and views, and I noodle my way to a storyline by running interviews."

"Interviewing competitors seems not right," says Dominique. "This is a film about Severin."

Ruth places her clicker down on the table. "You will be highly interested to know some of the iconic persons who have enjoyed our world-famous perfumes. Princess Grace of Monaco, a very beautiful and important woman, wore our famous Evening Star. Brigitte Bardot and Carla Bruni, wife of the French President–"

"I'm looking for something new, that the public doesn't already know."

They look stunned.

Maybe they need me to be more specific. "How about I start

by interviewing your mother, Dominique, Madame Catherine?"

They exchange nervous looks, eyes darting back and forth. "My mother unfortunately . . . is indisposed. She's an older lady, very frail." He crosses his arms.

"I believe she was CEO right before you."

"She is a marvelous lady," says Ruth.

"You worked with her?"

She colors. "I can be here because Madame Catherine Severin funded my education," she says.

"Public relations?"

"I'm the first person in my family to go to university." She casts a look at Dominique to check if she can go on. "I used to help with parties at the big house."

I'm intrigued. The cuttings tell me Catherine was a strong leader. Is Dominique a chip off the old block, or has he trained himself to be the opposite of her?

That white shirt and silk cravat thing Ruth wears shows how buttoned up she is, but those red butterfly-shaped glasses say she's got oomph, something a bit counterculture. "Great glasses!" I say.

"*Merci bien.*" On her inner wrist floats a tattoo of two tiny butterflies.

I point at it. "Sweet."

She blushes. "I made it the day I graduated."

"Ruth, this is great. I want to know what the business means to the town, how it shapes the lives of its people."

"My mother and my grandmother and all five of her sisters worked in the fields picking the early morning blossoms that are at the heart of Severin excellence. We've had a woman working for Severin as far back as we remember."

Finally, we're getting somewhere.

"Severin is as essential to Grasse as bread is to France. May we discuss our three hundredth anniversary of Severin Frères on 7th September this year? This will be a very grand and beautiful party."

"Stories are always about people. You're part of this community, so you're part of the Severin story."

"I'm merely the PR director. Now we must talk about the business." She flips open her binder of Severin press clippings, *Le Monde, Corriere della Sera, The New York Times, The Times*. "In France, we do things methodically. Our Palace of Versailles took forty years and thirty-five thousand people to build it. My father bakes the bread according to a three hundred-year-old tradition. I, too, must follow my recipe. Perception is reality to consumers, employees, and investors. It's a critical part of the business. We must stay on message . . ."

What the heck? "If your mother isn't well enough, can I meet Jacqueline, the Nose, today?"

"Jacqueline is extremely busy," he says. "Today is out of the question."

"Madame, I would like to present you our iconic scents." Ruth reaches into the middle of the table, where glass bottles sit on a silk-lined tray. Each has its own intricate shape and color. Each bears a name, Evening Star, Eclat!, Voyage . . . She picks Evening Star, opens the glass stopper, and hands me the bottle.

A waft of who-knows-what overpowers me. Now I'm back in my mother's room with the array of scent bottles on her dressing table. When I was small, my mum smelled of sweat and coal tar soap. She was about hard work and plain dealing. When we moved to New Jersey, Mum turned into a hollow-eyed shell, leaving a trail of sickly floral scent that reeked of social anxiety. Later we lived in Southampton where Mum would fly out to ladies' lunches. Suddenly it was Pilates, designer clothing, and hosting charity dinners. She was no longer steady in a crisis but high-pitched and nervous–everything drawn too tight, like the strings on her tennis racquet.

"No, thank you." I thrust the bottle back at Ruth. "I don't wear perfume." No perfume. Soap does the job.

"We'll work together," Dominique says. "I am absolutely available to you."

Nope. I'm not going to be mollycoddled like this. I'm not going to be fed his PR story.

"I'll be your guide. There's so much I look forward to showing you," he says. "It will be my pleasure to take you around personally. I'm available at any hour."

Houston, we have a problem. It wasn't just jet lag and champagne–my instincts were right. Handsome physique, but he intends to control this story.

I reach into my bag for a pack of Juicy Fruit. I unravel the teeny red string. I remove a stick, open the foil. Do I spell it out here and now–I tell this story, not him? Or do I show him by setting up my own interviews?

I can't afford to alienate him. I need his inside knowledge and access.

Foil is bad for the planet. I slide a fresh stick of gum into my mouth. *Chomp, chomp*. This fluff will not win me *Climate* because no one will air it. Four months to make this doc is crazy tight. I can't waste time.

I reach under the table to retrieve my bag. I sling the strap over to my left shoulder.

"Thank you. I need those interviews to do my work. Now, I'll head down to pick up my rental vehicle."

He and Ruth stand. "Is that necessary? I can drive you around," he says.

"No thanks. I'm going to Nice to meet my crew." I'll do this my way, not his. "We need to recce locations."

He thrusts his card at me. "This is my private mobile number."

This is my story.

"Call me anytime."

"Of course." I slide his card into my bag.

"Anytime, you understand?"

"Absolutely." Outside the office, I hail a cab.

This is day three.

It's perfume.

Can it be this hard already?

I had my eye on a moped to get around, ideally a Vespa Elettrica. There are far fewer carbon emissions in the making of the Vespa than in making a car. Plus, it doesn't create greenhouse gases or pollution because it's not powered by gas. But CNM insisted I rent a car. Some business about their insurance, in case I get knocked down.

I need a sense of this place, so I roam around for a couple of days, gathering facts and trying to embed myself in this culture, this way of life. I dig, I follow leads looking for interesting characters and story lines. The gems of a story are usually buried deep out of sight.

Eventually I cool off from sodding Monsieur Severin. I drive over to Grasse and at 6:30 p.m., I'm standing on the doorstep of his *Nez,* his Nose, unsure about what to say to get in her door. I cock my head. "I came to say hi."

You can just about smell the pheromones pouring off Jacqueline Lacroix–her voluptuousness knocks me for six. She's curvy, womanly . . .

"At this time on a Friday night?" She runs a hand through her thick blonde hair, cut to the shoulder. She's bloody Catherine Deneuve.

I need an interview. I'm on the hunt for what I say about perfume in this documentary. "You're the beating heart of perfume. The Nose is everything." Crass, but it comes out of my mouth. "I thought at home, we could have a more relaxed conversation."

"Or you get away without Dominique Severin knowing you're here?" She quirks an eyebrow.

All the Noses I've researched online are effete men, wearing makeup and velvet jackets–androgynous creatures living in an impeccable world of fine taste, food, clothes, and travel. Or white-coated matrons, Margaret Thatcher style.

Not this bombshell with smiling almond-shaped eyes and impeccable teeth.

"Dominique told me not to talk to you." She cocks her head. "And you know it!"

"I can't make this movie without you. Could I come in for just a few moments?"

She looks me up and down. "I wanted to relax in a hot bath but it's the Gare du Nord here tonight. Dominique is in my conservatory."

My heart plummets. "Excellent. He needs to know I mean business."

"You're very naughty, which . . . I happen to like." She takes a step back and ushers me in with a flourish of her hand.

Along the dark-green passageway towards the back of the house, I say, "How do you start? Walk me through your steps."

"My dear, I have two thousand bottles of absolutes in little drawers. I divide them into nine groups: Flowery, fruity, woody, herbaceous, spicy, soft, animal-like, marine, and mineral."

"How do you keep track of them?"

"I developed a system to find my way through my memory of scents."

She stops. "Look here." She points to an engraving of a woman on the bookshelf. "Tapputi of Mesopotamia, the world's first *parfumeur,* a woman."

At the back of the house, we come into a hexagonal, glass-walled conservatory.

Dominique sits at the table in the center. Looking up, seeing me, a dark look comes over his face. He clenches his fists.

He's frightening me. I stand taller, pretending poise. "*Bonsoir*, good evening, Dominique."

"*Bonsoir*, Zandy. I said Jacqueline is busy."

"She was too persuasive." Jacqueline beams. "Let Zandy visit for ten minutes." She gets a wine glass from the sideboard and shoots him a look.

"We'll have one glass of wine, then we get back to business."

I'm going to tough this out. I take a seat on her side of the table.

"I'm telling Zandy that smell is a complex chain of events." Jacqueline pours me a glass from the bottle on the table. "Our limbic system picks up odors reminding us of people, places, things that happened . . ."

Bless you, Jacqueline. Between us, on a plate, black olives sit in a puddle of oil with a sprig of rosemary.

"Even as a child, I loved tastes and smells," she says. "I had no toys. I was fascinated with flowers."

I prompt her with questions, while I feel him busting to leap out of his seat, shut her down.

"Fragrance is like music. I create small chords and put them together to make a bigger composition. If the chord is incorrect, the fragrance will not be balanced." She's on a roll. Her hand movements are large, round, gracious. "There can be similar ingredients in twenty different fragrances, but they won't smell alike. Maybe the proportions are different or the quality of the raw materials. I took my degree in analytical chemistry before starting as a lab assistant to my late father."

"A great *parfumeur* who created our world-famous Evening Star," says Dominique in a small voice. "Antoine Lacroix, who was perhaps the greatest Nose of the twentieth century. Present company excepted."

"Your father worked for Dominique's grandfather? He was his Nose?" I ask Jacqueline.

"Yes, Antoine worked with my late grandfather," says Dominique. "Now, there was a character."

"And now you two work together?"

"*Et voilà*! Yes, it's fabulous," she says.

We sit in a sea of plants overflowing from pots, the scent of flowers, framed photographs, botanical engravings, sketchbooks. It's a place that makes me want to lounge and luxuriate.

"Now, tell me about you," she says.

Dominique grips his chair.

"Me?" My cheeks burn.

"I give you my story, you give me yours."

I wish he'd leave, then I'd open up with her.

"Why documentaries?"

I know she won't let me off the hook. I'm both enchanted by her verve and nervous about revealing myself. Here goes.

"Erm . . . I got an innocent man released from jail because of pieces I wrote for my college newspaper."

She claps her hands. "Bravo."

"Righting injustice with my laptop . . . I was on fire. There was no way back." The truth. But not, of course, the whole story.

"Passion is everything." Her eyes gleam.

I turn to Dominique. "Stories matter." This isn't an advertising game. "The truth matters."

He opens his mouth to reply. His phone rings. He glances at it on the table. "Excuse me." He rises and heads towards the door out to the garden. "It's Camille. I need to take this."

"Composing a scent is to imagine a more beautiful world, to create more harmony," says Jacqueline, "and perhaps a new truth."

Woo hoo. I'm getting a whiff of the story I might tell.

"He's a good egg. He'll come around." She reaches for a cigarette and lights it.

"You smoke? Don't you have to protect your senses?"

She blows out the smoke and laughs. "I only take a few puffs. My little pacifier, for pressure. Where is your lover, *chérie*?"

Heat flames up the back of my neck. Yet, I'm not foolish enough to think she'll continue talking to me if I don't give as good as I get. I shrug. "Single." I dribble out my pathetic story about Luke.

She stubs out her cigarette. "Beautiful young woman like you with no lover–a waste."

I writhe on my seat. "I'm fine, really . . ."

"*Au contraire.* We have to do something about that. For me, weekends are for love. Friday nights, I usually take the little plane to Roma."

"Rome?"

"For my lover . . ."

I wish I had her ease. She's flamboyant but doesn't take herself too seriously.

"Who is he?"

"He lives in Roma. It's perfect, don't you think, to work in one place and to love in another . . . in the greatest city in the world?"

"Are you lonely sometimes?"

"Of course. But I need to experience every facet of life. Anticipation of coming together, the regret at parting. It's exciting. It's moving. I need to feel moved."

She's fabulous, this Jacqueline, so engaged.

"You want to know me because I have the perfect life." A throaty laugh as she tosses back her head. "I have to use my imagination, to have fantasies, to feel instinctively. If I am not passionate, the fragrance will not be interesting."

I get a wave of her scent as she gesticulates with her hands. Is that jasmine? "Go on."

"When I travel to Roma, when I experience art or love, when I travel through Botswana, Andalucía, or Herzegovina, I'm working because I'm expanding my imagination, experiencing our world and what it is to be human."

I've got to use who she is, and how she creates a perfume, in my storyline. If only Mr. Fancy Pants would allow me. He opens the conservatory door and returns.

He stands over me. "Your ten minutes are up." He's treating me like a child.

I stand. "I have a documentary to deliver on time and on budget."

"Jacqueline and I have urgent work to do."

I want to stamp my foot. This is gridlock.

"You put Jacqueline in a difficult position tonight. If you want to talk with my staff, you ask me first."

I scowl at him and tramp down the passageway towards the front door.

Jacqueline follows inches behind me. "My dear, everything is about love. Unless you make love to this man, you won't get the story you want."

"You must be joking."

"There is no person, no company in the world that understands perfume the way a Severin does. You need him on your side."

I stop dead in her corridor–hung with watercolors, hats, overcoats, and old walking sticks. "He's impossible."

"*Non, non.* Be a woman. Be clever. You hold all the cards if you want to."

Do I take her advice by spending time with him, letting him lead me through his PR frippery, letting him chaperone me, trying to enter the story his way?

"Come, *chérie.* You want to make this film or you wouldn't have come all the way."

She thinks I want to spend my time on perfume? It's utterly beneath me.

"He wants it too."

Huh. I'd like him to see me talking to his competitors, to union leaders and political journalists. That would give him a fright, and I might find out what he's so secretive about.

"Work your feminine charms on him. All men are susceptible to flattery. Women, too, or I wouldn't have invited you in," she says. "Be softer, get him on your side," says Jacqueline. "You'll find a way." She smiles before closing the door. "And then you'll get just what you want."

Chapter Eight

DOMINIQUE

Jacqueline sees her out, but Zandy's presence hangs on in the conservatory–like the sound of gunshot on a crisp day in the woods.

When Jacqueline returns, she's got a vase of water in one hand and the flowers I brought in the other. "If you two keep fighting, you won't have a documentary."

"I don't want her digging here, digging there." I can still pick up Zandy's smell . . . pepper and cucumber.

"She's just a filly," says Jacqueline, placing the container in the center of the table.

"Next thing, our formulas will turn up in Malaysia."

One by one, she arranges the blooms in the vase. "Let her work off steam."

"You know why I'm here. I can't leave until I've persuaded you to reinvent Evening Star." I watch her artistry, admiring how she turns the vase this way and that to find the presentation that most pleases her.

"We've never had a reason before to take a risk like this–but with the documentary we do. We need younger buyers. Without them we can't survive." She's not making this easy. "Don't you think you should obey your boss?"

She throws her head back and laughs. "I'm twice your age."

"You're impossible . . . Jacqueline Lacroix."

It came to me in the shower this morning, that Linda's death is the challenge but also the opportunity. I need to work towards it slowly. Not frighten her off. "Jacqueline, who are the women you admire, women who are changing the world?"

She takes a seat just to my right.

I sip my *Côtes de Provence.*

"So many wonderful women–Malala, Greta Thunberg, Noor Haddad . . . "

I narrow my eyes. "Haddad?"

"The Jordanian woman in microfinance. She helps Middle Eastern women start their own businesses."

"Right. Her brother was at Harvard with me in the family business program."

"She's marrying Prince Karam in the autumn. Big splashy wedding. It's all over Instagram."

"She's raised millions in grants for the ultra-poor to start their own businesses."

"It's admirable . . . and Linda, your Linda, was admirable." A photo of Linda in a silver frame sits on the table. She's in dressage gear, wearing a hard hat, navy jacket and white jodhpurs, leaping a huge fence on her Hanoverian. I reach for the photo, place it between us. I run my index finger around the frame.

"Recreate Evening Star as a homage to Linda . . ."

She plucks a lilac from the vase and inhales. Behind the bridge of her nose, millions of sensors receive its molecules, which bind to nerve hairs on the cells. The cells send messages about the odor to the limbic system, which transports her to a memory. She's thinking of Linda.

She locks eyes on me.

"Is that too painful?"

She shakes her head. "I don't want her memory to fade. Even hurting means I feel her in my heart again."

"Bring me Evening Star as Linda would have worn it. You owe it to her memory, to who she would have been in the world. It'll be your best perfume, because you will be truly inspired."

She crosses her hands over her heart.

"How old would she be today?"

She bows her head. "Thirty."

I nod. "A woman stepping into her prime." I lean towards her. "Immerse yourself. Give it fourteen days, fourteen long days. See what you come up with." I sip the *rosé*. It's lovely. I must ask her where she bought it.

She returns the lilac to the vase. "If I'm in the lab day and night . . . what will you be doing with Zandy?"

"Not her again."

"Relax. Let her develop her story."

I grind my teeth. Camille threatening to walk out, Annabella and her tantrums. Now this Zandy.

"I like her idealism, her determination. Anyway, you're as stubborn as she is," says Jacqueline.

"*Pas croyable*. Why are you fighting her corner?" I look out into the garden beyond the conservatory–the grouping of chairs under the tree–the way of life that is in my blood.

"Not hers, ours." She pushes back her chair and stands. "Mount an *opération seduction* on this Zandy. You'll have her eating out of your hand."

She can't be serious. I twiddle the stem of my wine glass.

"Imagine you're enchanted by her. You want her. Whatever it takes, you're going to have her."

I stand. "You're telling me to woo her?"

"You don't know how to do that?"

"This . . . creature in her 1940s airman's getup?" The idea is preposterous.

Jacqueline quirks an eyebrow at me.

Infuriating.

"Get under her skin. Show her what we're made of." She paces around, touching and aligning the mass of framed photographs on the side table. "You do that, and I'll try to reinvent Evening Star."

"An ultimatum?" I watch her, immobile.

Do I agree to 'woo' if, in return, Jacqueline will reinvent Evening Star? It's ridiculous. I don't want that Zandy coming close to my family. She's quite the opposite of gracious or elegant. We've invited her into our lives, and all she wants is to trample all over us.

On the other hand, if I agree, Jacqueline will do the work I need. And that will give us something marvelous to promote. This is my plan and what I need to achieve. Every morning these days, I have a waking dream that the factory and the office are engulfed in flames. I'm fighting to put out the fire, but it's useless. The blaze is too large. I watch, helpless, as everything is razed to the ground.

The charm offensive is . . . an extension of our craft. It's making something beautiful with artistry. It's what we do best in France.

I take a last sip of wine, allow it to slide cool and crisp down my throat. I feel the alcohol spread its warmth though my body, radiating outwards. And for a fleeting moment, I see the sheen on Zandy's chestnut hair, its delicate waves.

She wants me to play Romeo? She isn't saying pretend you're in love with her. Jacqueline is saying dazzle her with glamor, make something beautiful with artistry–just what Severin Frères has been doing for three hundred years.

Outside, the sun tries to linger a tad longer in the sky. But already the nightingales whistle and gurgle outside the conservatory. "You will tackle Evening Star?"

"You will work your charms on the filly?"

"I'll show her our jasmine fields. . . . She'll be enchanted."

"*Fabuleux*." She kisses me on both cheeks.

I choose the locations. I set the agenda. I control where she goes. Genius idea.

She sees me out. At the door, she says, "And have sex." She pinches my cheek. "Not with her. But how can you do your job if you don't relax sometimes?"

I raise my brows. "Thanks for the tip . . ."

"*Serieusement*, pull the bow too tight, it will snap."

I nod. I'll take a delicious walk across my beloved Grasse. Once I get home, I'll pump up my music and take myself through my favorite dance moves. I need to prepare for this adventure.

Chapter Nine

ZANDY

In New York, I fast until noon, which gives me energy and focus. But a cloud of yeasty smells overpowers me as I walk by the bakery, so I join the queue for a morning croissant on my way to the office. Bodies are rammed so close to me in this minuscule space that I feel their warmth, as my fellow villagers await their *pains au chocolat* and *baguettes.*

As Ruth's father, one of the two village bakers, reaches into his glass cabinet to serve me, I sense a jostling from behind. I turn to find Dominique smiling at me.

I inch away. What's he doing here?

Dominique raises two fingers.

The baker slides two croissants into a paper bag.

Ching-ching. He taps the cash register.

Dominique insists on paying. "Shall we?" He shepherds me out across the cobbled street, guiding me towards a stone bench outside the twelfth-century church.

We sit in a pool of sunlight and I breathe in the bright toasty aroma of the croissant, which sits atop its bag on my lap. "The village is enchanting," I say.

We bite into our croissants.

Mine melts on my tongue. I lick the buttery flakes from my

fingers. I'm calling this indulgence "research." Tonight, I must exercise. I'll roll out my mat and do a body-weight workout. Burpees, pushups, squats.

"How about we take a break this morning, and I show you the market?"

I still don't know what to do about this Dominique. I like Jacqueline. She intrigues me, but I'm irritated by her ridiculous challenge of last night.

I nod. "Fine." For the moment, I haven't got a better idea.

I scrunch up the paper bag and shove it into my pocket. I spot a yellow recycling bin behind the church. Good. That's where I'll put my plastics.

We stand and make our way into the main square. The Tourrettes market is coming alive, like New York waking up on a day in May, only softer, sweeter, slower. The scent of lilac and jasmine wafts through the air.

I let him take the lead as we meander through the stalls. Sunlight spills into every nook, old stone underfoot, a green canopy of tree leaves overhead; a day from heaven.

All about us, the square is a hive of activity. In every direction, sun-worn locals barter, gesticulate, laugh. "*Bonjour,* Marie," calls out one voice. "*Fous le camps,*" another. And "*Déplacez votre vehicule, s'il vous plaît.*"

Long trestle tables are laden with dark glass bottles of olive oil and open bowls of glazed tapenade. We're a mere twenty-five minutes from the glitz of the Riviera.

I pick up a glass honey jar, turning it in the sunlight to admire its amber translucence.

The stall holder, a youngish woman with a nose piercing, offers me a sample scoop on a mini plywood stick.

I take it in my hand, raise it to my mouth. Rich flavors of mountain flowers melt on my tongue.

We amble. My hands hang at my sides. It's beautiful here.

Sensual, real, earthy, almost mystical in its commitment to the traditions of past centuries and a slow way of life. Warm, nutty smells fill the air as we pass a man with deep lines on his tanned face, sliding *socca* pancakes in and out of his oven.

Dominique stops at the largest stall, which is shaded by a canvas awning. Jewelry, purses, and lightweight shoes are arrayed on white cloths covering long trestle tables. He shuffles in close to my side. "I want to apologize. We got off to a poor start. My fault."

A weightlessness flies through my chest. His apology has disarmed me–it's so out of character. I reach for a dun-colored Greek sandal and twirl it in the sunlight, encircling my index finger with the strip of leather. A silver buckle holds it together.

To my right, linen dresses in pale colors hang on portable rails, crammed alongside silk coverups and marginally edgy, lightweight, summery clothes.

"I have somewhere I'd like to take you," he says.

"For the story?"

"*Absolument.* But something private, something special."

I root my boots into the stone paving underfoot and drop my shoulders. "Work your feminine charms on him," said Jacqueline. "You'll get what you want." I run my fingers along the row of hanging garments, which are silky soft. Do I take Jacqueline's advice and enter the story his way, let him chaperone me and lead me through his PR frippery? I reach out and pick up a hanger. I raise it up and look at the lilac silk sheath it carries. The flyweight silk puffs and waves, billowing in the warm breeze.

Her suggestion was absurd. Men like me because I'm spunky, and I get things done. Not because I dollop on the eyeliner and prance around catlike. I'm no Brigitte Bardot, naked but for a man's shirt. I don't bat my eyelids and flick my hair around. I don't smile when I want something. I don't play games. Anyway, flirting and work don't mix.

I look away to my left towards the thudding of metal boules

landing on the sand court. A group of men are playing, smoking, talking, rapt in attention for the game.

Dominique makes small talk with the stall holder. Everyone here knows him.

I finger a jumpsuit in parachute-weight silk. Fast fashion is disastrous for the planet, but I'm stifling in these 1940s airman's wool trousers.

I slide my hand into my bag to reach for my credit card.

"Allow me." He presents his card.

"I can't possibly." This is business.

"No ties. I promise."

"You're sure?"

"And this." He grabs the lilac sheath dress I'd looked at. I have never worn a garment with spaghetti straps.

"A gift for a better working relationship?" He hands it to the stall holder.

She folds it in tissue, her fingers covered in knobbly silver rings. She reaches towards a pile of plastic bags.

"No bag, *non, merci.* Save the planet. One bag at a time?"

"*Oui, la planète,*" she says.

"Thank you," I say to Dominique and mean it.

"You accept my invitation? My place will interest you, I promise." Warmth and also a tender melancholy inhabit those chocolate-brown eyes. Eyes which draw me to their depth and make me curious about his sadness, his soft center. "Let's walk up the hill to my car."

I nod in agreement. It's time to be less confrontational with him. Alright, Jacqueline. I'm in.

We leave the market and begin to climb the hill up the narrow Rue St. Jean. He's a new man today, softer, easier to deal with. Jacqueline, did you lace his wine with a magic potion?

He rests his hand on the small of my back. Why is he touching me? My ears prick up. Is that a French thing or something else? I take a breath and decide it's gentlemanly and gracious. I allow it.

We pass the florist, the newsagent, and the post office. Everyone smiles, touches their cap, or calls out some greeting to him. I'm thinking if I let him talk, show him I'm open to his ideas, he'll start to relax and trust me. Once he trusts me, I'll explain why I need to spend time with Jacqueline and ask him to set up an interview with his mother.

He opens the passenger door of a teeny mustard-colored Smart car. What's this? One moment he's Debonair David, driving the Alfa Romeo, now this? "You changed your car?" I say.

His eyes dart to the right.

Whoa. Darting eyes.

"More practical," he mumbles, looking at the ground.

Look me in the eye, dammit. A shudder reverberates through me. Is he lying about the stupid car? "Really?"

"These back roads are too twisty," he says.

He drives them every day. What's changed? "The sports machine seems more your thing," I say.

"James Bond?" He lifts an eyebrow. "You can still call me James."

Alright, that was funny. He opens my door for me, and I climb in. He shuts my door, goes around to his side, and we both buckle up. We pull out of the lot, the little mustard tank juddering.

Maybe I overreacted. I'm still jet-lagged and out of my element. Maybe he wasn't lying. "Where to, James?" Gold star, Zandy.

How can I trust him if he's . . . Drop it, Zandy. Be. Here. Now. I focus on my breath, willing my heart rate to slow down. In . . . out . . . in . . . out. Just for today, I'll let him take the lead. We're making progress, and sports cars are crazy gas guzzlers. This Smart car is way better for the planet. I force a smile.

The Route de Grasse winds around the mountainside into the interior of the country. Hillsides are carpeted in flowers. Torrents of water cascade over rocky crags, under a blue, blue sky.

The light makes everything sharp and clear. Perched medieval villages with terracotta roofs heave into view.

"Did you always want to make documentaries?"

"Always. The truth matters. Especially in this fake news world."

He sighs. "Indeed."

The narrow road dives down a steep incline and curves through a picturesque village set in a gorge.

"The Pont du Loup was once a fashionable resort. Your Queen Victoria used to come here by train, on the Provence Railways line. So, you went to university in the States?" he says.

"Yes. SUNY, that's New York. Then I got my MFA in film arts from Brooklyn College. I worked my way through college. It took a long time, but it was worth it."

"Impressive."

"Thank you." He's different today. Jacqueline is an alchemist.

We pass an aqueduct picturesque enough for Wordsworth. "This bridge was blown up by the Germans in the war," he says.

"Interesting, and so beautiful."

"Isn't it? There are so many places I need to show you, like La Bastide Aux Violettes, the violet museum in Tourrettes."

"I want to see them all."

"And the olive mill. I want to show you how artisanship is at the heart of France. People think of luxury brands and mega yachts off the bay in Cannes. But it's about connection to place and tradition that is the real France. The *confiserie* in this village transforms the fruits and flowers of our region into confectionary using copper vats and traditional methods."

Phew. This is better. My heartbeat slows. My shoulders soften. The mood is easy now, and he must pick up that I've calmed myself because he says, "I think we understand each other better now. Am I correct?"

I smile and nod. Is this my moment to ask for access to Jacqueline? I take in a long breath and let it out slowly. "Our difficulties yesterday . . . it's my fault too. I can be . . . overeager."

"Not at all," he says.

"It's just I want to make a success of this."

"*Absolument*," he says.

"I shouldn't have turned up at Jacqueline's unannounced. I apologize."

"Thank you." He explains that she's working on a new scent in time for the documentary.

"Sounds interesting . . ."

"She needs her peace. We mustn't disturb her creativity," he says.

Take a breath. "I understand." Another breath. "I'll wait." For the moment, Jacqueline is a "no."

We arrive in front of a huge set of metal gates, closed with a padlock. "Is your mother better today?"

He stares ahead. "Unfortunately, no."

His face is taut.

And that's a lie. The grocer told me Dominique's mother came into his shop in the village yesterday. I grasp the edges of my seat, squeezing tight.

He presses the handbrake and turns off the ignition. "Wait for me a moment, would you mind?" He opens his door, climbs out, and walks around the front of the car.

The seat covers stink of that chemical they put in new cars. My heart thumps in my chest, *da boom, da boom, da boom,* its rhythmic beat fills the car's interior, clanging against all four sides.

Eighteen years ago, three members of the FBI had spent a long afternoon at our house–two burly ones and the short guy with albino hair. I was twelve. All afternoon, I sat at the top of the stairs while my heart thumped so hard, I thought it would fly out of my chest. When the front door clicked shut behind them, I bolted downstairs, out the back door, to tell them that Mike *had* been at our house on Sunday the twelfth. To tell them my father was lying and that he'd pressed me to lie about it too.

I ran around the house, the gravel crunching underfoot.

They were sitting in that red Toyota, the engine turning over. The albino one still had his front door open.

I got halfway to the car and stopped dead, my torso alight with volcanic matter. Mike and his daughter Rita *had* been at our house that Sunday, but Dad had begged me to lie about it. Should I or shouldn't I tell them? Should I, shouldn't I? In my throat a burning sensation. Tell them, tell them, tell them. But he was my dad. He was my dad.

I pressed my body against the cool stone of the house, hiding from view. Bile rose up and hit the back of my throat. I couldn't tell them. I was spineless. I knew nothing of insider trading laws. But I knew that my father had lied in a terrible way. The red Toyota pulled away.

For months after, I stared at police cars. Should I, shouldn't I? Should I, shouldn't I? Time after time, I didn't. The trial came around. Mike got ten years. My dad got off scot-free. I got the weight of my decision: the burden of my inaction and cowardice.

But I'm not back there. I'm sitting in this car, today, breathing. Slow down, Zandy. I close my left nostril with one finger and begin alternate nostril breathing to calm my nervous system. I inhale through my right nostril to the count of four. Do I call him on the lie?

Exhale through the left to the count of four. I mustn't break the fragile bond we've built today. I don't want to go back to square one, fighting him and hating this assignment.

But I can't make this doc if Dominique is lying. Hold to the count of four. Inhale to the right . . . exhale to the left. I have to trust him, or I'll never get this film made. Stewart wants to see my storyboard tomorrow. I will ask again to interview Maman another day. For now, I'll overcome my pique and let him lead the way.

Chapter Ten

DOMINIQUE

At the front of the car, I bend down and set aside three large signs saying *Chien Méchant*. In fact, we have no dogs here. I undo the padlock and swing open the gates.

Inside, the field stretches out before me. I raise my face towards the magnificent outline of the Alpes Maritimes soaring just beyond it.

This Zandy is like a difficult dog. My shoes stick and squelch in the mud as I shuffle toward the group of jasmine pickers working on the east side of the field. I'm embarrassed Zandy caught me fibbing about the car. We need cash for the new scent, so I sold the Alfa Romeo. We're scouring everywhere, selling anything we can–furniture, jewelry, old plant equipment. It's interesting she understands that I'd never choose a Smart car myself. It's got no beauty or engineering, no kind of coherence. It's about price, not excellence.

I trudge the furrows between the jasmine bushes, determined to maneuver her away from Jacqueline. How sneaky she was intruding on her like that, at home, in the evening. Does she have no breeding?

To design, produce, and market a new scent in three months is like climbing the Khumbu Icefall of Everest. I'm going to distract her by introducing her to our jasmine pickers. Decent, hardworking, wide-hipped women clustered in a group just over there.

I brush my hand along the low jasmine bushes, allowing myself to be wrapped in their scent, which is warm and sweet but never cloying. Jasmine has a sophistication that always intrigues and surprises me.

Each time Zandy mentions Maman, I see myself a small boy, trying to haul my mother, limp and hungover, out of bed in the morning. Each time she mentions her, I endure a battle to keep my equilibrium. Zandy must leave Jacqueline in peace and also Maman.

The women in patterned headscarves, cotton aprons, and rubber boots step forwards to greet me. I explain about the documentary and ask their permission to bring Zandy over and introduce her.

They nod, their weathered faces brown and lined.

I return to the car and maneuver the wretched bathtub to the corner just inside the gates, mud flying up in all directions. The thing jolts to a halt as though we're in a dodgem car collision.

I go around to Zandy's side and open her door for her.

She swings her legs over the door jamb and steps out. She's tense because I said no to those interviews. I've known her three days, and already I can read her.

She follows me along a furrow. I've got to guide her in a different direction, navigate her towards a different story.

We make our way over to the jasmine pickers. They bend at the waist, inspecting the blooms and plucking them one by one. "This jasmine, and you ladies, are at the heart of our business." They gather in a semicircle around us.

Zandy walks from one to the other, making eye contact and shaking the hands of all ten women. She stations herself beside Nathalie, holding herself erect. Any moment she could turn into a cat with claws again.

"This lies at the very heart of Severin Frères," says Nathalie. "It's one of the things that sets us apart." She raises her forearm to her brow and uses it to wipe away perspiration.

"Do show me." Zandy's voice is relaxed and rich. She extracts a moleskin notebook and pen from her crossbody bag.

"We begin at dawn." Nathalie's nails are thick and cracked with lines of mud under the tips.

"We handpick the blossoms until 1:00 p.m. The sun mustn't burn the fragile petals."

Zandy scribbles notes.

Coline steps forward. As she opens her mouth, we see a black hole where her front tooth is missing. "We separate the mature flowers from the green foliage and the stem."

Zandy's face is open now. She looks more relaxed. But what if she's playing a game? I have to stay on guard.

"We have to be precise, detaching the jasmine flower without damaging it." Nathalie's cornflower-blue eyes shine.

A smile plays around Zandy's mouth.

"The work is tiring."

"I see that." Creases appear at the sides of Zandy's eyes which also smile. Here and there she looks around the field and makes sketches and diagrams. Zandy tilts her face towards the sun, soaking in the warmth and the genius of the place.

"We must bend low to pick two kilos of petals per morning–about 16,000 flowers."

Zandy leans over and peers into the baskets into which the pickers have dropped their blooms.

"Gosh. And ladies only?"

"Women are considered more precise, less likely to damage the plants," says Nathalie.

"See how you like this." Nathalie squeezes a bloom between her fingers and hands it to her.

Zandy twirls it beneath her nostrils. "It carries you away." She inhales, seeming to savor it. She seems more at ease here. Who wouldn't be in this landscape? The beauty, the flowers, the sea air work their magic on all of us.

Thank goodness for Jacqueline. This is a good direction to lead her in.

"Floral and musky and green?" says Nathalie. "In some cases, Severin sources jasmine from Algeria, Egypt, and India, but for Evening Star, the *Jasminum grandiflorum* is grown right here."

Zandy gestures towards the corner where we entered. "Why the high walls and locked gates?"

"The climate here, the soil, the topography–like the *terroir* of a special wine, the combination is unique." I drop down and gather a clump of soil. I rub it between my fingers and invite Zandy to do the same. "Also, the balmy microclimate and the gentle sea breezes . . . We keep this private because our competitors would love to have this place."

I address the ladies. "Thank you, all. We mustn't disturb you any longer. With permission, I'd like to show Ms. Watson the processing plant." I point to the barn-like structure at the north end of the field.

Zandy starts up the furrow ahead of me, divots of mud sticking underfoot. That tension I've been holding onto since she mentioned Maman dissolves into the blue sky. There's a clarity about her like the light here in France–something unique. I watch her hips sway from side to side. I want to rest my hand on the jut of her hip. No. What am I thinking?

I swing open the huge wooden doors.

We enter and I close them, sliding the oversized bolt into its housing.

"We process the jasmine within ninety minutes of picking it." I explain that the Bastides who own this property and run the plant have worked for us for eight generations.

"Like 250 years?"

"Absolutely."

I reach into the shelving, pull out two folded paper gowns, and hand her one.

We shake them open and don them over our clothes.

We sit on the old wooden bench and cover our shoes so as not to contaminate the area. "We 'wash' the blooms three times with two thousand liters of hexane solvent in that vat." I point to the oversized cylinder in the far corner. "We line the flower petals on trays before immersing them in solvent. This is how their fragrance is transferred. If the mixture steeps for too long, nonfragrant molecules in the flowers could migrate to the solvent and disturb the signature jasmine scent, so it is critical to get the balance right."

"Next, we evaporate the solvent, and that gives us yellowish-brown waxy 'concrete,' which is used in some perfumes. Or we take it one step further by adding grain alcohol to the 'concrete.' We heat it and cool it to remove the color and wax. We evaporate the alcohol, and *voilà*, we have the pure 'jasmine absolute.' Come, we'll go upstairs." I indicate the iron spiral staircase to our right. I avert my eyes from her rump as she climbs ahead of me.

It intrigues me that there are facets of her which seem unknowable. She thunders around, in those woolen pants of hers. I can't get a read on her–as though she harbors cachets of gunpowder, explosions that might go off at any time.

Up high on the upper walkway, we lean over the iron railing and look down across the barn. "Quality is everything. It's critical that once we create a special fragrance, it never changes. So it's vital for us to retain the ongoing production of this famous Grasse jasmine, the *Jasminum grandiflorum*."

"I love that this has been going on for centuries–the same families living here, working the land," she says. "And you, did you always want to come into the business?"

"Of course. But maybe not so soon."

"What else would you have done?"

"I'd like to spend time in Japan with the Nakazato family. They are an unbroken line of family potters stretching back thirteen generations." Interesting how she drew that out of me. Annabella never asked. I miss your curves, Annabella, but not your marriage agenda.

"The Nakazato family is known as a National Living Treasure of Japan. I took over Severin earlier than I had wanted–when Maman became unwell." Even mentioning Maman makes me nervous. "Duty to my lineage is very important."

She seems wounded behind that brittle façade. I asked about her father on our first day at the Château Saint-Martin, and she shut me right down. I'm not proud of my own father, who fled Maman's problems, abandoning us for Paris.

"And what do you do for fun?" she asks.

I punch the air with a fist and twirl around. "I love to dance."

"No. I bet you work all the time."

I almost reach for her hand. I manage to restrain myself. "One day I'll take you dancing."

She shakes her head. "Good luck with that."

From nowhere, a bee swoops down and buzzes around her ear.

I reach out and swat it away.

She startles.

"I didn't want you to get bitten." I place a reassuring hand on her shoulder. The bone is firm and the flesh around it soft. She's beautiful. I didn't see that before. A ripple of excitement runs through me.

"Thank you."

She stands on her toes, leans over the railing, and waves to one of the workers downstairs. I love how respectful she was talking to the jasmine pickers. I see a different side of her now. What if I give her exclusive permission to film here? It's risky because the Chanels and Diors of this world would kill to have a jasmine source like ours. We've kept it secret for good reason.

But Zandy is our pathway out of total collapse. Camille says I must give, in order to get. I don't know what I'm going to do about Maman, but I'll play for time. This will distract her from digging into Maman for the moment. "No one has ever photographed or filmed here. I'd like to offer you an exclusive for the documentary."

She swivels towards me, beaming. "Marvelous."

Excitement spurts through me.

"This is real. I can work with this."

"This is what we do best in France–tradition, craftsmanship, the pursuit of excellence." Meanwhile, I need to make sure Jacqueline is on task. Our timing is razor tight. "Camille will arrange all this for you. You two will enjoy each other."

Chapter Eleven

ZANDY

I spend time visiting the big commercial perfumers, Fragrance, Riviera, etc., so I can see how different, how artisanal Severin Frères is in comparison. I contact journalists from local papers and TV stations, rooting around for story angles. I make connections in my lovely village with the butcher and the *pâtissier*. I roam its cobbled streets, and pop into the Mairie and the Café du Midi.

It's Wednesday when I meet Dominique's sister, Camille, in the office foyer at 7:00 a.m. I explain that I'll need time before filming the jasmine fields. I need to build my script and tee up the crew.

Camille tosses her head, unfazed. "So, let's head over to our library-archive in the west wing of the complex."

We enter through her grandfather's office, which she says they keep "in its original condition as a piece of history." We pass through a set of French doors into the adjacent library-archive. Camille opens the cupboards, which flank an entire wall. Inside, floor-to-ceiling shelves are packed tight with box files, organized in alternating lavender and rose-colored paper. Labeled by year, they begin in 1721, the year Severin began, and run through the current year, 2021.

"You can come here whenever you want and read up on our history. I think you'll enjoy the old newspaper cuttings and photos."

I run my hand over the cardboard folders–smooth but also grainy. "I can use the photos for my stills?" It's easy to talk with Camille.

"Of course. If the library is locked, Alain, our janitor, will open up for you."

She's not hiding things. She doesn't resist me. Quite the opposite.

Ten minutes in, after pacing up and down to calm myself, I risk explaining the difficulties I've had with Dominique–how he says no to my requests and seems on edge.

"My brother is nervous about Maman because of the drinking. Do you know about adult children of alcoholics? They're nervy. My brother has it worse than me."

Okay. That explains things.

She closes the cupboard doors, and we walk side by side back to the east side of the complex. As she shows me around the marketing department, she says, "You'll like Maman. Between her father, Grandpapa, and our father, who was never home, she had a rough time of it. But she's a good person."

She makes me an espresso from the machine in her office and sketches her early ideas for the new scent they're producing.

Now I'm getting excited. There's something live and real here. I ask if I can follow the creative process–be a fly on the wall as it unfolds.

"Come on, let's go to the lab." She dabs a paper napkin to the corners of her mouth and paints a swathe of vermilion lipstick across her lips.

As the lab door whirrs open, I finally feel hopeful we can figure this doc out. The jasmine fields were good. And this could be great. We step inside the vast white space with its high ceiling.

Dominique and Jacqueline perch on stools at the long workspace. They swivel to face us.

"The heart of the documentary will be our creative process." Camille holds herself erect, with hands akimbo looking like she owns the world. Her deep black eyebrows stand out against her pale skin. "Zandy can follow Jacqueline as she reinvents Evening Star. A fly-on-the-wall account."

Camille is fabulous.

Dominique rises and comes towards us. Under the white lab coat, an open-necked shirt and navy pants, composed and smooth.

I feel alive and alight and hopeful this morning. I love Camille. The jasmine fields were good, indicating the artisanship angle. I'll bet anything he noticed me as a woman, in the field yesterday. It was right there when he put his hand on my shoulder. Or are there perfume molecules wafting about this lab that are landing on the sensors in my nostrils, doing things to me that I'm not conscious of?

I see it now–after what Camille told me about him. He's protecting the wounded part of himself. That's why he's all buttoned up and why I have to tread gently. I understand him more now that Camille has told me his problems. So I have a tightrope to walk. I need to get this work done. But I do see I have to be a little less headstrong. Tricky, but this is the skill of my job.

"We think Zandy's story arcs from the special blooms at the jasmine fields, through the creative genius of Jacqueline, all the way to the design of the bottle." Camille flings her hands open.

Jacqueline removes her glasses as she walks towards us, nude court shoes squelching on the linoleum floor. "*Pas mal.* I like it."

"From tentative beginnings to masterpiece at The Fifth on Fifth," I say. "The evolution of a new perfume." *Voilà.* I've got my story. "I show Jacqueline as artist with a unique vision."

Dominique's mouth hangs open.

He's nervous, but I'll win him round. "A unique look into the heart of a legendary *parfumeur*." I pace about in a circle. "That's my emotional center."

"*Loooove* that." Jacqueline wears a red dress under her lab coat, her blonde hair coiled in a French pleat.

"What does that mean?" His voice is deep and sultry.

"You're not interested in thumbtacks, right?" I say.

He nods.

"I show you a man with arthritic hands who works into his eighties to support his autistic daughter. Are you interested now?"

He nods.

"Documentaries don't work on intellectualism. My audience needs a person to root for." I make my voice small and even to calm him. "When we get under Jacqueline's skin, the viewer will feel like they're creating their own perfume."

"But Jacqueline may have days when she's failing to find anything." His voice is musical and regal.

"Yes. I want to film her struggling. My subject is creativity. How she turns the mundane into beauty. Perfume is . . . alchemy. That's what this movie is about." I've got it!

"Yes, I see it." Jacqueline paces. "An adventure. I use this filming to keep me on deadline. Every day I must come up with something new to show Zandy."

"Sounds risky," he says.

What if I flirt a bit to help him relax? I cock my head. "No crew. Just this little thing." I reach into my bag and hop the handheld onto my shoulder.

I pivot to Jacqueline. "Walk me through your steps." I hit the red RECORD button. "How do you start?"

She looks at Dominique.

I'm surprised he doesn't stop me.

He shrugs.

She begins.

"Last night, I sat in Linda's room. I ran my hand across my daughter's clothes and the objects on her dressing table, absorbing the scents and textures of her life. I allowed myself to bathe in my memories of who she was."

My throat clutches. I don't want her to go here–and this is exactly what I want.

"Linda was headstrong, talented, capricious–like you."

I raise my eyebrows, "*Moi*?"

A laugh tumbles out of her. "Evening Star is elegant, sophisticated. It's about nobility and the patriarchy. It's perfect for the Duchess in her *château*, but too haughty for younger women. Last night, I imagined Linda maturing, softening the extreme parts of her nature. The idea of 'balance' came to me."

Keep going, Jacqueline. I don't move a muscle.

"Last night I gave myself the fantasy of what I will never see."

"How do you make that into a harmony of smells?"

"Come." She beckons us over to the long desk on the side of the lab.

At the desk, Dominique picks up a brass paperweight and clasps it in his palm.

Jacqueline flips open an oversized iPad and presses the home button. The LCD screen on the wall above her desk wakes up to reveal a scrabble of words, bubble maps, equations, symbols–almost like a painting.

A weight descends on the space, a tension.

I keep filming.

"I want a balance between work and pleasure, strength and vulnerability," she says. "Neither too masculine nor too feminine. Strong and vulnerable at the same time. This is Evening Star, reincarnated for Linda and Camille and you!"

"Me?"

"Indeed."

Camille steps forward. "For marketing I'm looking for

someone glamorous to be the face of our scent, its spokesperson . . ." she says. "Someone young women can rally around."

Dominique fingers his lapel. "The timing is tight, but it's worth a try."

"I'm going to work my contacts," says Camille. "If necessary, I'll have to crash the Sotheby's evening."

What a world I've walked into. I can see her swanning in, wearing a Gagaesque outfit, pretending she owns the place. A room full of high rollers and celebrities. Just what I dislike about the South of France. But she's impressive, and I see the point.

"As I was saying, Zandy, scents can be flat, horizontal, vertical . . . thick or thin." Jacqueline gives a flourish of her hand. "I want this one to be light but interesting, medium intensity, and last a long time." Her face lights up. "I want it to feel like the promise of dawn and of dusk. It represents the turn of the Earth, the mystery of being alive."

"We'll name it after Linda," says Dominique.

"We can?" There's fire in her eyes. "Pour Linda, or For Linda or Lindissima? How about Lindissima?"

"Yes." He looks at me. "Meaning, very Linda, extremely Linda, the most Linda."

Jacqueline claps her hands in jubilation.

Camille twirls around on the spot. "This is *fabuleux*!"

Jacqueline swipes through pages at speed. Diagrams and doodles dance before us, like a Leonardo sketchbook. This is an intriguing blend of art and science that reminds me of medieval alchemy–a far cry from that department-store salesperson spritzing me with some synthetic blend of acetone, benzyl acetate, and phthalates.

"The limbic system creates sexual desire, rage, fear, and joy. That's why fragrance is such an emotional experience."

"Our sense of smell is ten thousand times more sensitive than any of our other faculties," says Camille.

"How will you evoke this idea of balance? What absolutes will you use?" I ask.

Dominique's eyes dart from her to me, to the screen and back again.

"I'm sensing a blend of orange and grapefruit, and for middle notes pepper and pelargonium."

I'm picking up tension from Dominique, like a force field over my left shoulder.

Jacqueline is in her element. I love her for it. "I want it to be neither too masculine nor too feminine, so I need to discover the bridge between them. As for base notes–"

Dominique leaps between us and slams the iPad shut. "Turn the camera off."

I press the END button. He's fibbed about his car and his mother. Now he's covering up ingredients. My body goes cold, like he's flipped a switch in me too.

I lower the camera to my side and squeeze it tight. "What are you hiding?"

Camille, Jacqueline, and Dominique exchange looks, their eyeballs zigzagging back and forth like a game of table tennis.

His hand stays clamped on the cover of the iPad. "Formulas we do not reveal."

I don't want his formula. I step forward. "What's all the cloak and dagger stuff?"

Camille places a hand on my shoulder.

I remove it. There's another story here he's not letting me in on. He's shutting me out. "I can't make this doc unless you trust me."

Camille rests her chin on her hand. "Nothing here has to be secret."

I ignore her. I look hard at Dominique. "You keep doing weird stuff. I think you're lying to me." I will not be lied to. I'm weak; all the energy has drained out of my body. Everything around me is black and white.

His face blanches.

"The more you hide, the more I want to find out what you're hiding." Heat flares up my back. "Until yesterday, I thought it was a trashy piece about the beauty business. Now I've found a fabulous angle about creativity. I'm giving you the chance to tell the world about your new scent, but you're determined to obstruct me with your coverups and lies." Perspiration trickles down my spine.

I cram the camera into my bag and shut the flap. "You don't make cheap perfumes. I don't make cheap movies."

I sling the strap of my messenger bag onto my left shoulder.

"You decide if you want this movie . . . or not." I stride across the white linoleum floor. As I reach the door, my back prickles from my shoulders down to my tailbone. I sense the magnetic field I am leaving–like a cape trailing behind me.

Outside the building, I lean my back against the stone wall. I'm hollowed out. Should I just paper over my commitment to the truth and make this stupid fluff piece? It's what Stewart wants. It's what Dominique wants. It's how I earn my stripes and go home to make *Climate.*

Nope. I can't work like this. I have committed myself to truthtelling. I slide down the wall and slump onto the ground. Cold, hard ground underneath me. Cold, hard, and unforgiving, like New Jersey was to me when we moved to North Caldwell from Tower Hamlets, East London. I was ten. My Dad had sold his chain of shops. He was rich, ambitious, excited. I was lost. We staggered around Jersey and New York looking for our touchstones.

I noticed Rita my first week at Lincoln Elementary. I couldn't take my eyes off her–black hair, pale skin, huge, searching eyes. I was immediately drawn to her. She looked neat and put together on the outside. More than her looks, what I discovered over time was that she was calm–whereas I was on edge about everything, especially since our move to the States.

Rita made my world feel stable, as though everything was mostly in its right place, not uprooted and transported over the Atlantic as I had been. Rita was earnest on the outside, and a lot more fun than she looked.

Rita was everything to me for the next three years. Then came the day at West Essex Middle School. Snow was piled up on the sidewalk. We only had four days left until Christmas of our eighth grade. We'd just finished our last math period. She stormed up to me in the hallway, where I was unzipping my backpack to stack my books in my locker.

"Whoa. You okay?" I said, sensing that something big was blowing up. I could feel it in the atmosphere.

She was washed out, sunken-eyed. Those beautiful big black eyes of hers looked haunted. "I hate you." She spat in my face. "I hate you, I hate you, I hate you."

I dropped my pack. Books splattered out, skidding in a circle across the tiled surface.

She turned and ran towards the stairwell, her trainers squelching on the floor. That mini-tartan kilt she always wore over black leggings swung over her backside.

I belted after her as fast as I could. Catching her on the top step, I grabbed her hand.

She yanked it away from me. "It's your fault. It's your fault." She was crying and hyperventilating.

"What is, Rita? Slow down!"

"My dad's gone to jail. Your dad got him put away. He's a liar, a liar, a liar."

I shook my head. "What are you talking about? He's not a liar. You're wrong. This is all a mistake." A chill ran down my spine, even as I said those words.

Now my back against the wall of the Severin Frères office, I can still feel the chill in my spine that I felt that day. The same chill I felt in the lab when Dominique slammed the iPad shut.

First he fibbed about his car. I let it go. Next, he straight up lied about his mother. And now he's covering up something about his perfume. Speaking my truth is the only way I can make peace with what happened back then, with my part in it.

I squeeze my fists, feeling the tightness in my chest. Walk, I tell myself. I leave by the entry gates and wobble towards the old town of Grasse.

That man isn't being straight with me. I'll do some digging. Unless I find out what he's covering up, I can't trust him or the story. I climb narrow cobbled streets, flanked by stucco walls–Italian yellow, ochre, burnt brown. I've got ninety minutes until I need to check in with Stewart. I pull out my phone and dial Jenna, my roommate in New York, who's a consumer products analyst at Morgan Stanley.

"What d'you think he's hiding? Animal cruelty, carcinogens? I think it's an ingredient he doesn't want me to know about. And something else is going on. One day he was driving an Alfa Romeo, which he suddenly swapped for a Smart car. When I asked him why, he got all shifty, wouldn't make eye contact, came up with some cock-and-bull story. It was obvious from his body language he was lying. Why would he lie to me about that?"

"I'll check it out."

Twenty minutes later, I'm seated under the *bigarade* orange trees in the garden of the International Museum of Perfume and she's back on the phone.

"No one knows the precise formula for Evening Star. He could be covering up all sorts of things," she says. "People have tried reverse engineering it, but natural essential oils and other complex mixtures make it hard to be precise."

"So . . . ?"

"I only had a quick look. But you might be on the right track."

"Go on."

"Oakmoss has been banned in the EU, and so has one type of lily of the valley. Lots of perfume companies are scrambling now. Plus, there's always commodity shortages because of political and other upheavals."

"Which means . . . ?"

"Maybe they're trying to replace some ingredient in short supply."

I dig the heel of my boot into the fine sand-colored gravel underfoot and draw circles with it. What in the heck am I dealing with here?

"This could be a big story, right?" she says.

"What about money?" I ask.

"I looked at his financials, as best I could. But Severin is privately held, so I can only see the annual filings."

"What d'you think?"

"I can't see how they're surviving in this market."

"Are you saying he could be in financial trouble?"

"Independent perfume houses are few and far between these days. There's Tweed, but they're designing signature scents for Lady Gaga and the music crowd. They've got that as a cash cow."

"You just scored lunch at one of your ridiculously overpriced Wall Street haunts. Soon as I get back."

We end the call. I stand in the shade of the orange trees—now in blossom with their delicate white flowers. I tear off a leaf and crush it between my fingers. I know there's something bad here. My instinct tells me there is. I can't believe I let Dominique touch me. He will not touch me again. Not ever.

I need to walk and think. I leave the garden and wander into the International Perfume Museum. Inside, it's cool and quiet. I love these raw brick walls and open-plan staircases.

At 3:00 p.m., I dial Stewart.

He opens with, "All set for the walkthrough with marketing?"

"Yup. There's something I need to talk to you about . . ."

"Whatcha got, Zandy?"

I describe my hunches about secret ingredients and money troubles. "I don't think we can work with a guy who's running circles around us."

"Keep moving ahead with lifecycle of a perfume. I like it."

"You're not getting this," I say.

Weighty silence. "Glamorous façade but trouble at mill?" he says.

"Plenty of trouble round here. I'm on the ground. I see the lying tells."

"You need to stick to the brief," he says.

"Shouldn't I dig a bit?"

"Zandy, it's a mess here. The new director of marketing is throwing around fancy ideas about beating the internet. I'm losing editorial control."

"What if this is a major scoop?"

"Stick to the brief. Don't piss this guy off. I'll take a serious look at *Climate* if you do a good job on this. You reading me, Zandy?"

"Yup. Great."

I have a lump blocking my throat, like I swallowed one of those bath bombs my flatmates leave on the side of the tub in Brooklyn.

"Am I wasting my time with you, Zandy?"

Bath bomb exploding inside me. "It's fine. How's Al?"

"He had a meltdown at work. They won't take him back. He's home all day."

"I'm sorry, Stew."

"Yeah. Get some sleep. Start a new page tomorrow."

"Got it, Stew." After the call I pace the hallways. Overhead, industrial piping hangs in the rafters, part of the complex machinery of distilling perfume which took off in the late nineteenth century. Complex, like my mind at the moment.

Do I stop filming until I persuade Dominique Severin to be honest with me?

I enter the section called "Elegance and Classicism." Peering into glass-fronted cases, I admire the simplicity of alabaster pots in which the Romans stored their scented oil. The artistry of the bottle traditionally mirrored the value of the concoction it contained. Ceramic vases for "low-end" products and faience vials for luxury scents.

I can't let him lie to me. Next, a suite of rooms devoted to the "Magic and Dynamism of the Middle Ages" and the development of distillation techniques invented by twelfth-century Arabic doctors.

I'm a doc maker. I have to trust my instinct to discover the truest story.

Gosh, the museum has Marie Antoinette's traveling vanity case, a large valise with lots of silver and glass containers, each housed in individual pockets.

I won't abandon *Climate*. Nor will I abandon my commitment to the truth. The middle ground is to smoke Dominique out. I'll wait for him to come to me. He will. Because he can't help himself. He's a control freak.

I enjoy the imaginative designs of nineteenth-century perfume bottles and stoppers. In the 1910s, François Coty commissioned master craftsman René Lalique to make opulent glass bottles for his perfumes.

Over the next few days, I film with the crew. We get some great footage at the jasmine fields and location shots of the Alpes Maritimes in the soft evening light.

I spend days watching archival footage and interviews, giving myself an intense education about perfume, family businesses, Grasse and its environs, and creativity. I work on getting the clearances and permissions to use archival material. I cannot afford to run into copyright infringement violations.

Time is our vital resource in this business. We refine our schedule for shooting. We allow for hiccups like bad weather on an outdoor shoot day, which could blow my budget.

The following Sunday, my crew is off, and everything is closed. I decide on a long drive–a regrettable emission of greenhouse gases on my part–but driving is the only reasonable way to get where I'm going.

For some reason, Dominique texts. Can he take me out for the day?

I decline and tell him I'm going to take a day trip. I'm heading to the Camp des Milles near Aix-en-Provence.

Because it interests me.

Because the long shadow of the Nazi past would make a good B story for this film.

Because it'll scare the heck out of Dominique Severin.

Chapter Twelve

DOMINIQUE

The Camp des Milles is a former tile factory where, during World War II, thousands of Jews were housed before being shipped to Drancy and on to their death at Auschwitz. What can she be up to here? Is she thinking of using this in her film?

As I walk through the cool, airconditioned space with its smooth concrete floors, I'm thrown off guard, thinking of the many internment camps in France, camps which bolstered anti-Semitism and "the Final Solution." I make my way through an exhibit on the rise of Nazism and the events that led to World War II.

I spot Zandy in the far corner and tense. I don't know what I'm going to say. I'll read the situation once we get talking. I want to build a bridge of some sort, then explain that I'm doing my best to give her access, but some areas of the business are off limits and cannot be open to public scrutiny.

I'm sure she's going to go off like a rocket, probably accuse me of stalking her. I clench my hands at my sides and gird myself. I don't want a row in public. But I must override any feeling of embarrassment. I come up behind her. "*Bonjour*, Zandy," I say, in the most even tone I can muster.

She looks me dead in the eye and says nothing.

I feel ridiculous. I'll have to make the next move. "I . . ."

"I knew you'd follow me." She tilts her chin with haughtiness.

I don't move a muscle for fear of betraying how powerless, how crumpled I feel inside.

All about us screens flicker, broadcasting videos of survivors who speak of their experience of this transit camp.

"You have an interest in the war?"

"I can't craft a story about France without understanding the legacy of the Nazi occupation," she says.

"This will be part of the documentary?"

In the nanosecond before she replies, I sense that she is in control here, not me.

"No."

"Definitely not?"

"I'm here as a tourist," she says.

I release the breath I was holding tight. I'm relieved, but can I believe her?

The fine scent of old stonework hangs in the air, bringing the period alive. This hall dedicated to the idea of resistance is well lit with overhead spotlights. Huge boards ask big questions: "How did this happen?" "What would you have done?"

"I remember the day our teacher taught us about the camps and showed us photos of emaciated Jews herded onto cattle cars. It was devastating to me." I don't reveal that I'd asked Maman at the dinner table, "Did you know that seventy-five thousand Jews were sent away to be gassed during the war?" Maman had brushed off my question. "That was a long time ago. The Severins are Catholics. We keep to our own kind," she'd said. "What about our Christian feeling?" I asked. She'd responded, "It's better to forget and move on."

Zandy and I shuffle forwards, reading a banner asking, "What can people do to resist when they see something going on that is not right?" We watch video clips about individuals who resisted the Nazi occupation. "Do any of us know what stance we would have taken if our own lives had been in danger?" reads another banner.

"It's extraordinary how the story was buried for so many years," says Zandy.

I wince and am grateful that she's not rubbing my nose in our shameful past. We pass through rooms whose walls are covered with inmates' drawings and writings. Interactive displays show photos of the old Les Milles tile factory. We are side by side reading panels about what life was like in the camp when I pluck up the courage to broach what I came for. "We're stuck, Zandy. That morning in the lab . . . you and I can't go on like this."

"I agree. Whose fault is that?"

Alright, hardball, but I'm not backing down either.

We continue through the exhibit in silence, emerging from the bitter darkness of the Nazi story into bright sunlight. I'm wrung out by that experience.

I point to the low wall across the gravel pathway, where we sit and turn our faces towards the warmth of the sun.

"What were you covering up that day in the lab?"

Her question goes to the heart of the matter. My jaw clenches.

She's wearing her WWII airman's combat gear again, and there's a set look, a kind of shield around her that says, "Don't mess with me."

I don't see how we can resolve this. "It's my duty to protect our formulas."

"I think it was an ingredient you don't want me to know about." She looks with determination down the memorial walk. We both gaze at the boxcar marking the site whence prisoners were deported to Drancy.

Tension flares through my shoulders. Of course I don't want her to know. Our brand is built on the concept of local flowers from which we craft the finest quality essential oils.

"It's an aldehyde, right? You don't want me to know you'll have an aldehyde in the new perfume."

I'm like the spider trapped in a glass jar by the schoolboy. I'm surrounded by a glass wall on all sides, with no way out.

"I don't care about your formula. Your formula is your business," she says.

"So what's the fuss?" We're going round in circles.

"Don't cover things up. Don't fib about your car. Don't block my interviews." She swivels and looks me hard in the eye. "I think Evening Star contains an aldehyde, a synthetic. I think you don't want me to know that."

She's like a dog with a bone. She's not going to let go.

"I have zero interest in revealing your formulas. Here's how this works. You tell me what's commercially sensitive. Then you trust me, or I can't make the kind of doc you and I both want."

Sacré Dieu. What a day. I'm shaken up by the exhibit, which is not only a story of our past, but also reflects the hate and extremism that overhang our society today. And now I have a journalist right on my doorstep asking if we use synthetics.

Shall I be open with her? She's being decent and honest. My eyes travel around and around her face. There's no aggression today. She has a lovely expanse of porcelain skin covering that high forehead. Smooth, inviting, grand. The skin translucent in a way that makes it look valuable, precious, cared for. It makes her look vulnerable, like a creature who walks lightly on the earth. Maybe I judged her too fast? She's so unlike those brittle, perfectly formed women who buzz around here–always wanting to get married.

But she's a journalist! I squeeze my fists. She needs a scoop, and I need to protect everything we have. I must shut away whatever it is I'm beginning to feel for her. I have to keep my sangfroid for this movie. I can't let her near Maman, who'll likely be drunk, because she's got to that stage where the alcohol never really leaves her body. "You ask me to trust you, but we barely know each other."

"That's right."

"Get close with her," Jacqueline said. "Ask her outright, 'Please do not reveal this information.' She'll have no choice but to do as you ask. Think about the bond between lovers. It's like that." Lovers!

I got this Zandy wrong. She's shown she's a decent person, just hurt and vulnerable. That's what the brittle outside is. Maybe there's something to be said for her quirkiness, her gruffness. It threw me off my stride when I first met her. I didn't know who I was in relation to her. Somehow it made me stiff and formal. Like when I'm in a business negotiation which is going wrong, and try as I might, I can't read the other side, so I close ranks and stand my ground.

And most important: I need her to tell the world about Lindissima. Our survival depends on it. I can't afford for her to walk away. Our future teeters on this headstrong woman promoting Lindissima with the documentary. This is our plan. There's no turning back.

"You will not on any account reveal our formula. You will not reveal our ingredients. We agree to this, yes?"

"Absolutely 100 percent. You can trust me. It's of no interest to me. It doesn't help the story."

I take the plunge. "Everyone uses synthetics. The industry has used synthetic molecules since the end of the nineteenth century. Guerlain adopted vanillin as soon as it was created in 1870. It became their hallmark. Thanks to synthetics, perfume is truly an art, because we now have scents which you cannot find even in nature."

She rolls the twill of her pants through her fingers and looks up at me as though she's taking this in, processing it.

"Jacqueline might want to evoke the idea of water. Water is

odorless but from just a few molecules she creates the effect of water, the illusion of water and the emotion associated with it. There is no combination of natural ingredients that can fully suggest this."

"I don't understand . . ." A shadow crosses her face that suggests bewilderment. "Why did you slam shut the iPad? Why hide it?" she asks.

"It's an industry secret, this use of synthetics. We know that the public would be disappointed, angry even . . ."

She rolls her lips around her top teeth.

"Yes, we use an aldehyde. Everyone does it. Everyone knows about it. We just don't talk about it." There, it's out. She holds an axe over my head. She could destroy everything that Severin stands for. "For a twenty-first-century *parfumeur*, whether a scent is chemical or natural is not important. Synthetics, in fact, make for a smaller carbon footprint and less animal cruelty."

"Really? Synthetics are better for the planet?" She extends a leg and traces a circle in the gravelly path with the heel of her combat boot. The high color in her cheeks tells me she feels foolish, embarrassed.

For myself, I feel lighter, like I don't have to hold on so tight. "What matters is how the perfume affects the wearer. It's alchemy. A truly great perfume carries a sensory message so emotional, it moves the heart of the wearer and stirs the senses of all who come into contact with him or her."

"You know I'll check this, so there's no point in your lying about it."

I nod. "I know you will. Our industry thinks if the public knows we use synthetics, it could damage our image. I'm happy to tell you more about it, but I'm asking you not to put it in the film."

"Okay, Dominique, I believe you. And you can trust me. No mention of synthetics in the film. I promise."

I proffer my hand. We shake on it and agree she will return to film in the lab with Jacqueline.

"Excellent."

At this moment, we're not in an office with all its power structures. We're just two tourists, members of the public sitting on a low wall on a Sunday, a little dehydrated, with museum fatigue.

"You'll be straight with me going forward, tell me what's on your mind?" she asks.

"I will."

She high-fives me.

The touch of her skin, cool and soft, zings through me.

To have been open feels like a relief, not a defeat. Now I have the pressing need to let off steam. A whim overtakes me. "Seems like it's exactly the time for me to invite you dancing."

Tilting her head back, she laughs. "Definitely not!" Her chestnut waves bob up and down.

I look her straight in the eye. "You know I'm an excellent dancer?"

"The jacket comes off?" she smiles.

Something inside me melts. "Let's go dancing," I say. "We've both been working too hard."

"You don't want to see me dance. . . ."

"Anyone can dance. You just need to practice. I won't take no for an answer." I stand and hold out my hand to help her up. "Maybe you're not up for a challenge?"

"A challenge?" She raises her eyebrows. "Just try me."

Chapter Thirteen

ZANDY

We enter the Caves du Roy nightclub in Saint-Tropez, making our way through the purple and blue light beams crisscrossing the space. Earlier today, Dominique told me they use synthetics–and was willing to talk about the Nazi past. He trusted me. Tonight, I want him to go further. I want him to explain why he lied about the car and what's going on with his finances. And just let me get to the inner story here.

I'm wearing the strappy silk shift he bought me and wishing I wasn't. I pull my leather jacket around me tight.

He drapes his arm across my back, placing his hand on my right shoulder. Does he sense that I feel vulnerable walking through this crowd?

Electric music booms through my head, hijacking the command center of my brain. I'm working, but this is a sexed-up place. What am I doing? Have we crossed a line?

As Dominique carves a path through the horde, I notice he's wearing an electric blue shirt under his shiny black leather jacket, plus flares and pointy tan boots. *Okaaaay*. Straight-up seventies like John Travolta in *Saturday Night Fever*. And a good third of the throng here is wearing similar garb.

He pulls out a chair for me at a table on the edge of the dance floor. Everybody here is preened, shaped–every object colorful, sparkly, loud. I take my seat. We order drinks.

To our left, the entrance is flanked by bodyguards wearing black and fingering their radio earpieces. I'm about to ask questions about his car and his finances when the place is bathed in an explosion of lightbulbs. A herd of paparazzi, half squatting, backs away from . . . Ye, formerly Kanye West, striding forward, head held high. Onlookers part in front of him, all smiles, gold and jewels glittering under the lights.

"Glitzy here, I know," says Dominique. "But you can't come to the South of France without visiting the Caves du Roy."

I take a breath, in . . . out. I'm in sensory overload, but I can do this. As long as he doesn't invite me to dance, everything will be fine.

I'm wondering how to talk with this deafening beat going on all around when the atmosphere changes again. A posse strides across the dance floor, bodies parting in front of it. A tall, handsome woman glides past our table. Tremendous thick black hair, down to her waist, heavy as a bushel of corn. Huge black eyes with a tinge of violet. The large nose, the one imperfect feature on her face, handsome as it is. Full lips. A slender dark man at her side, with a neat moustache, his hand on the small of her back. She slides on by to a booth at the back of the room.

"Wow, that's Noor Haddad."

"You're a fan?"

I clutch the table, to make sure this is for real. "She knows women can change the world. And so do I."

"That must be Prince Karam, her fiancé, with her." Dominique beckons a waiter. "The lady in the booth over there?" He points.

"Mademoiselle Haddad?"

"Just so. Kindly ask Monsieur Michel to send her a magnum of Crystal with my card and my compliments." He hands him the card. "Thank you, Aziz. Everything good with you?" He slips a folded banknote into his hand.

He nods. "Thank you, Monsieur Dominique."

I'm having a hard time staying in my seat. I'm getting over-excited about Noor Haddad. Groupie excited. She's a big role model for me. Settle down, Zandy. You're here to ask what he's hiding about his finances. I swallow . . .

"On September 22, Noor will marry Prince Karam at Petra," he says.

"Right," I say.

"By then we'll have a scent worthy of an icon. What if we offer her Lindissima? She can be the first woman in the world to wear it."

"On her wedding day?"

"*Exactement.* The public would love that."

I can see the romance. The storyteller in me gets that. "But why would she agree?"

He shakes his head. "I don't know. Camille will have to come up with something, Jacqueline will . . . or you will." He flashes me a smile.

What was that? Definitely personal. "Not me!" Discombobulated, I look around the room, anything not to look at his eyes. Heat sears through me.

"*Le moment que vous avez tous attendu,*" blasts through the sound system. "Ladies and gentlemen. The moment you've been waiting for, *Soirée Club aux Caves du Roy* . . . Club Night at the world-famous Club du Roy."

The room vibrates to heavy bass notes.

Now that my heart has stopped galloping, I feel warm, expansive, and flattered a little by his including me. At least he's not blocking me–quite the opposite now. "I totally love WomenUP," I say. "What could be better than the women of the Middle East creating their own businesses? In a culture in which so many women are denied education and trapped inside the home?"

"*Saturday Night Fever*!" A woman's voice slices through the air. We swivel towards the DJ–a Black androgynous figure with a shaved head, blue-shadowed eyelids, and fiery rouged cheeks–a Grace Jones lookalike.

Dominique raises an arm and spins his hand in celebration. I've never seen him excited like this. "These are classics." He tilts his head towards the floor and beckons me. "Come on. This is fun."

I feel awkward and small. "I'm no good at fun."

He takes my hand, his skin cool and smooth, lifts me off my seat.

He leads me onto the floor.

Yikes, this is getting too personal, but he's oblivious. The crowd pulls away and forms a circle around him while he struts and spins, hips gyrating, arms flying to the side, punching the air.

Others in satin shirts with wide lapels join him, striding, clapping, jumping. Everyone is pumped, egging them on.

My insides fall away as Dominique grabs my hand and pulls me onto the center of the floor, showing me the moves, encouraging me to copy him.

I tumble, tripping over my feet.

He catches me, guiding me into the next move.

He beckons for the whole circle to join in. We're in a sea of bodies, pumping up on the diagonal, diving down. He smiles, lost in the rhythm, a Dominique I've never seen before.

"You Should Be Dancing" fades out. He guides me back to our table–his hand is warm and comforting. Eeek! Is he hitting on me, or just holding my hand?

Everything in me is pulsing with life, from my skin through to the pathways of my nervous system.

At college and grad school, I went to techno raves where I'd jump up and down in a mass of bodies. This was foreplay to a heavy snog with someone unsuitable, followed by a silent walk back to his dorm room and sex, be it acrobatic, sweaty, good, or disappointing sex. I'd stumble out of their dorm room in the early hours and head back to my quarters, where I'd stand under a hot shower and erase the experience.

This isn't a techno rave. This is actual dancing, which feels good, like working out.

"Where's that buttoned-up CEO gone?" I burble to fill the space between us. "Where did you put him tonight?"

We sit down. "This is how I relax. Here, I don't think about business, I just enjoy."

In front of our table, two women hold each other, locked in a kiss. One tall, dark, angular, the other petite, with straight blonde hair cut to the shoulder.

I'm enjoying this too. Part of me wants not to be "on" tonight, not looking for my opening but just to relax into this sound and light show. But I have work to do. We're both relaxed–so this is my moment. "Can I ask you something?"

He locks those brown eyes with mine in a way that seems more steady, more comfortable than I've seen him before. "Try me."

My heart picks up. "I know you hate that little car. Why lie about it?" Am I going too far? Will he shut down as he always does? "My sense is that Severin is . . . under financial pressure." There. I let it hang in the moment.

He doesn't flinch. He's calm. "Why d'you ask?"

"There's an elephant in the room I keep sensing. What is it?"

"All businesses go through ups and downs." He swivels his flute round and round. "When I took over, the business was not in the best possible shape."

He sets his eyes on mine. "This is not for the film, a private conversation between . . . friends?"

I nod. "Off the record."

He explains that the business is on the brink of collapse and that he's relying on our doc to boost sales. Severin's survival depends on it.

I believe him. "Thank you."

"I sold my car to make the new perfume. We're down to our last *sous.*"

There. He said it. I respect him for taking the risk. One last thing: I need access to Maman. What if I tell him I won't show anything about her problems with alcohol and the havoc that it's caused? Should I trade access for privacy? Or is this a slippery slope? Will I regret giving up editorial control if I discover something I need to reveal?

But Maman is central to the Severin history. I can't make this movie without spending time with her. He trusted me. I need to give something in return. "One more question."

"Ça suffit." He looks out to the floor. He's tapping his foot to "Stayin' Alive."

"Why all the cloak-and-dagger stuff about your mother?"

His face tightens. "*Oh là là. . .* she's not well."

"The drinking?"

He nods.

"You know I have to meet her. How about you chaperone me? I promise not to reveal the drinking, the mistakes . . ."

"I want to dance!" he says.

"Fifteen minutes with Maman tomorrow–with you in attendance?" I ask.

"Fifteen minutes, not more. Mamselle Watson, we've got a long drive home. I insist on one last dance." He doesn't ask my permission. He grabs my hand and pulls me onto the floor. "*How Deep is Your Love?"* fills the room. He pulls me in towards him.

Everything around us melts, fades into a closeup of us. I am tipsy from the evening. I shouldn't be letting Dominique Severin hold me close and glide me around this floor.

I'm letting him do just that.

He's being honest. I could bloody well kiss him for it. For me, with men, something clicks, something mental. And suddenly we're having sex. (After that, it gets messy, like it did with Luke. And I get out fast.)

There's something soft and tender in the way he's holding me. I move my face back from his shoulder and tilt my head. I reach up onto my toes and plant my lips on his.

His lips are warm. And his breath is warm. It tastes sweet in a tobacco kind of way.

He squeezes my hand.

I float in the moment.

He leans in. His lips are on mine, staying there, kissing me properly.

I'm thirty. I haven't kissed a guy in ten years whom I haven't then slept with. But that is definitely *not* happening. You do not sleep with the subject of your movie when you're a doc maker. Never.

"You're lovely," he says into my ear.

A thrill zings through me. It's hard to imagine what he's like in bed. Nice body, but is he a control freak? One of those who jumps out of bed straight after to wash his privates?

He pulls me in tighter.

This is crazy. I let go of him and step back. "We should go, right?" What the heck? Did Jacqueline drug me too? It's been weeks and weeks and weeks since I slept with Luke. Maybe I need to have sex.

Maybe I should go drinking with the crew one night–see who I can meet out there.

"We should go," he repeats in a singsong way.

Outside, we wait in silence for the valet to bring over his Smart car.

The night is warm and fragrant with jasmine. The tang of sea air shrouds us. We clamber into the car and open the windows to receive the sparkly black expanse of the heavens. This place is magical.

We navigate the winding roads of Saint-Tropez and pick up the autoroute. I should be worrying about the carbon emissions made by the sound and light shows back there in the club and the limousines idling outside. All this unnecessary driving we're doing. The waste of it. But I've gone soft. I'm enjoying it–all of it, as the cocoon of music we've been in falls away. No more rainbow-colored light beams and lasers, just this tinpot car and the heavy urgency of the motorway that sucks in our concentration.

"That was a mistake," I say.

"I apologize." His voice warbles.

"My fault."

"We won't do that again." Our words tumble, one over another's.

I must be out of my mind. My job, my salary, my reputation, this documentary. My eyes are fixed on the road. "Back to work," I say.

"Never again," he says, looking dead ahead.

"Never again," I say. "No more nightclubs."

"It was my fault," he says. "We shouldn't have come here tonight. It's good we trust each other more. It's good we enjoy each other's company. But we stick to professional places."

"We leave what happened inside the club. And get back to work."

Chapter Fourteen

DOMINIQUE

Camille and I sit on the grand patio of the Villa Ephrussi de Rothschild on Saint-Jean-Cap-Ferrat. We're surrounded by the columns of pink marble Beatrice de Rothschild installed *à la* Renaissance. What parties she is said to have given here. We wait and we wait in the enormous silence of this triple-height room, while sunlight pours down from the galleries of the upper floors.

It's a miracle we're here. For days now, Camille and I called around the world. Finally we reached Noor Haddad's brother Zaid. (He and I had taken a class together at the Harvard Family Business Program, so he persuaded Noor to receive us.)

We long to have Noor be the face of Lindissima. It's an inspired, brilliant solution to our problems, a way to put a rocket under our sales. Camille is decked out in wild prints: a multicolored cotton skirt that flares from the waist, a hair bandeau of red and pink silk peonies. She's Frida Kahlo. "Couldn't you have opted for something more restrained to wear today?"

"Meek, like Carla Bruni in Dior?" As she gesticulates, her hands dance with colored rings on three fingers of each hand.

"Yes." I nudge her in the ribs. "Noor will take us for gypsies."

She tosses back her head, jangling the little bells that hang from broad silver hoop earrings.

Elaborate displays of flowers pour out of oversized urns. It's like the foyer of a flagship hotel in a European capital. The grandfather clock ticks away. Noor is keeping us waiting, like the princess she is.

"Did you make peace with Zandy?"

Oh my gosh, Zandy at the club, in that silk shift we bought at the market. I couldn't take my eyes off the skin on her shoulders, and her gleaming chestnut hair. "I told her the whole story about synthetics. She was taken aback."

"Good." Reading my mind, she adds, "You're fine. You did the right thing. To get trust, you have to give trust. This way, we can be collaborators, not antagonists, in this documentary."

"It's done now." I clench my teeth. "I admitted we're under financial pressure. It seemed to elicit her sympathy." Zandy's sea-green eyes flecked with hazel bewitch me. I want to know and understand her. I'm aroused even thinking of those three kisses–as though I were sixteen, seducing a girl on a hot summer's night.

No. I grip the sides of this velvet chair. I can't let Zandy get under my skin. I won't allow that to happen again.

"Is this a power play, keeping us waiting like this?" I ask Camille. "This feels like her throne room."

"Dom, let's just do this. Okay?" says Camille.

I'm nervous as a schoolboy sitting for the Grandes Écoles. I selected a handmade navy suit from L'Atelier Hoche. I jiggle my foot, admiring the lilac socks I wore for good luck.

Noor glides in, brilliant and regal in a tightly tailored skirt suit–Roman purple. Her ink-black hair falls in waves about her shoulders. The eyes, the prominent nose, the full lips command attention.

A bevy of grey-suited men form a semicircle around her, like a swarm of bees.

She sits opposite us in a highbacked chair. Intricate carving on its woodwork rises behind her head, like a crown. Her Prince

Karam, a major general in the Jordanian army, a slender figure with a neat moustache, stands behind her, as though they're posing for a formal portrait.

My heart kicks into a trot. "So good of you to receive us." Channel Grandpapa, I tell myself. Grandpapa with his cigar-chomping swagger, who exuded an I've-got-it-all certainty, to the level of Donald Trump.

"The pleasure is mine." She speaks in the Queen's English, the consonants so crisp she must have been educated at Benenden and Lady Margaret Hall. "So good of you to send me your perfume, which I of course love. How can I be of assistance?"

I describe Lindissima and ask, "Would you do us the honor of wearing Lindissima? We are creating it entirely with you in mind." I look up into the Prince's eyes. "Perhaps Prince Karam could, shall we say, 'commission' it for your wedding day?"

"What a very charming idea." They met at Oxford, and his English is as clear-cut as hers.

She turns her head and looks up towards him.

He bends and speaks into her ear. There's animation in his figure. He seems to like the idea. They move off to the side of the grand patio and stand in front of a trompe l'oeil from a Venetian palazzo.

I tremble with excitement.

They return and take their places. She sits so erect, you'd think she has an iron rod holding up her spine.

"We are so flattered," she says. "But I avoid publicity. I'm sure you understand."

I raise my eyebrows. "Of course. It's just . . . with the publicity around your forthcoming wedding . . ."

Long, tapered fingers dance through the air as she brushes aside my suggestion with a wave of her hand. "I agreed to a big public wedding to further the cause of my people. Fifteen percent live in poverty. Prince Karam," she turns her head and looks up at him, "he works tirelessly to attract foreign investment into Jordan, in IT and communications."

"A noble cause." Camille stands and walks around. "I imagine your winning the British Fashion Award this year was an excellent way to attract attention and . . . more foreign investment."

"That was unwelcome." Noor's face is implacable. "To be associated with Cassandra Bojangles and Boo-Boo Market. I have no interest in being draped across the pages of *Hello* magazine." Her hand circles the air with the grace of a prima ballerina. "You'd be pushing me further into the realm of fashion and style. It's the last thing I want." She quirks a definitive eyebrow. An eyebrow dark like Camille's but with five centuries of Royal hubris behind it.

Camille steps towards her. "It would be subtle. Perhaps a single line drawing on the bottle. Just a suggestion of your person, in the best possible taste." Camille gives her a broad smile.

"I am most honored. However, I cannot associate myself with a commercial enterprise . . . I'm sure you understand."

A short, thickset man in a shiny grey suit crosses the space. Bending at the waist, he whispers in her right ear.

Looking straight through us, her face impassive, she nods and rises.

"I'm extremely flattered." She places a hand on her heart. "But I'm a *fanatically* private person." A slight upturn of the lips. "*Shukraan jazilaan*. Thank you sincerely." She gives a little bow. And she's gone.

Like a puff of smoke, everyone else has gone too.

She's a celebrity who doesn't like publicity? My heart plummets.

Camille and I look at each other. Her eyes swim with disappointment.

"It was based on her wanting publicity."

I look down at the adamantine marble floors.

I take Camille's hand in mine and we traipse back out into the sunlight. We wait on the front step surrounded by impeccable walkways and rare fragrances. Behind the house stand gardens designed in seven different styles: French, Florentine, Spanish, Japanese, Provençal, exotic, and lapidary. I am no one. I have no significance.

A bodyguard drives our tinny little car round to the front of the property.

Giant men in black uniforms open the car doors for us. We slide into our seats.

Hands on the wheel, I depress the accelerator pedal. The tin-pot car jerks forwards. We pull out of the main gates and along the curving coastline. To our right, luxurious villas nestle in lush vegetation–and narrow stone pathways lead down to private beaches where the salty Mediterranean slaps against stone walls.

"I can't believe that." Camille chews on her bottom lip.

I reach out and place my hand on the smooth cotton of her skirt.

She rests her hand over mine and gives it a squeeze.

"We move on." I stare through the windscreen. Dragon, palm, and carob trees, jacarandas, hibiscus, and cycas guard the rugged coastline, which is punctuated by creeks and coves. Here and there we see the water, turquoise, then azure blue, and the rich green of overhanging trees and shrubs.

"But with Noor as our face . . ." She swivels towards me, pulling her legs underneath her on the seat. "D'you want to call her brother? Try again?"

Now with a break in vegetation, a flash of sunlight dances off the glassy sea. "We don't have time to chip away at them. The question is do we try and land someone else?"

"Or we accept the timing is too tight," says Camille. "We drop the idea of a signature scent."

Curving around the bay of Villefranche, we are met with a

panoramic view of white-hulled sailing boats, bobbing at anchor in the cerulean sea. It's not my fault that we've had to swim upstream since Maman's problems. I do the best I can–and that's good enough. "We've got to keep trying." My moment of optimism surprises me. It must be last night's dancing keeping me aloft. "*C'est utopique* but you come up with a list and we'll brainstorm access."

Chapter Fifteen

ZANDY

I spend the next days shooting interviews and following our subjects. At night, I make a detailed record of our shot list. I create clip reels and send them back to Stewart. I always film two or three times more footage than I expect to use. I can pare it down later.

The next time I'm with Dominique, he takes me to his late grandfather's office. They've left the place as a museum piece, as it was in the fifties.

We're both doing our best to be businesslike, no touching, no nod to those kisses at the club.

He opens the door. Maman sits behind a green leather-topped desk, smoking. She is fragile–bony in her Chanel suit. Her well-lined, papery skin carries layers of face powder. Finally I meet her. She and her late father loom–as icons–over Grasse.

I take a seat across the desk from her.

Dom perches on the oak window seat, looking intently at his mother as though by looking hard he can control with puppet strings what she might do or say.

I try to fend off the tension emanating from him by focusing on my job. I start with questions about the good old days when the company was flourishing. I ask about Evening Star; its sales soared in the late twentieth and early twenty-first centuries, thanks to lavish advertising and promotion.

I can use her sponsoring Les Voiles de Saint-Tropez, a regatta featuring classic sailboats, to add the kind of glamour Stewart wants. Not as my main storyline, but good for enticing and enchanting the viewer.

"Wonderful times." Her voice is husky as she looks up and off to the right.

Her hair is backcombed and sprayed stiff, but I smell the whiskey coming out of her pores. The teeth are bad.

She swivels in her chair.

"How did you two meet?" she asks.

Whoa, where's she going with this?

He leaps off the window seat and rushes towards her. He places a hand on her shoulder. "Maman, Ms. Watson is a journalist. She's here to ask you about your years as CEO of Severin, and about Grandpapa."

She leans forward over the desk towards me. "He's a good boy, my Dominique. Mind you look after him. When are you getting married?" she asks.

My chest tightens. I've been trying to erase the memory of what happened at the Caves du Roy. Now all I can think about is those three kisses on the dance floor.

Dominique jiggles his leg, exposing a pale lilac sock, showing the creative, sensual side of this man underneath the impeccable navy.

I'm transported back to that dance floor where I rose onto the balls of my feet, luxuriated in the sweetness of his breath, and placed my lips on his. Warm and smooth. He pulled me in closer . . . . Stop it. This is the last thing I want to think about. I stare at the wood-paneled walls. Breathe, Zandy. This too shall pass. "No, no." I say.

He rearranges the inkstand and the paperknife on the desk.

He's trying not to look at me. "Maman, Zandy and I aren't . . ."

The smell of whiskey, the fact that she won't look me in the eye or stick to a subject; she's an old soak. That's why he didn't want me to meet her. The knowledge washes over me, like the sea seeping over sand. And with it, a churning feeling of anxiety. For her, for Dominique, for me.

I wanted to hear her vision for the company, what her key decisions were, what drove her forwards. I find a sad woman, soaked in a jumble of memory, old before her time.

Dominique makes eye contact with me. "Maman, I'll take you back to the house." He reaches for her hand and just about lifts her out of the chair.

She wags her finger at him. "No, dear boy. I'll walk myself."

Oh, for this to be over. "It was wonderful to meet you, Madame. I thank you most sincerely for your time today."

She plants a kiss on his cheek. "You two go out and enjoy yourselves." She patters out in her leather pumps, singing to herself.

Behind her, a leaden silence hangs in the shafts of sunlight slanting into the room. I play with the parachute silk of my jumpsuit, bought in the market at Tourrettes. I feel the featherlight weave against the pads of my fingers. I rock back and forth on my Converse All Stars.

I've read the cuttings. I know she fell off the stage at an annual meeting and was carried out by her chauffeur. I'd imagined a health crisis but not this.

I would trade a drunk for my scumbag dad who shopped his colleague in order to evade jail time for himself.

"I'm sorry. This is tough." And it has left an intimacy between us I don't want.

He shrugs.

"This won't be in the doc, I promise."

"Thank you."

"You're very snazzy in your navy suit," I say.

His face is tight. "Camille and I met with Noor."

I'm still buoyed by her energy, by seeing her sweep into the club. Her purpose flowed off her. "It would be incredible if she were the face of Lindissima."

"She turned us down." He looks at the floor. He nods and gives a little smile. He's being sweet and gentlemanly, but he's withdrawn.

I get up. "What happened?"

He turns away, looking out over the view of Grasse that falls away beneath us.

"She thinks we're beneath her."

"No way."

He clenches his fists at his sides. "Said she doesn't want to be associated with the fashion world."

I stand to his left. "I get that."

"You don't win a business deal in five minutes. It takes months, sometimes years of relationship building, but I'm disappointed. Now we have to find someone else."

I'm also disappointed. "When I got home that night, I googled her: She's helped 335,000 women start their own businesses. For every woman she reaches, five people benefit. She's helped over 1.5 million people rise out of poverty." Last night, I wondered if she could be the B story for this doc. "Wonderful work and celebrity pull . . ." I feel a buzz of excitement. What if I pitched Noor myself, with the clout of CNM behind me?

I run my finger over the warm wood of the window seat. With Noor, a social justice warrior, as part of this story, the doc would rise above fluff. It would make this work meaningful to me.

No. Calm down, Zandy. I film what I see. I don't try to change the reality. A doc maker stays on the outside as observer.

But it's a genius idea that I can't resist. Noor would be a win-win for both Dom and me. Noor is a viewer magnet. She could make this film into a big success. "She won't turn me down," I say.

He half turns towards me. "What d'you mean?"

"I can wing this." I elbow him in the ribs. "What are you waiting for? Let's go."

Minutes later we are barreling down the autoroute. We're in his tinpot car, but it's electric and better for the planet.

"This is madness. Why will it be different the second time around?" he asks.

"Because CNM has 1.5 million viewers," I say.

"I doubt she'll give us the chance to explain that."

"I'll persuade her." I fist punch the air.

He shakes his head.

Neither of us mentions Maman. We pull onto Cap-Ferrat, a finger of land between the two bays of Villefranche and Beaulieu. It juts into the glassy Mediterranean just before the Italian border. "Home to the greatest villas in the South of France," he says. "In all shapes and sizes: huge, elaborate, elegant, and vulgar."

I don't know whether to be repulsed or impressed as we arrive at the Villa Ephrussi de Rothschild, a stately pink Italian palazzo. We hear a grating sound and watch the iron gates swing open. A sleek black Mercedes glides out. Actually, three in a row, a caravan of black Mercedes.

In the middle car, I spy Noor in the back seat. "She's leaving?"

"Zandy, it's useless," he says.

"Follow that car!" I yell.

He hits the accelerator. "She won't change her mind."

"*Psshh.* I'm good at this."

Dominique accelerates around the turning circle and screeches down the narrow lanes leading off the promontory–like we're in a James Bond movie. Looking up, I see the Alpes Maritimes soaring, then dipping into the sea.

Down the Basse Corniche, through the Italianate old port

of Nice, onto the autoroute. "I'm not going to tone down the hero-worship here," I yadder on. "Noor Haddad is changing the world, culturally, economically, politically. When women step into their power, everything changes. I *have* to meet her."

I hope, hope, hope I can pull this off. He's going to be watching me deliver. We're racing to keep up with the Mercedes. Life behind the camera is easier. Under the spotlight is scary. A juggernaut shoots past us with inches to spare, creating an earpiercing shriek as our windows are sucked away from their rubber seals. It feels like we're doing 180 km/h, not 90.

Finally, off the autoroute, we climb into the hills. We follow her along a road that snakes up to the medieval hilltop village of Saint Paul de Vence. "She's headed for the Colombe d'Or," says Dominique.

"What's that?"

"A small hotel where Matisse, Picasso, and Chagall paid for meals and rooms with their paintings. You'll see their work on the walls," he says. "During the war, many artists took refuge on the Riviera and stayed here."

Dominique hands over the car for the valet to park. We enter the hotel via a heavy wooden door in an old stone wall. Inside the courtyard, an outdoor dining terrace is hemmed in with trees and flowers of every possible sort. Waiters bustle through the packed tables. The place is crammed with arty A-listers.

Noor sits on a banquette facing the terrace. She's in a pale rose *shalwar kameez* and matching *dupatta.* Next to her sits Prince Karam in a long white robe topped with a red and white *keffiyah* headscarf. At her actual table, chatting and laughing are. . . Steven Spielberg and Kate Capshaw.

Disaster. Walking up to pitch someone cold is embarrassing. I've done it a zillion times but I start at ground zero every time. My mouth parches. And this is of a different order; this is impossible.

"You're going to approach her?" says Dominique.

"No," I whisper. A waiter sweeps past us into the hotel. I nudge Dominique. "Let's go inside."

He guides me, his hand hovering over the small of my back. I'm so shaken up, it feels comforting. The bar is cool and darker than the outdoor dining terrace, a Hobbit-hole of a place, like the inside of a tree trunk. I sink onto a cushioned bench.

Dominique sits at my side.

"What now?" he says.

"I have no idea. I can't accost a celebrity relaxing at lunch. That's tacky beyond belief. She'd never say yes. She'd hate me forever." My body is limp. My confidence is gone.

"You tried." He makes eye contact with the waiter and raises his hand. "Let's get a drink."

"First, I need to pee." And to compose myself.

Dominique guides me across the tiny bar, down a narrow flight of steps to the basement. I push open the door marked *Femmes*. Inside are two loos, one to the right, one to the left. In the center is a room with two hand basins and a large mirror on the wall. Handmade tiles decorate the walls. Severin perfume bottles sit on the countertop–Evening Star, Eclat!, Voyage.

I realize that Noor will likely have to pee before she leaves. I text Dom to wait for me. Time ticks by, ten . . . twenty . . . thirty minutes. Women enter, in twos and threes. Finally, the door opens and in comes Noor filling the space with her presence. She's taller than I'd thought–probably five feet, ten inches, a good five inches taller than me.

I pretend to fiddle with my hair while she finishes her business. She emerges from the loo and stands to my right.

Go. Go. Go.

She rests her clutch on the side of the handbasin, runs the tap and washes her hands–taking care not to soap the massive emerald-cut diamond, which glitters on her left hand.

This is my moment. I thrust my press card in front of her.

She shakes her head.

I explain the documentary, how it follows the creation of Severin's new perfume, how wonderful if she would agree to be the face of Lindissima.

"No thank you, Ms. Watson."

"CNM has 1.5 million prime-time viewers. Think of that."

"I avoid publicity."

"But the PR for your wedding . . ."

She places a hand on her heart. "I'm *extremely* flattered. But I'm a fanatically private person. *Shukraan jazilaan.* Thank you." A little bow. "Excuse me, I must get back to my guests." She slays me with a million-dollar smile.

Dammit. I blew it. My legs are leaden as I follow her up the narrow staircase. On the top step a preposterous idea spurts through me.

I don't have the authority for it. I need to run it by Stewart. He might well say no. But I'm out of time. And I've imagined the new movie with Noor as my B story. I can't erase it from my mind. I can't go backwards and make a movie about just perfume. This is my one route to truth plus meaning–plus ratings–in a single movie. Good for me personally and good for my career.

I'm right behind her at the opening out to the terrace. "I'm offering WomenUP three minutes of prime time. Our viewers are aged twenty-five to fifty-four, with disposable income to invest in your cause."

She pivots to face me. Noticing Dominique, she raises her eyebrows. "You're with him?"

"That fills your pipeline with 1.5 million potential donors." Dominique taps figures into his phone. "I'll run the numbers on conversion rates and your fundraising potential."

"We'll show your website in the credits," I say.

"We'd have iPads at the display counters in perfume stores,

and the public could buy the perfume and click on your crowdfund link to donate right there." Dominique stands close to her, his chest puffed out. "With your face on Lindissima, they'll be reminded of WomenUP every time they walk into the bathroom. Continual reinforcement of your brand."

"We'll link each young woman buying a bottle of Lindissima to her peer in the developing world." Whoa. This is way beyond my remit. "This isn't about capitalizing on your wedding. It's publicizing your foundation."

She fingers the edge of her headscarf.

I nudge Dominique in the ribs. "What if Monsieur Severin donates a percentage of profits from Lindissima to your WomenUP?" I stand tall. "Perfume as a vehicle for social justice."

Noor shines her black eyes on me–powerful, deep, and mysterious as a cat's. She switches her gaze to Dominique. "Pull your figures together, then come and see me at the villa. No moonshine. I want hard data. If those figures are real, we might be in business."

Chapter Sixteen

DOMINIQUE

Noor hasn't said yes, but I think, I believe, it's going to happen. I take Zandy's soft hand in mine, and lead her skipping to the inner courtyard. We must mark the moment, celebrate, away from prying eyes.

I grab her by the waist, lift her clean off the ground, and twirl her round and round.

She roars with laughter. When I put her down, her eyes sparkle with excitement. Joy radiates. A joy that meets my own head-on.

"You did it. You wonderful, brilliant woman." I've told her we use synthetics and we're in financial distress. She's seen that Maman is a drunk. Things I've been at pains to keep behind doors for years. Now that she knows, I'm free. I don't have to strain to keep the door of my life closed tight with all the bolts.

"What if Noor doesn't like the data?" she says.

"There's no danger of that." Behind her, the pool, a perfect emerald green, glistens. "I'm a master of data." I lean into that delicious neck of hers. "I need to check on something, Mamselle Watson. Are you wearing jasmine? Is there a hint of rose buried in that fantastic deal you've just pulled off? You, Mamselle Watson, are wearing Evening Star. And you vowed that you never wear perfume." Evening Star is called stately and traditional, but it has an enticing blend of femininity and promise that enchants me.

"A master, are you?" She tilts her head in that come-hitherish way women have. "Talk to me of mastery."

My body zings. She's flirting with me. I think of our kisses on the dance floor a few nights ago. I've been trying to keep them out of my mind this whole day. I can smell her body underneath the scent. It's turning me on. There's a whiff that tells me she wants me.

"It was luck," she says.

"It was skill."

"Tell me about skill," she teases.

This is dangerous. I should have more self-control. But we just landed the deal of a lifetime. Or nearly did. Right there is the majestic Calder mobile. We are surrounded by trees bearing early summer blossoms, old stone, fine wine, good paintings, and the promise of a long summer ahead of us.

I love that Zandy is foolish, fresh, spontaneous, and true. That spontaneity pours off her.

"People can change, you know, when they come under the spell of a master . . . a naughty master." She squeezes my hand and then raises it to her face. "Vetiver?"

I'm on fire with desire and the danger of this. "Very impressive. You're a fast study."

My body relaxes. My ribs open to the delicious pleasure of breathing. Those three enchanting kisses at the Caves du Roy. Like I was sixteen again, kissing a girl in a club on a hot night in the South of France, without a care in the world.

Back on the terrace there are seventy diners clamoring for their lunch. Everyone knows me here. In one hour they'll all be around this pool. This is madness. I'll be the talk of Grasse.

And I don't give a fig. I lean into the scent of her skin. "There is something that a perfumer tries to capture, but which is forever elusive . . ."

"What's that?"

"The scent of an accomplished . . ." I plant a kiss on her collarbone, "and very beautiful woman." I lay a suite of kisses up the delicious curve of her neck. I press her against the ivy-clad stone wall and place my mouth on hers.

Her mouth, soft and warm, tastes of butter and fennel.

I must stop. This is going to complicate matters. I can stop. I *have* that self-control.

She breathes deeply, rhythmically, her intensity building in the dance with me.

I can't stop.

She wants this too and I'm not harming anyone. There's the summer breeze. I'm alive under the blue sky. I have everything to live for, health and hope and dignity. . .

My hand wanders down to the jut of her hip. God is there anything as beautiful as the curve of a woman's naked hip? "I can see the bottle for Lindissima!" I say.

"A moment of inspiration?" she asks.

Her breath is fast. She is panting. She stands on her toes and kisses me long and slow, rich and deep.

I feel her lips imprinted on mine. "Mmmm. Deep purple with a hint of burgundy." I'm beyond stopping this now.

I see a cleaning cart poking out just beyond the corner of the wall. I have an idea . . .

I squeeze her hand and pull her around the corner. "A heavy burgundy glass bottle for Lindissima!"

The door to a room on the ground floor stands open. The bed is unmade–the bedsheets crumpled and pulled back, the chairs and dustbin awry. The guests have left, and it hasn't yet been cleaned.

I pull her inside. I snap the lock on the door.

A disheveled breakfast tray sits on the small round table. The scent of bitter coffee and warm croissant lingers in the shafts of sunlight.

"Really?"

"Certainly." I push an armchair against the door with my foot, to block anyone opening it from the outside.

"I can see the bottle." I lean my body towards her. My lips hover over hers and her breath flutters over my face. "A line drawing suggesting Noor, that is simple, elegant, subtle."

We face each other square on. A tantalizing inch of space between us.

Do I let myself fall into this, enjoy one moment of freedom? Can I be me, not the CEO of Severin Frères, and leave my cares outside that door?

I hesitate. So much hangs on this documentary. This will damage . . .

No. We understand each other now. We are partners in this project with Noor Haddad. That was incredible how she pulled it off.

Zandy waits for me to move on her, inviting me with her poise. Standing tall, she juts out her chin with a haughty look that drives me insane. Desire and anticipation burst alight inside.

I drive and push and hustle day in, day out. But without sex, without connection, it is hollow, impossible. I'd never get through my days. I need this release. "A single line drawing, as innocent and God-like as a late Matisse." My words cast a gossamer veil over what is happening between us in this room.

"I can see perhaps the curve of her eye?" She plays back.

I focus my gaze on her neck, the most sensual, vulnerable, inviting part of a woman's body. The skin creamy. "I'm a little busy right now to get into that . . . detail." I lean in to kiss it.

"Good." She tugs at the zipper on her parachute suit, peels it down the length of her torso, until it stops right above her pubic bone. She's breathing faster, through her nostrils.

I need to know what she most wants. I press my body against hers. I'm aching to pin her on the bed.

"Nuh, uh. Naked first." She rolls a shoulder, slipping the silk down her bare arm. One side, then the other. "I need to know if you're actually wearing vetiver or something more potent." The vixen is taking control.

I shrug off my jacket, drop it on the floor, and unbutton my shirt, holding her gaze.

A smile curls the corners of her lips. There's also a rim of perspiration at her brow. She's suffering, too, with the pleasure and anticipation of this.

I undo my belt, drop my pants to the floor, and kick them away.

It's striptease.

Me, then her. One move at a time. I'm on fire. She's putting me through hell. I love her for it.

She drops her jumpsuit in a puddle on the floor.

Sacrebleu, the confidence.

I drink in her body, which is straight up and down, gamine, vulnerable. She makes me feel strong and manly. The hell with control. I couldn't muster it if I tried.

Flat at the tummy and pale brown. The breasts, perfect little mountains, pert and youthful. My body has taken command. I'm at its mercy, at her mercy. I walk her backwards to the bed where I straddle her. I want to please her, I must please her.

She presses her knee into my thigh and flips me over, laughing.

Now she's on top.

Each of us wrestles for control. I love her playfulness and abandon. She's willing, open. She trusts me, and in the rush of adrenaline and excitement that overwhelms every part of me, I feel alive and . . . free.

Afterwards, I lie curled around her back, her body naked against mine, absorbing the delicious smoothness of her skin.

An early summer's afternoon, in which time is suspended in the scent of starch and rosewater and a silky 400-thread-count sheet. I allow myself to bathe in this feeling of closeness, in the cool smell of the brown floor tile, the lemon beeswax of furniture polish, the waft of lilac from the vase on the dressing table.

"That was lovely," she whispers.

"Mmmmm." I can be myself. I don't feel she's after marrying me, like Annabella and all those other women have been for years, making me want to bolt. But not Zandy. Quite the opposite. "We might have to do it again . . ."

Chapter Seventeen

ZANDY

My body thrums, vibrating in tune with the universe. God, I needed that sex to work off the tension. I thought I was going to fail with Noor Haddad–in front of Dominique.

I pulled a rabbit out of a hat and now I deserve this lovely, zinging feeling. I want this moment to last and last–his warm body spooned around my back. A summer's afternoon, light beating through the shades, his breath on my back. I feel calm and centered. I don't want to go home and get my presentation together for Stewart. Plus, he's got all those dudes from upstairs he's bringing in.

I flip over to my tummy and lay my head on his chest.

He strokes my hair in a rhythmic way as I curl myself around his brown body.

The sex was hot and tender at the same time. Yummy combination. I love how he dropped the power thing in the bedroom. I was surprised he let me take the lead. Out there he has to be in control. In here, he's willing to let that go.

I curl my foot around his ankle. I want to do it again. If we do it again, is it a 'thing'?

"Welcome to the South of France," he teases.

"I think I finally arrived." He's no longer blocking me. We're making this deal with Noor Haddad together. It's nice to feel part of a team, not out on my own–I'm always out on my own.

With Luke, we'd have great sex, then he'd pull on his jeans, walk over to his computer, and edit something. But I can luxuriate in this, lying here, drugged with pleasure, feeling the muscles of his shoulders and his chest.

"Can I ask you something?" he says.

"Depends what it is . . ."

He half raises his torso, resting on an elbow and looking down at me. "I'm always answering *your* questions," he says.

Do we have to talk? Can't we stay submerged, a pair of dolphins spooning under the smooth Mediterranean. Do we have to break the surface of the water? "*Okaaaay* . . ." I say.

He plants a row of kisses on my head. "Who hurt you?"

I freeze.

I hear his breath, watch the regular rise and fall of his chest.

"I think someone hurt you."

My eyes are pinned to his clavicle.

"Your father?"

"You're clairvoyant, now?" He's zooming in on me. I don't like it.

"My mother's an alcoholic. I feel everything in the room."

Don't feel me, I think.

He strokes my shoulder.

"You're even more touchy about your parents than I am about Maman. You just about leaped out of your chair when I first asked you about your father."

That pleasure zone vibrating from my solar plexus has gone, replaced by a sphere of pain. I look away down to the left.

He circles my breast with the pad of his index finger. "I think that's why you're sometimes a bit . . . headstrong, superior." He runs his finger over towards my collar bone. "That's not who you are underneath."

My eyes prickle. He sees me. I want this and I don't want this. I might cry. I don't want to cry. This isn't like Luke where the sex was transactional–leaving me bereft, but this is too . . . too . . . something else.

He shakes his head. "That was clumsy. I shouldn't have asked."

"It's okay."

"I'm an idiot." He runs his knee up my legs. It hovers over my skin, creating a layer of warmth over me. "I could . . . make amends?" He leans his face over mine, shrouding me with his warm breath. I smell vetiver.

I tingle all over. That sphere of pain has gone. He strokes me, lighting me up. His skin is smooth. Must be all the swimming they do round here. If I push away what he said, I can sink into his gorgeousness. If we have sex again, I can delay writing that presentation for Stewart. We can submerge ourselves in all-encompassing pleasure.

I wrap an arm round his shoulder.

He kisses me, his tongue hot on mine.

We shouldn't do it again. Friends is one thing, lovers quite another. This will mess up the work.

But I want to stay here curled up next to him. I don't want to find the words to persuade Stewart that Noor Haddad as my B story is what he's looking for.

He strokes my hair.

I should go. I don't want him saying that stuff again.

"We don't need to talk."

I definitely want to have sex with him again.

He nibbles my ear.

He traces circles on my thigh with his fingers. Any minute now, it'll be too late, I won't be able to leave.

My body is on fire, but I've got that wriggly feeling inside that I don't like. I flip onto my side. "This was lovely." I kiss his chest. "Let's not . . . mess up this film?" I whisper. "We need to be careful, right?"

I caress his shoulder as I pull back and sit up.

He makes a sad, puppy dog face.

"We should go," I say.

He groans and sits up, pulling the sheet up to his waist–a beautiful man, lean and toned, the skin smooth and brown. He tugs on my arm, guiding me back towards him. "Stay . . ."

"The housekeeper will arrive any minute now."

He leaps out of bed and drives the grey velvet armchair away from the door with his foot. He places the "Do Not Disturb" sign on the outside handle, shuts the door, and locks it from the inside.

"Dealt with."

I'm out of bed, standing in the middle of the room.

He places his hands on my shoulders and runs them down the outside of my arms.

I cock my head and give him a smile as I step into my underwear. "Gorgeous afternoon." I stand on my tiptoes and plant a kiss on his forehead. "Seriously, I've got work to do."

He wraps his hands around my buttocks and slides my underwear down with a finger. "All work and no play makes Jill a dull girl." He kisses me from my neck down to my collarbone. "And you're not dull . . ."

"Good." I twirl my bra in the air. I slide it on and hook it up. "I don't want you getting bored of me." I bob down, pick up my parachute suit with one hand. Standing, I step into it.

He runs his hands through my hair, sweeping it back off my face. "Do I seem bored?" He asks in a low voice.

I step back. "Dom, we mustn't complicate this."

"We're grown-ups. We can handle it." His lips are warm as he kisses me.

Chapter Eighteen

Back in my flat, I'm high on the afterglow of sex. Everything is light and tingly, everything seems alive and possible. I like to work after sex. I like to work out after sex. I like to do anything and everything after sex, to think about it, to go back to the beginning and remember every delicious detail.

When I first met Dominique, he was all so James-Bond-Look-at-Me with his sports car. But now I know him a bit. How wonderful that he was so tender, so giving in the bedroom. Usually I have sex first, get to know after. Or skip the get to know and move on to the more sex. Certainly in New York, and with all the apps, hooking up is easy. And unmemorable. Like eating takeout food from a cheap polystyrene box. I wonder if Dominique knows what a hookup is. How do you say that in French?

I was definitely doing too many hookups before Luke. Luke. My chest tightens. Sex with Luke was good, hot, potent. But hurried in the sense of uninvolved, unwilling to linger. Whereas Dominique Severin is Mr. Linger in the Moment.

Now I can relive the deliciousness. But, thank God I got out and escaped any complication.

The next morning, a small package of vetiver soap arrives on my doorstep with a note from Dominique: "From the market."

Nice. That was so naughty, doing it in a hotel bedroom that

wasn't ours. In a room where the staff could come in at any moment. Forbidden fruit. Deliciously forbidden.

I spend a couple of days in my sherbet-colored flat, preparing my presentation for Stewart. Work helps me calm down and get some clarity. Dominique is a man I like in the bedroom, but we're not going to have sex again. I don't have sex with a coworker after too many shots in a bar, followed by a tussle to forget the whole thing and move on. No. I come to the sensible decision that Dom and I will not do that again. Mixing work with pleasure is *no bueno.*

Dominique texts me updates about his meeting with Noor. Noor is IN. I work on rethinking my core story points. I write each element on 3x5 index cards. I lay out my storyline, shuffling and reshuffling my cards.

Actors on film sets have sex with each other because of the intensity of the shared experience. I can see what happened there. I'm not blaming myself.

Dominique texts to say that Camille will hammer out the details with Noor's people in NYC.

I'm pumped about showing Stewart how I'll weave the face of Lindissima, Noor Haddad, and WomenUP around the Severin story. He's going to love it. It's everything the advertisers want– and me too!

At 3:00 p.m. on Thursday, I log on to Zoom and find it's not just Stewart at this meeting. Two of the upstairs executives are also staring through my screen at me.

A bit tight in my chest. Should I be alarmed that he's got the big boys joining us or flattered that they're showing interest in my reel?

"I want to introduce Euan Robertson," says Stewart. "He's joined the Executive Team as Director of Cross Digital Content. He and John MacDonald, Director of Marketing, are eager to hear your storyline."

I take a breath. Lamar, my trainer, always says, "Forget the other guy. Stay focused on yourself, your footwork, your technique."

I give an overview of the Severin story, highlighting the romance and talking about my focus on the creation of a new perfume, Lindissima. "I'd like to introduce a subplot that I think will give the piece more depth and much more reach."

I compare Noor's WomenUP story to the *Girl Rising* documentary. "The Noor story invites engagement to a cause, showing how we can harness commerce to change attitudes and make the world a better place for the nearly eight billion humans who share our planet."

"I love that, Zandy," says MacDonald. "She's a big name, which will make this a cash cow. She also happens to be a somewhat cool character," he says.

"I'll interweave the Noor story, drop in an interview with her, and cut away to archival footage," I say. "We'll have shots of the new bottle with her face on it. There's the segment about WomenUP and stills of Petra, where her wedding will take place, mere days after we air. I love that hook!" The marketing peeps are going to love this 'perfume as a tool for social justice' which I promised her.

"As a channel, we're leaning towards something edgier," says Stewart. "Which is why John and Euan are here today. Go ahead, guys. Euan, what's your take on this?"

"We're seeing increasingly hard-edged material in the market." I see a smooth operator, with a wide, passive face and a sheen on his skin that says he's a gym rat. He raises his hand to his chin. Is he checking his messages on that Apple watch?

They subject me to a barrage of data on actuality footage, viewer numbers, and crossover developments. Should I be interested or as skeptical as I feel here?

"Stay with us, Zandy. This will all make sense in just a moment," says Stewart.

"Our competition isn't the other channels anymore." Euan's accent is broad Aberdeen. "It's the internet algorithms that are pulling the public towards ever more sensationalist content. More violence, more sex, more 'aliens just landed in my backyard' kind of stuff." He keeps thrusting the thick mop of ginger hair off his forehead. "The Noor story is cool. It pulls in a whole new demographic–angry women with hairy legs demanding 'justice.'" He grins.

Whoa, Houston, who is this jerk?

"Millions of them out there. The blue wave," says Creepy Euan. He's an actual toad. I don't want him anywhere near my movie.

I raise my hand. "As I understood your brief, the advertisers want a romantic foray into the world of perfume," I say.

"Actually, they want viewers, because viewers mean buyers. They don't care how they get those viewer/buyers, as long as they get them," says MacDonald.

"We also need to keep robust as a channel. And that depends on numbers of viewers. Or we won't be here to have this conversation," says Euan. "We have to think of the CNM brand, as well, of course, as thinking of our advertisers' brands."

"Zandy, we've just completed a new strategic plan. It's been a huge exercise to align ourselves with the social changes being driven by the digital/cross-channel arena," says MacDonald.

"I don't see why we shouldn't give a bit of zing to a softsoap lifestyle piece. We're not in the *fifties* anymore. Ha ha ha," says Creepy Euan.

"This is very interesting," I say. Not. "I'm not quite sure how this relates to my Severin reel."

"Absolutely, Alexandra," he says.

"Thanks, it's Zandy," I say.

"Stew, how about you take it from here?" MacDonald waves goodbye. "Zandy, Stewart will explain where we're headed." He and Euan leave the meeting.

Stewart nods at me. "It's written all over your face, and I agree. We all take Euan with a pinch of salt. I'm not after sensationalist stuff. But I do want you to add something more hard-edged, and that's right up your alley, Zandy."

"Didn't you tell me when you sent me to France to *stop* being so political?"

"You want your Noor Haddad subplot. You want to raise money for WomenUP. That's highly political. I just want you to add another layer, something a bit grittier."

He ordered me to make a soft-soap reel about Severin to please the advertisers, and suddenly he wants gritty?

Taking in a long breath, I lean back in my chair. I can barely make sense of this.

"Let's brainstorm. You've got ninety minutes, so you can go deep and layered with this reel."

I reach for the pack of Juicy Fruit on my desk and pull the tab.

"Synthetics, union problems, financial pressures for starters."

I pull out a stick and slide it out of the silver wrapper. I'm giving up gum as soon as I get back to NYC. "I've tried synthetics. There's nothing there. And financials. He's not hiding anything."

I chomp on my chewing gum, extracting the burst of flavor, rolling it around my mouth.

"What about the Nazi backdrop?"

Dom would freak if I dropped that into the back of his film. Plus, I promised I wouldn't. "I don't know."

"I thought you'd jump at this, Zandy."

"It's just . . ."

"Severin has got to you."

He knows we had sex?

"This is the challenge of documentary making. Getting close enough so they open up, but not so close that you go native."

Easy to say from a distance in New York. I want to get off this call right now. I chomp on my gum.

"I've been in that fix myself. You can dig yourself out. Disengage a bit, and finish your job like a pro," says Stewart. "I thought you were all about the Nazi backdrop."

I feel sick. I'm cornered and I don't even know who's cornered me, Stewart or Euan or Dominique. This is bad . . .

"Or find something else," he says. "Euan wants the ugly side of the perfume business, the cat and dog fight among the rival companies. It's a billion-dollar industry. The stakes are high. Show us how they race to the finish line."

I pull the gum out of my mouth and roll it in the silver wrapper. It's taking all I've got to listen to him.

"Interview his competitors. It's a small town. Someone hates Severin because of something."

I can't feel my body. I'm looking at the screen with my mouth open.

"Out front, it's jasmine and lavender. In the backroom, they're stealing each other's Noses and hacking into their rivals' computers. A documentary is a true-life story. We make documentaries to remind ourselves what it is to be human–the beautiful and the ugly."

"Ten days ago, you said steer clear of ugly."

"The brief has changed."

Briefs change, but not at this stage of the game and never with an assignment as cut and dried as he gave me.

"Call me as soon as you've found something." He smiles.

My throat parches. I need to end this call right now.

Thirty-five days I've been floating around in a lavender-scented world; now he tells me Dom is the enemy–and I just slept with him.

"And about *Climate*–I've set aside some budget for it. There's talk Bill Gates will give an interview–presuming all goes well with perfume and we assign you *Climate*, etcetera, etcetera. It's heaving into view. Something to look forward to, potentially for the fall."

Has Stewart changed? Has the business changed? Or have I been deceiving myself about what working for a network is like?

He waves goodbye.

I manage to raise my right hand for the signoff wave.

There's no point in trying to persuade Stewart to stand down. The big guns from upstairs want meat, so he's dangling *Climate* in front of me–as a bribe. He's saying, "Get me the grit on perfume, and I'll get you *Climate*."

Do I betray Dominique like this so I can produce and direct *Climate*? No. That's underhanded and it repulses me. I press my hands onto the arms of the chair and force myself to stand. He's trusted me with his secrets and I promised I wouldn't use them against him.

My legs wobble as I make my way to the bathroom. I pick up the soap which Dom delivered and raise it to my nostrils. Immediate time travel–the vetiver transports me to his side, naked under the sheets. I will respond with integrity. I want to and I must.

But Tourrettes sur Loup is just a brief moment in my life. I turn on the cold tap and splash my face with water. Stewart as good as promised me *Climate*. The stakes for humanity couldn't be higher–the survival of our species versus a little film about perfume. Plus, I *will* be telling the romantic, beautiful, creative Severin story. That will get most of the airtime. It's just that I'll add another strand. Won't that strand, whatever it is, make the film closer to the whole truth?

I dab my face dry with the hand towel. No. I'm not sending him to the dogs. If I do that, I'm as bad as my rotten father was when he betrayed his colleague, Mike.

I can't breathe in here. I grab Paddington from the dressing table, slide him into my messenger bag, and head out of my flat. Downstairs, tantalizing smells float out of the bakery. I cross the village square. It's coming to life after the afternoon siesta. Locals play boules on the sandy courts in the middle.

I hike up the steep Rue St. Jean. A group of walkers with packs and hiking sticks coming down off the mountain passes me. I want to find the time to get up there one day. Halfway up the hill, at the ledge, by the shrine to the Virgin Mary, I stop to look over the terracotta roofs of the medieval village and at the green hills that roll down to the sea.

I'll ask Dom how I can add something spicier–maybe competitor rivalry–without harming him.

Do I want constantly to be digging for lies and not trusting? Or when people confide in me, do I repay them with probity? There has to be honor in this profession. I clasp my bag, silently asking, I'm right, Paddy, aren't I? Who owns this story, me, the network, or Dominique? It'll never be black and white but there has to be a way to act with integrity and that's the way I choose to take.

Two adolescent girls come down the hill, giggling. One, aged about twelve, has curly, dark hair–like Rita. Rita has never aged in my mind, even though we were BFFs when we were twelve, and I'm thirty now. I squeeze Paddy tight through my canvas bag. I can't bring Rita back, but I can confide in Dominique, tell him what happened on that call. He needs this movie, and so do I. He can find me something gritty but not damaging. I can do what's right. And I will.

Chapter Nineteen

Early the next morning, Dominique drives me up the steep, winding road that leads to the Domaine de Courmettes. He wanted to update me about his meeting with Noor and how the partnership will develop. I agreed to come hiking so that I can tell him what happened on the Stewart call. Together we'll find something to include that's gritty but not damaging.

The Smart car judders up the incline, which must be 15 percent in certain parts. Deep green shrubs with an ancient feel line the side of the potholed road. Here and there, gnarly branches reach out and narrow the road. That's when I hold my breath, hoping we don't encounter someone coming down this mountain in the other direction.

As we get higher, the stone walls and houses behind them disappear, and heartstopping views of mountains that drop to the sea sweep in on us. I throw myself into these views, so I don't think about us being naked together, having sex, a few days ago.

Anyway, it's not happening again.

We park. He releases the trunk with the remote, and the boot opens. He hands me a pair of walking sticks he's brought for me. "That's sweet of you," I say.

We pull our day packs out of the trunk. I yank my water bottle from the side pocket and take a few hearty glugs.

Dominique raises an arm and points up to the left. We set

out, passing a grand house, faced in cream stucco, crumbling, but impressive.

"Built as a sanatorium for TB. Now it's a Christian foundation that offers classes in bread making."

"Looks like an English estate, with this parkland," I say.

A slight incline leads us up a rocky path, which opens out onto flatter terrain and wider views of meadows and surrounding mountains. The silence calms me. Much needed after the intensity of the last few days. This is good. The more relaxed I am, the better I will be at finding a creative solution to this problem–with Dom, of course.

My shoulders loosen, and my breath finds a steady rhythm as we walk side by side. Up here, this beautiful air is cooler and rarer. "I've seen hikers coming down off this path into the village. I've been longing to climb the Pic de Courmettes."

"I've wanted to bring you up here since the first day we met." I'm grateful he doesn't mention us having had sex.

The path climbs, demanding more energy as our mitochondria build density. We climb in step. "I had no idea this was up here. It's *magnifique*."

I stop to retrieve an empty plastic water bottle. I swing my day pack around, undo the drawstring, and stuff it inside. Minutes later, he does the same. Bravo! He's learning that climate matters.

Thirty minutes in, he guides me out onto a rocky ledge to the left of the path. The Gorges du Loup plunges away–with its craggy rock hollowed out by the river down there. Fir trees cant off the bluff into the abyss below. It's romantic, dramatic, Wordsworthian. Hang gliders like enormous bats swoop by, silhouetted against the azure sky. I take out my phone, and he shoots me with the mountain peaks as backdrop.

We rejoin the path. I'm fired up by the incredible landscape and by the energy from the long, slow climbs. This is a good moment. I feel open and free. I'm going to tell him right now about the Stewart problem, but he launches right into details of his meeting with Noor. The whole machinery whirring. Camille is now on a plane to New York to hammer out the details with Haddad's team. Then she flies on to Taiwan to organize the production schedule and oversee the marketing materials. "We're thinking some elegant, simple, powerful line drawing of Noor. Not at all vulgar. Taiwan can deliver in a fraction of the time compared to the West. Without you we wouldn't have arrived at this point," he says.

I bow my head, humbled, tender, proud of myself. This is the win-win I so wanted.

We pass through a gate and descend through a dark wood, so overgrown it feels ancient and mystical. Forty minutes later, we come out into an old stone village in the belly of the valley, silent and, it seems, deserted. He leads me to a meadow with long grass and daisies. We drop our day packs and walking sticks onto the ground and sit a few feet apart, our sit bones resting on outcrops of rock.

Stopping is an event as my blood zings around my body, which feels alive and oxygenated. We reach for our stainless-steel water bottles. I swig on mine. The cool water goes down like the pure spring that rushes through the Loup riverbed and wends its way from the Alpes Maritimes to the sea.

Dominique retrieves two sandwiches from a paper bag. We chomp into them, mozzarella and tomato in half a baguette.

We lie on our backs with our heads resting on the mounds of our packs. Red and purple wildflowers carpet the meadow. The grass, sweet and damp, tickles the back of my neck. The sun warms my skin, which tingles–I can almost feel it browning.

"Wait here a moment." Dominique stands and brushes crumbs of bread from his pants.

I push myself up a few inches, half propping my torso on my elbows, and watch him walk across the road to the little Auberge de Courmes. The stone-paved terrace is shaded by umbrellas. A black cat slinks around terracotta pots of orange-red geraniums, which skirt the length of the old stone house, now a restaurant and bed and breakfast.

Dominique disappears inside. I bask in sunlight.

He reappears and returns with a brown paper bag, out of which he slides a piece of wine-red cherry tart. "*Clafoutis* for the climb back up." Smiling, he offers it to me in the palm of his hand.

I take it and bite into the narrowest angle from the center of the cake. It's tart and mildly sweet. The buttery, firm pastry melts in my mouth.

I hand it back and lick the remaining flakes off the palm of my hand.

He locks eyes on me.

My insides melt. No, no, no. Stop it, now.

"Time to go," he announces.

We gather ourselves and our possessions, muscles tight and joints creaky from the rest.

Dominique shows the way and I follow up the narrow, winding, rocky path, dappled in sunlight and patches of cool shade. Where the path is overgrown, he beats the tangles out of the way with the metal tip of his walking stick.

The air is fresh and warm, perfumed with wildflowers. Dominique climbs just ahead of me–neat and muscular. I'm inches behind him. His butt is shapely in army-green hiking pants and the navy T-shirt shows the ripples of his taut body.

He stops and turns back to face me.

I look up at him. I tingle. His face, released from care by hiking in the mountains, is open and relaxed. I want him. A woman, a man, on a heavenly mountain. I lock eyes with him and lean towards him, closing the space between us. The musky smell of him ricochets through my torso and spurts through my arms and my legs, permeating all of me.

I plant my foot on a rocky mound and step up to him. I raise my right arm and run my forefinger down his cheek, outlining his cheekbone, drawing the pad of my finger around the rim of his jaw.

He swallows. He wraps my hand in his palm and guides my forefinger through his lips.

His tongue encircles my finger, housing it round and around.

My groin thrills. I plunge my finger in and out of his mouth. I perspire, wanting him. Here. Now. Nothing else matters.

I tug at his T-shirt and pull him off the path. Taking cover behind an ancient oak, I yank his T-shirt out of his trousers.

He pants. I thrust my hands up his chest. I lean in and kiss the curve of his neck. It tastes of salt, sweat, and lemon.

We tug, stroke, press, and knead each other. He walks me backwards and positions me against a tree trunk. Standing entwined, we stumble, then find our footing. Our bodies fit one another's. We've been here before. It's easy.

Afterwards, we lie on the rocky ground, our legs encircled in a pretzel. We breathe in the loamy, earthy smells and the blanket of white wildflowers surrounding us.

Time stands still until we come to, a tangle of limbs and clothes and leaves and rocks.

I should tell him about Stewart now. It's why I came hiking. I stand, hitch up my pants, fasten the zipper and the waist stud.

He too stands. He brushes leaves and crumbles of rock off my tank top and shoulders.

No. This isn't the moment for the work talk. I want to bathe in what just happened. I bend to retrieve my walking sticks. They clank together as I pick them up off the ground.

He brushes twigs out of my hair. I'll take a few minutes. I'll tell him when we get to the top.

We wend our way back up, clambering on small rocks, right foot, left foot, using our poles to steady ourselves.

From behind, he plants his warm palm in the small of my back, half pushing me up the hill. My legs are alight. My lungs are smooth and open, and the climb is weightless.

Here and there, I tilt my head back and gaze at the patches of clouds scudding across the blue sky.

I look down at the rocky path and focus on the tilt of my boot on the incline, pushing off with the ball of my foot. Choosing the next rock and planting the other foot. My lungs inflate and deflate in rhythm with my steps. The sun pokes through, beaming long slashes of light into the woods.

He needs to know sooner rather than later. We reach the top, a few hundred feet above the estate where we parked the car. The view opens out. We stand side by side, leaning on our sticks and gazing down across green meadows. Beyond the vast, tree-clad vale, towards the inky silhouette of the Esterel mountains which dip themselves into the slate-blue sea with their bony hands. Bathed in warmth from the climb, I feel masterful–tipsy on oxygen and sex, my limbs warm, stretched, relaxed. Not now. I can't spoil this moment. When we get back to the car, I'll say something.

We reach the car, parked under a line of bulbous oaks. We deposit our packs and our sticks in the trunk, climb into our respective seats, and buckle up for the drive back down. Sitting beside him in the passenger seat, the climbs, the views, the cherry tart, and the sex shrink away behind us. In the silence, I fold into myself. We'll talk in the office, when the fact and feeling of sex isn't spreading its wings across the day.

He stares straight at the road as the little Smart car tips and rolls down the steep incline.

"How did we let that happen?" I ask.

"It happened. We won't do it again." The bathtub car bends and weaves down towards the Route de Grasse.

"Definitely not." I focus on the tarmacadam of the road. We'll see what we can agree on, something about unions or maybe a climate angle. We'll figure this out.

Early the next morning, I head to Dominique's office. I really must have this conversation about the new brief with him today.

Dominique is nowhere to be seen. He was here earlier, and now no one knows where he is. His assistant thinks he's driven Camille to the airport to talk about production before she heads to Taiwan. I text him about meeting up–making it eminently clear this is business, not personal.

I will not think about sex with Dominique. And we are definitely, definitely not doing that again.

I find an empty office and get working to set up my shoot with Noor for Thursday. Thirty minutes later, I'm on my way to the library-archive in the old wing of the office. I need the marketing materials from when the shop belonged to Pereira et Fils and the stills of the boutique on the Avenue Montaigne.

To enter the library, I must pass through Grandpapa's office. I open the door–and startle. Maman, Dominique's mother, is seated at the desk, in her father's swivel chair.

Her skinny body is housed in a lavender linen dress with matching jacket, Jackie O style.

I've come many times to use this place as my office. She's never been here. What's she doing here now?

"Good evening, Madame. I hope I'm not disturbing you."

"You're the journalist."

She remembers. There are some brain cells firing in there.

She shuts the *Vogue Italia* she was leafing through. "Sit down, dear."

"I'm going through to the library."

"Take a seat. We can have a talk, now."

I know how sensitive Dom is about her, but I can hardly

refuse. I pull out the chair in front of the desk and sit. "I came to get some photographs of your boutique on the Avenue Montaigne." I sling my messenger bag on the floor. "Nineteen-thirties Paris seems so romantic and atmospheric."

I don't know if I'll get anything sensible out of her, but I may as well try. I want to ask her about Grandpapa. It was under Grandpapa that the business grew exponentially. That's a story I haven't yet mined.

I look at his portrait behind her. Big man, Churchillian with his elegant hat, waistcoat and cigar. He looks nothing like Dominique. The prominent nose yes, but not the character. This one is all swagger and showmanship. He could be running a circus. And she grew up with him so she carries him in her head all day.

"What was your father like?" My phone vibrates in my pocket. Must be my crew. I ignore it.

"Talented . . . clever, powerful." She taps the desk with her pearly, manicured nails.

"Powerful men can be difficult to live with, especially when it's your father. What was he like with you?"

"Powerful men often have big weaknesses," she says.

This isn't alcohol speaking–parts of her brain are working just fine. "Like what?" I move my chair closer into the desk and lean towards her.

"He was greedy and vain."

No one round here has dared say that.

"That must have been hard to live with."

She has a full head of white hair, swept back off her face, coiffed into tidy waves that end above her shoulders. There's a beauty in the evenness of her features. "Yes. He had a big ego. He was very invested in his own success. A success that was not 100 percent his own. It takes many people to make a success. But he was never willing to acknowledge that."

I don't know what she means by that. "Your father wanted

a Paris boutique, right? That's why you bought the Pereira business, with the Avenue Montaigne shop?"

"My father could have taken on a boutique anywhere he wanted, Faubourg Saint-Honoré, or the Avenue Montaigne–he had the money. No, it wasn't the shop. It was Evening Star he wanted."

"But your father created Evening Star . . ."

She shakes her head. The brow furrows. She gazes out of the window.

What's she thinking about? Have I lost her?

She slides a cigarette out of a mother-of-pearl box and lights it with a gold lighter. She turns her face back to me and makes eye contact. "*C'est une histoire*. It's a myth that Papa invented Evening Star."

"What d'you mean?"

"Pereira created that perfume, which at that time was called Bijou. It means jewel. After the war, Papa took their formula and renamed it Evening Star. He commercialized it with clever marketing, that was his success. When America opened up as a market, he persuaded The Fifth on Fifth to sell and promote it, that's how Severin went international.

"He'd bought Pereira, right?"

She leans towards me and lowers her voice. "He bought Pereira, my foot."

"What do you mean, Madame?"

"Better not to ask. Shhhh, shhhh." She giggles, raising her finger to her mouth as if to say it's a secret. "He stole the business from his old chum."

"He stole it?" The room seems to be spinning around me.

"We don't talk about that," she says. "We're not allowed to talk about that. Shhhh. They were on the run, the Jews. Fleeing *der Führer*, darling." She's as refined looking as Marlene Dietrich, blowing smoke circles into the air.

I shiver thinking of German generals buying Bijou for their mistresses from the boutique on the Avenue Montaigne. "You have proof?"

"Papa wouldn't leave evidence lying around."

"Are there any living relatives who might remember the old business?" I ask her.

"Most are gone. Exterminated in the camps."

Do I believe what she just told me? I focus on my breath, in . . . out . . . in . . . out. I need to calm down. Like, really calm down.

She seems lucid today, but she's an alcoholic. She might be making this up. Why would I trust her? "Why are you telling me this?"

She looks straight at me. "I'm an old woman now. I won't go to my grave holding this. I won't."

My phone buzzes again in my pocket. "Madame, thank you so much for your time today." I reach across the table and shake her hand. "Would you excuse me?"

"*Absolument.*" She smiles and flips open her *Vogue.*

I feel sick and hollow. Like I'm twelve with an essay to write, and I can't think of a single word to say. Is this why Dominique has taken pains to keep me away from her?

I'm a documentary maker with a job to do here. I need to check this out.

Chapter Twenty

I text Jacques, my cameraman. Twenty minutes later I'm sitting in a van on a side street of the old town, squished between him and Jules, the lighting tech. "We can't shoot this afternoon," I tell them.

"But we're behind schedule . . ." says Jacques.

"I need to find a family called Pereira." It's the only way I'll figure out if Maman's crazy story is true.

He shakes his head. "Then don't complain about going over budget."

"Okay, Jacques. Why didn't you tell me Pereira was a Jewish name?"

"It's obvious, isn't it?" he says.

"Sounds Portuguese," I say.

"Exactly." He grabs a can of Coke from the shelf above the dashboard. "Sephardi." He takes a glug. "What's up?"

I google "Pereira Grasse." It produces 1,380,000 hits, many of which are property realtors. Only eighteen hits contain the word "Pereira." "You take half. I'll take half. Start calling," I say.

"Good evening, my name is Zandy Watson," I say in my politest voice. "I'm a film maker researching the perfume house of Pereira. Do you have any connection to this business?"

I'm powered by adrenaline. I've picked up a scent. Now I follow it, chasing it like hounds to a fox.

Pereira Julia is a fifteen-year-old national snowboard athlete.

Pereira Anastacia is a landscape designer.

Pereira Fernando is a mason.

Pereira Pascal is a business trader.

Pereira Ruben cleans buildings.

Pereira Sylvie runs a day care center out of her home.

Twenty minutes later, we've covered eighteen names and found no connection to the Pereira perfume family.

"There are twenty-five thousand Jews in the region, mostly North African immigrants who came in the 1960s." Jacques scrunches the Coke can in his hand. "Are we calling all of them?"

"Who do you know who is Sephardi?" I ask.

"I told you I'm nonpracticing. I don't hang out with them."

I sigh. "What about your family? Surely there's someone who's connected to the community?"

"Uncle Louis," he says, "but he's deaf as a post and I'm not going in. Can't stand those places. We'll pick up your car and you can follow me down there."

Forty-five minutes later, my heart is in my throat as I stand at the desk signing the visitors' book at the Maison de Retraite ORPEA, 89 Corniche Fleurie, on the western side of Nice. I'm confused and overwhelmed. All circuits are busy–sex with Dominique, Stewart's new brief, and now Maman's story–how much can one brain process at a single time?

Louis Cardoso lives in room 49. I jog along bleach-smelling, pastel-colored corridors, my shoes squelching on the grey linoleum floors. I knock and enter a narrow room. A flimsy curtain serves as partition between the two hospital beds.

Cardoso is slouched in an armchair watching a tiny TV. Small, sunken, and whiskery, he has white hair combed across his pate and 1970s-style sideburns. Potted spider plants on the windowsill. Is this what awaits us all?

I introduce myself, shaking his cold, smooth hand that is limp and almost lifeless. Could I have a few moments of his time? I pull up a chair. He comments on the football scores and the weather. "I'm wondering if you might help," I say. "It's very important that I find a member of the Pereira family who was involved in the perfume business before the war."

"What's that?"

"The war, Monsieur Cardoso."

"Yes, the war."

"Did you know anyone in the perfume business?"

"Perfume? Not at all. Haberdashery was our line. Linens for the table and the bed. Fine cottons from Egypt and Italy. Hand embroidered in those days," he says.

"Right." Dead end here. At the end of a long, long day.

"Only two-thousand survived." He shakes his head. "We were the lucky ones."

Don't give up yet. "Yes. Tell me more."

"It was the police, you know. The French police. They sent seventy-six-thousand Jews to the camps. Only two thousand survived."

In my mind I'm back in the Camp des Milles, in the presence of violence and genocide. "Do you remember the Pereira family with the perfume business?"

He shakes his head. "Stay a while, Mamselle. It's a rare day I have a visitor. Isn't that right?"

There's nothing here. I take my leave, return down the maze of corridors and staircases, and stand at the desk. I lift the pen attached to the visitors' book with a shoelace, to sign myself out. I see the names of two visitors since I arrived. One written in spidery hand is Rose-Marie Giaume. She signed in and out . . . visiting room 32, resident Sylvie Pereira.

My heart leaps. "I left my phone with Monsieur Louis." I jog back down the corridor. One flight up, I give a sharp knock on number 32.

Please be there. Please be compos mentis and *pleeeeease* Sylvie, be a member of the Pereira family who owned the perfume business. With those eighteen calls that went nowhere two hours ago, that's about as likely as winning the lottery. Jacques tells me that's one in thirteen million.

Dust motes dance in the beams of sunlight which traverse the room. In front of a small sea view, Sylvie Pereira sits in a chair, her hands making crochet, a blanket over her legs. A walker beside her. Medical equipment all around.

She's in her late sixties, with a pleasant round face, framed by fine hair which hangs in a braid. Bright, clear blue eyes. Long white fingers, bearing a number of rings, like a psychic at a traveling show.

I introduce myself. I say I'm researching the fate of Jewish families during and after the war. I go easy so as not to frighten her off.

Her lips and nail beds are tinged with blue. She seems weighted down with fatigue.

She does not invite me to sit, so I stand.

She coughs in a way that seems to engender a lot of pain.

"I'm sorry, you seem to be in discomfort," I say.

"Emphysema," she says.

"Very challenging," I say.

"It's the flour dust. I worked all my life in a bakery."

"Yes." I nod, turning on my handheld camera. I establish that she is Jewish and ease my way towards the treatment of Jews in Vichy, France. "People think Jews were treated well because the Nazis weren't in power down here. Can you tell me what happened to your family during the Nazi occupation, Ms. Pereira?"

She points to a chair.

I pull it close and take a seat.

"Most of my family died," she says. "Caught escaping to Switzerland, arrested at the border by the French police and sent to the camps." She wheezes.

The hair on the back of my neck stands on end, hearing it from an individual, an actual family member.

"No one in my family came back except my father. He was eighteen when he returned in 1945."

"How did he survive after that?" I say. "Having seen his whole family murdered."

"He had a difficult life."

"The trauma. I can't even imagine. D'you mind my asking, are you related in any way to Rodrigo Pereira?"

She looks at me out of the corner of her eye.

"Who did you say you were?"

I repeat my credentials and show her my press card.

She's tentative, nervous . . . I've lost her, lost the thread. But she has a son. "Maybe I could talk with him?" I say.

Yes. He can come over. Now she remembers he's a machine operator in a textile factory and that he's moved to Normandy. She calls him. No reply. He's at work.

My insides are scrambled. I don't know what to think, what to feel. Just keep going, I tell myself, one word, one foot in front of the other.

"Madame Sylvie, my area of research is Jewish property. Were Jews able to get their houses and businesses back, if they returned?"

This triggers something.

Her misty eyes meet mine.

"Many lost everything and had to start from scratch," I say.

"My father's family were wealthy before the war. They had furs and jewels and houses."

My heart rate picks up. Is there something here? "Exactly. D'you know what property your family owned?"

She looks away into the distance. Out beyond that boxlike window, the Mediterranean shimmers under a perfect blue sky.

Heat bounces off the cement pavements. "I'm not a wealthy woman. I worked all my life in a bakery. And the flour dust, that's what's given me this emphysema."

"Might I ask if you are related to Rodrigo Pereira?"

"Why d'you ask?"

Come on, Sylvie. Don't back away now. "I'm making a TV documentary about Severin. I believe there is some confusion about the merger that took place with that business and Pereira et Fils." I hold my breath in anticipation.

"My father was Jose Pereira."

I keep silent. Is something coming here?

"My grandfather, Mamselle, was called Rodrigo Pereira."

My throat parches. "The Rodrigo who owned Pereira et Fils?" I ask.

"Yes, Mamselle. He owned Pereira et Fils, so my father always said."

A small bomb detonates inside me. "What happened to the business after your father returned?" I grip the arms of my chair.

Silence.

My throat parches. "Madame Sylvie, do you know anything about your family's perfume business?"

"The Germans took Paris on 22 June, 1940. My grandfather had heard about Kristallnacht in Germany. He didn't wait to see what would happen. He rushed round to Yves Severin's office and made the deal with him."

"Your grandfather sold the business to Yves Severin?"

"No. They agreed that Yves Severin would hide the business inside his own, just as long as the war lasted. The agreement was that when my grandfather returned to Grasse, Severin was to give the business back to him, my father said."

The thrill of uncovering something. And leaden dread. I want this–or do I?

"Did your grandfather lodge a contract with lawyers or bankers?"

"There was no time," she says.

"Of course." But without evidence, all I have is the hearsay of a needy woman. There's nothing here I can use.

"My father tried to get our business back, but he had no proof. His word against theirs. He searched everywhere for a contract. There was nothing. He challenged Yves Severin while he was alive. The man denied it, and my father gave up. He had no document to prove it, no money, no big lawyer."

I'm pulled every which way, like a puppet in a show with some larger being pulling on each of my strings. Who am I, a documentary maker hunting down a story, or a friend–dare I say lover–discovering who she just slept with? I can't figure this out. I jiggle my right foot, as though that will give me clarity.

"Did your father ever mention the name Bijou?"

She's at her crochet, feeding the hook in and pulling it out, in . . . out, in . . . out. A frown pinches her brow. "The formula for Bijou was ours," says Sylvie. "Severin promised not to look at the formula, to return the unopened envelope when the war was over. Severin made a killing with their perfume, Evening Star. My father said Evening Star was our Bijou with a new name. The Severins stole our business," she says.

I get the chills. My body shakes so hard my teeth nearly chatter. "How do you know they did?"

"My father told me over and again. Why would he lie?"

"Didn't he go to the newspapers? Why didn't they publish his story?" I ask.

"It was chaos after the war." She wheezes. "My father had no home, no dignity, no identity . . . He'd lost his whole family. His life was not a . . . stable one. He often turned to drink or the open road."

Meanwhile, everyone and his wife demanded reparations as the country was putting itself together again. I remember the video from the Camp des Milles–even after the Nazis left, Parisians marched through the streets, demanding that Jews be sent to the crematoria.

"Madame, let me ask you again. You have no proof of this?"

"No proof. No good. It's too late," she says.

I need to get out of here and think.

"Why did you come here?" she asks.

I don't have an answer. "You've been of great help." I cross my hands over my heart. "Let me think about this. I'll be in touch."

"That's right." She tosses her handiwork onto the table to her right and doubles over. "I need to rest now," she croaks.

Do I hunt down that contract or pretend this never happened?

Outside the building, I stand in the rays of the setting sun, letting the moist sea air coat my body in salt. I'm tempted to sit a moment. Here in front of the car park sit round metal tables surrounded by palm trees. But the chairs are splattered with bird poop, so I make my way over to my car.

As a documentary maker, it would be incredible to find this contract. I would be fêted at CNM. *Climate* would be mine for the taking.

I sit in the driver's seat, my finger on the ignition button. I can't pretend I haven't heard this story–from two people now. I wish I hadn't heard it. I don't know whether I'm betraying Dom or he's betrayed me. There's no way I'll find this contract. It's too much of a coincidence this story has come to me just when I need it.

But burying my head in the sand isn't right. I uncover the truth and show it to the world. It's my job, and it's what I was put on this earth to do. Like Stewart said, I'm not taking anything away, I'm adding. And I'm not adding anything–yet. I'm investigating. This will probably lead to nothing–and then what? What about Stewart and Euan and his layer of grit? I don't know. I'm not making any decisions. I'm just doing my job, trying to stay open-minded to the truth of all this.

I start the ignition. I'll hunt down that contract, and then I'll talk to Dominique right after that.

I pluck my phone from my bag to find a text from him asking if we can meet up now.

I'm in no mood to see Dominique.

`me: rain check tonight?`

`Dominique: noooh. Why?`

`me: bit confused here. Want to see you but worried it'll complicate our work.`

`Dominique: ☹`

`me: regroup tomorrow?`

`Dominique: sleep well xo`

I pull up Amy Winehouse on my phone and blast her through the car speaker, so loud I can't hear myself think.

"Sorry, sweetie." I pat Paddington's head. He doesn't get Amy, whereas all that pain and genius is just what I need to get me out of my own funk.

I hurtle back to my flat. Inside, I roll out my yoga mat, place Paddington on a chair in front of me so we can have a good workout–for only the second time since I've been in France–squat, pushup, burpee.

I've gone soft, allowing myself to get out of shape. I'm confused about everything.

Squat, pushup, burpee. Bloody land of lotus eaters. Squat, pushup, burpee. Repeat, repeat, repeat.

At 7:00 a.m. the next morning, I jump in my car and belt over to the library-archive, hoping to slip in unnoticed. The archive is the first place I thought of to look for the contract–well, the only place.

I don't know how to do this, so I just put my next foot forward. The thought of sifting through the file boxes appeals to me as appropriate and calming. I need to do something physical to counterbalance the noise in my head.

I've got two hours until I need to meet Dominique and my crew to finish the interviews in the blending lab. I walk through Grandpapa's office where the ashtray on the desk bears three old stubs. A trail of ash runs across the tooled leather desktop–the only signs that Madame Catherine was here last night. I don't know whether to feel sad about her, or intrigued at what else she might be harboring.

I shut the door between the office and the archive and stand with my back against it. Blood rushes to my head, and I try to counteract this by welcoming the cool silence of the space.

Hands shaking, I lay my cameras out on the coffee table between the two sofas. I turn to the wall on the right of the door, which is lined with cupboards. Inside those cupboards are the box files.

Grandpapa acquired Pereira et Fils in 1940, so I pull out all the boxes dated 1939, 1940, and 1941. Eight of them. The Nazis arrived on French soil in 1940, and my heart catches as I remember that six weeks later they had taken France, Belgium, Luxembourg, and the Netherlands. I kneel and lay out the boxes across the floor. I need some kind of proof, some paper trail, showing the agreement between Pereira and Severin. With no training in business or accounting, I don't know what I'm looking for.

I start with the first box marked 1939 and lay the papers out across the sofas and the floor. One by one, I pick up bank deposit slips, receipt books, invoices for raw materials and manufacturing equipment. Petty cash slips lie between depreciation records and accounts of travel, transport, entertainment, and gift expenses.

I've been skimming boxes in this archive for weeks now looking for stills, flipping through marketing materials, old photos, data about flower harvests and essential oil quality, mixed in with receipts for Cuban cigars and for Paris lunches at the Café de la Paix, Bouillon Camille Chartier, Le Grand Colbert–the Severin corporate scrapbook.

I will myself to slow down, to search methodically, not rabidly. I need to keep my whole consciousness primed for this search. I cannot allow my emotions to overrun the process, or I'll miss something. Yet I must hurry too. I don't want anyone to surprise me here, and I'm cutting into our valuable shooting schedule.

I haven't eaten yet today. All I've had is black coffee and I'm faint with hunger. Why do they keep all this stuff? Accounting journals and ledgers, recording income, deductions, and credits. Old business checkbooks, payroll, sales slips, canceled checks. I don't even balance my checkbook, even if I should.

I pack up the paperwork for 1939 and return the box to its shelf. I slide out 1940 and spread that pile across the floor. The 1940 box is livelier with advertisement cuttings showing off Chanel N°5, "Every Woman Alive Loves Chanel N°5." I skim magazines devoted to the Grand Prix de l'Arc de Triomphe horse race.

The French *Vogue* cuttings show women with tightly cinched waists and full skirts to midcalf with multiple rows of pearls at the neck. They jut out hips and bare shoulders in evening gowns, striking come-hitherish poses, and vie with paper adverts for the perfume Shocking de Schiaparelli.

I'm an idiot. Why am I even looking? I slam my fist on the floor. If there were documentary evidence of this deal, Yves

Severin would have destroyed it. Keeping it could only incriminate him.

Slow down, Zandy. I return the 1940 papers to their carton and open up the lavender-colored drawer box housing the newspapers for that year, collectors' items for sure. I need to pee, but I haven't got time to go out to the loo at the end of the corridor. My stomach turns over as I review the huge black newspaper headlines, trumpeting doom.

> GERMAN TROOPS ENTER PARIS.
>
> PARIS THE GRAVEST HOUR.
>
> 1,000 BOMBS ON PARIS.
>
> PARIS FALLS MAGINOT LINE IMPERILED.

And a cartoon depicting the mooted Identity Registration System. Photos depict German generals in trench coats massed around the Eiffel Tower and ranks of soldiers filing by the Arc de Triomphe. Imagine being a Jew watching this unfold.

Holding the drawer open with one hand, I insert the newspapers back inside, careful not to tear any. The drawer was overfull, and it's hard to fit the papers back in. I'm sliding the overstuffed drawer back into its housing when my nail catches on something. It tears. A jab of pain spurts up my finger. Dammit. What is that? I'm about to remove my hand but I feel around to see what could have caught my edge. I hope I'm not dripping blood in there when my finger catches on something thick, stuck to the underside of the box top. I wiggle it until it comes loose and withdraw a bulky envelope which must have been glued inside the top of the container.

I yank at it. It gives way and comes out in my hand. I prize open the envelope, yellowed with age, and withdraw two sheets of superior quality folded notepaper, about four by six inches in size, thick and spongy to the touch. A circular stain, perhaps from a coffee cup, marks half of the first page.

Rodrigo Pereira. I whisper it out loud as I read.

My heart pumps hard. Stay calm, I tell myself. Stay focused.

Rodrigo Pereira: Je remits par la présente Pereira et Fils à mon ami Yves Severin. Cela inclut tous nos actifs, physiques et aures, y compris notre parfum Bijou et sa formule. La formule restera entièrement secrète et exclusive et tout ce qui précède sera retourné à Rodrigo Pereira à son retour en France.

Yves Severin: Je m'engage par la présente à protéger le commerce de Pereira et Fils pendant la guerre et à le rendre intégralement, y compris le parfum Bijou et sa formule, à mon ami Rodrigo Pereira à son retour en France.

Signé ce jour 23 Juin 1940

Rodrigo Pereira *Yves Severin*

I'm burning hot. Perspiration runs down the back of my neck. I understand the words but paste them into Google Translate just in case:

Rodrigo Pereira: *I hereby hand over Pereira et Fils to my friend Yves Severin. This includes all of our assets physical and otherwise, including our perfume Bijou and its formula. The formula shall remain entirely secret and proprietary and all of the above will be returned to Rodrigo Pereira when he returns to France.*

Yves Severin: *I hereby commit to keep the business of Pereira safe during the course of the war and return it in its entirety, including the perfume Bijou and its formula, to my friend Rodrigo Pereira on his return to France.*

My hand shakes. I read the signatures again and again.

Rodrigo Pereira's is a small, neat, artistic hand.

Yves Severin's is large and confident, splayed across the width of the page.

I came to find this, thinking I didn't have a chance in hell. Here it is . . . and now what? I stare at the pages transfixed.

Move, I tell myself. Right now.

I refold the two sheets of notepaper and return them to their envelope. I slide it into the inner compartment of my messenger bag and zip it up. I don't know why I do this, I just know I have to secure this letter until I've thought things through. I slip the strap of the bag over my torso. I feel like I've got a bomb in there. Which I have.

I return the boxes to the shelves and shut the cupboard doors.

My throat is dry and my hands are clammy. I walk across the room, shut the door behind me, and pass through Grandpapa's office. Outside, I stride towards my car, my head held high, trying not to attract attention. I slip into the driver's seat and speed out through the gates.

I've got a grenade in my bag. Like the charge I'd carried inside me for eleven days in eighth grade after Rita told me that her dad was in jail and it was all my dad's fault.

I didn't know whether to believe her or not. I consulted my diary and saw that things had been weird around my house ever since that summer's day when the FBI had come round and I'd lied to them because Dad told me to.

All year, Mum and Dad had been whispering to each other. Or I'd hear heated conversations from behind closed doors. More shouting. Doors slamming. That whole year, Dad went away a lot. Or he'd be home at odd times, closeted in his study, shredding paper. It was weirder than usual. He was coiled tight as a spring. No one came to our house anymore.

January 2 was crazy warm. The skies tipped everything they had in buckets all over us. I punctured the front tire of my bike at the park and had to walk home three miles in the rain. Soaking wet, I barged into my dad's study, told him what Rita had accused him of in that hallway, and demanded an explanation "right now!" I stamped my foot and water seeped out of my sneakers, making two brown stains on the carpet where I stood.

"Chillax, Zandy. Calm yourself." He took a white cotton handkerchief from his back pocket and wiped the sweat from his brow. 'Course it ain't true. Mike did some wrong things. He's making up these stories."

Mike was lying or my dad was. A black hole opened in my gut. Both versions were grim.

"Why did you make me lie to those men?" I asked.

"Don't be bothering yourself with stuff like that. You're too young to understand."

When school started back up, Rita wouldn't have anything to do with me.

After school, instead of hanging out at her house, I locked myself in my room, the curtains drawn, blasting Beyoncé on my headphones. I didn't know whom to believe. I blocked out the light, blocked out the day, blocked out the possibility of sifting through the story in my mind.

Now I'm thirty, barreling down the Route de Grasse and I can no longer hide in my room blasting pop music. Forty minutes later, still trembling, I've lodged the package in a safety deposit box in the teeny Credit Agricole bank in Tourrettes sur Loup.

Walking along the narrow pavement back to the village square as cars speed by is like balancing on a tightrope. Do I tell Dominique what's going on? Do I ask him, "Do you know your grandfather didn't buy Pereira, he stole it?" Or do I conceal it?

Of course I tell him. I make my way to the village square to retrieve my car. I can't keep this discovery from him. It's dishonorable.

I insert my parking ticket into the exit gate. As I wait for the barrier to rise and let me through, I focus on slowing down my breathing. I'm scared of how he'll react. If he was so touchy about hiding the use of aldehydes, he's not going to take this lying down.

I lodged the contract in that safety deposit box out of caution, fearful he could get hold of it, remove it from me, or even shut down the movie. Should I go for a drive and think this through before I reveal my hand? Should I text them all that I can't film today?

But I head back to the office. I can't bail on a shoot. I'm the director. Inside the foyer, I stand on the huge white floor, unable to move.

The janitor Alain pushes his cart of samples towards the elevator, whistling as he works. "Have you seen Monsieur Dominique?" I ask.

"*Oui,* Mamselle, he's in the blending labs with Madame Jacqueline and your crew."

I squeeze my fists tight. Get it together, I tell myself. I'm a documentary maker. I need to piece together this story by asking everyone all the questions and seeing how the different versions stack up against each other. I will ask, "Did you know your grandfather didn't buy Pereira et Fils. He stole it?" Then Dominique explains why I've got this all wrong.

We've come so far. I trust him. I know he'll know what all this is about. And he'll help me out of my fix with Stewart. I know he will.

I release a huge bag of breath I've been holding in and make my way to the labs.

Chapter Twenty-One

DOMINIQUE

We've been filming in the blending facility.

"It's a wrap." Zandy nods at Jacques. He hoists the camera off his shoulder, zips it into its black nylon case, and gathers up cables from the floor.

Now that we're finished, I want a few moments alone with her. Two days ago we were skipping up that rocky path from Courmes. In a trice she was naked, with her trousers around her ankles and her legs clamped around my hips.

No starched napkins, Michelin rosettes, or jewels. Those are nice. I like doing things properly–there is pleasure in that. But I can be myself with her. No fuss about dry cleaning, the weddings, the formality, the house parties. How sexy she was in cargo pants and a tight-fitting tank top.

None of the women I've been involved with in the past would hike with me. Some day after this documentary is over, I'll take her back-packing on the Grande Randonnée. We'll hike from here to Spain and sleep in huts. This is a woman who doesn't need to be pampered with breakfast on a tray in bed.

I can almost feel her boots digging into my backside as we leaned against the tree. I'm getting aroused just thinking about her. I was disappointed when she called a "rain check" last night and said, "It could complicate the movie." I'm drawn to her, to that fire in her eyes as she directs her crew. She's like Boadicea on horseback with her spear aloft.

"Well done. Thank you, everyone." Zandy files her script away in its binder. I like seeing her all commanding as director. It's sexy. I want to kiss that delectable mouth of hers, those plump, curvy lips. But not in the office.

Jacqueline, Camille, and I congratulate each other. "How did we manage to make all this come together?" Jacqueline smiles as they pack up and leave.

"We need to firm up the schedule for those outdoor shots," Zandy says to Jacques. "I'll text you."

They're a rough-looking bunch–the cameraman and the lighting and sound technicians–but decent and professional.

She swivels to face me. "Dominique, before you leave, could I have a word with you in private?"

Once we're alone, I raise my eyebrow and smile, hinting at our last meeting up the mountain.

But I'm met with a space of several feet–she seems to be keeping as much distance as possible. Her body language says she's closed off from me.

My thoughts of kissing her perish; like she's poured a bucket of ice-cold water over me.

"Can we talk about Pereira et Fils, the company your grandfather procured in 1940?" She stands with her feet apart, hands akimbo. Her combat boots peek out beneath her lab coat. Gone are her Greek-style leather sandals.

She seems determined to keep this strictly professional.

"Of course." Perhaps that meeting with Stewart has unsettled her. I understand–work deadlines make me anxious and tight. But look at her–she's more wound up than when she first arrived. She's making me nervous. I suppose the sex changed things.

She steps towards me. "Just to go over it again . . ." She recites the details of Grandpapa buying Pereira et Fils and the development of Evening Star in the fifties, pacing up and down in front of me.

It seems I'm being interrogated. I avoid eye contact, directing my attention inwards as I busy myself tidying up the new Lindissima packaging and the poster boards she's been filming. Noor's famous nose in a single line drawing is a strong statement full of character as well as beauty.

I swivel towards her. "What's this about?" We've been through this multiple times. I'm getting hot under the collar.

"What if he didn't buy Pereira? What if that's a story your grandfather . . . made up?"

That cocktail of shame, dread, and anxiety I live with washes over me. I worry Maman has been spinning her some tale. No. I overreact about Maman–she's my Achilles heel. Zandy is not talking about Maman. Besides, she's talking about Grandpapa, a great man, a man who was nothing if not honorable. "Zandy, this is a misunderstanding."

"I believe he stole the company. I think he promised to return the business to the family after the war, and he went against his word."

On three sides of this room, machines fed by an array of conveyor belts carry glass vials in and out from one process to another, under precise hygienic, atmospheric conditions–a vast complex arrangement of science and precision performed by ingenious electromechanical machines. Yet all I feel is chaos.

"This is preposterous." I try to arrange my thoughts, my emotions, my plan of action. "Someone's been spinning stories–local businesses are always jealous of our position. This is the union chief? *Allez,* Zandy. When you run a business of this size, countless people have a grudge against you."

"I'm not an idiot, Dominique. I know how to do my job."

"We have claims from employees we've fired. Marie Claire

Santon, publicly undressing in her place of employment. And Michel Barbue, undue profanity at work–"

"This goes way beyond the 'he said, she said' kind of spat."

"In what way?"

She cocks her head to one side. "Your mother told me about this." She looks steely; not soft or inviting at all.

"When did you see Maman?" The room spins around me. "What did she say to you?"

"We talked in Grandpapa's office yesterday."

I stiffen. How did I let that happen? Maman was surely making up stories to impress her.

"You know my mother is–unwell. The stories she tells are not always accurate."

Why am I panicking? I'm not responsible for this. Yet I feel Rome is burning around me. I have to clear this up, to convince her this is a misunderstanding. She holds that binder under her arm like she's got a dossier on us. I'd like to tear those script notes of hers into tiny shreds.

"Have you seen the documents of sale?" she asks.

This is preposterous. "No, Zandy. Have *you* studied the articles of incorporation of CNM Documentaries?" I grip the edge of the glass screen that separates us from the equipment.

She shrugs and throws her hands open. "You love detail . . ."

The glass is cool, almost cold but my fingers are moist with heat. "Do you scour the management's Discussion and Analysis of Results of Operation and Financial Condition?" If I press any harder, I might shatter the glass. "What's CNM's position on current financial condition and liquidity? Why should I review the documents of sale? There's never been any reason to." I shall hammer her with questions until she stops this nonsense. "Do you know what unrealized gains CNM holds on derivative financial instruments? Have you read their consolidated statement of equity?"

"This is your family business. I'm sure you've studied the records."

She stands tall, looks cocky even. There's a gulf that is unbridgeable.

"After the war, did Rodrigo's son Jose Pereira ask for the return of their business?"

I stamp my foot. "Is this some kind of game you're playing?" I took the risk of opening myself to her, and she's pulling this on me?

I pick up my phone and stuff it in my jacket pocket. Obviously, none of this is true. But she's deadly serious here. She's on a mission. I point to the door with my hand. I want her out.

"If you're so sure of this nonsense, why are you even asking me about it?" I'll have a technician come over here to ensure everything is in its correct place and working order, to resanitize it.

She stays rooted to her spot. "I find a story by doing 360 degrees of questioning. I ask everyone all the questions and see how the different versions stack up against each other. I'm waiting for you to explain why I've got this wrong."

"You're completely wrong."

She thrusts her head towards me and her chin juts out, like she's furious. "You're not convincing me of that. And, I have evidence."

She's a rocket that's going to explode at any moment. I don't recognize her, don't understand who she is or what's come over her. "What evidence?"

All around me the whirr and buzz of machinery. Metal clinking, the clack of interlocking rollers and chains on assembly lines, the hiss of an industrial press, intermittent warning beeps. I focus my attention on these rhythmical sounds and movements of my childhood, the heartbeat of my days, to get control of myself, of the madness that's happening here.

"Let's put the evidence to the side. I came because I wanted you to show me why I'm mistaken. To prove it to me."

I face her with my whole body. I need to assess this situation, try to sense what is going on here. "Show me your evidence and I'll show you that it's not valid."

"A contract has come into my possession implying there was an agreement to give the business back to this family."

"Who gave it to you?" I ask.

"I don't reveal my sources," she says. "Ethics . . ."

"Ethics! How convenient for you." I move towards her. Now I'm the one threatening her with my body, and rightly so. How dare she accuse me of this nonsense.

"Is this for the film or for your background information?" I ask.

She removes her lab coat and throws it on the table. "That's hardly the point."

This is like some conspiracy theory in Donald Trump's America. On the wall above the door, a digital clock ticks through the seconds and minutes. This is defamation. I need to get control of this. Shall I call the lawyers or the police right away? Or am I better off appealing to her personally?

I run my fingers along the edge of the metal table in the middle of the room. The cold smoothness of its surface cools my skin.

We only just had sex, dammit. The human bond is the best way through a tricky situation. I must appeal to the intimacy and assurance we have.

She strips off her rubber gloves and drops them on the floor.

I take my handkerchief from my trouser pocket and dab at the perspiration on my forehead. We have everything at stake–the business, our good name, our employees' livelihoods–everything. No. I was mad to trust her. I'm going big guns with the lawyers. I will leave no stone unturned.

"The truth matters." She glowers at me.

Before I can do anything, she shoots out of the door.

I follow in hot pursuit to see her off the premises. I will not have her contaminating my space and my life.

Chapter Twenty-Two

ZANDY

I stride down the narrow corridor needing him to come after me and explain why I've got this backwards.

There he is. I hear the swift *clack-clack* of his leather shoes on the linoleum floor. Relief. I need him to show me that Grandpapa *did* legitimately buy Pereira et Fils because I can't have got him this wrong. It's not possible.

"What's your agenda?" he says into the back of my neck as he comes up behind me.

I swivel back to find a pair of eyes bulging with anger.

This feels menacing, not reassuring. "The truth." My voice is small.

I see in the tiny movements of his jaw that he's grinding his teeth. A darkness emanates from him. His presence feels threatening. I want to flee, but the doors flanking us are all locked with keypads. Inside those glass-walled processing labs and blending rooms, employees bustle about their business like an alien worker race in their white coats, blue rubber gloves, hair nets, and plastic glasses. Behind those doors, Heath Robinson–style piping hangs over cylindrical stainless-steel vats. If we were inside one of those rooms, he might hurl me into a vat, into its boiling oil.

"It's impossible your mother didn't tell you about this. You're her son. She told me and I'm a stranger." If my account wasn't true, he wouldn't be angry like this. He would explain it calmly. "You're lying again," I say.

"I'm not lying." His neck flames crimson.

I don't believe him. "Dominique, you just need to show me you aren't."

His eyes narrow.

It's claustrophobic. I have to get out. I barrel down the corridor.

He keeps pace as I half run through the tunnel connecting the processing facility to the main office building. The scent of citronella sickens me, but I shorten my stride and hurry along.

At the foot of the stairs, he shouts, "You challenge my honor?" He's panting. "This is my family, my reputation. What about the jobs of all the people who work in this town? Do you know what damage you could do with these lies?"

Lies? He's gone mad. I'm racing, my feet turning over fast. My hand is on my messenger bag at my side to keep it from banging against my hip. I'm almost running now.

He jogs to keep up with me.

I sprint up the stairs to the ground floor.

At the top of the stairs I shout, "No. You're the one who's lying. I'm on the side of truth–and justice."

I cross the huge light-filled atrium.

He's right behind me. With his head bent over my neck, he shouts, "You're damaged."

It's a shocking personal attack, like a knife through my liver.

Staff crisscross the foyer in groups of twos and threes. In the center of the atrium, I swivel to face him. "How dare you . . ." He's trying to throw me off by attacking me. I won't allow it.

"You don't know what's real from unreal." His accusations come at me like an avalanche. "You have no sense of reality.

You're using us for your own profit. This is a game for you."

"Prove it's not true." That's my parting shot.

He circles me, stomping round and around. "I certainly will. This is some personal drama you're acting out."

Look, the neck flames again. He's definitely lying. I must report the Pereira scandal to Stewart. This is about justice. It's about one family profiting while another, a Jewish family, withered.

That tightness in my chest reminds me of my promise that day at the Camp des Milles that I wouldn't bring the Nazi story into this doc. And my other promise not to reveal his secrets.

No, I'm being weak. This isn't about whether he's run out of money. This is about truth and justice. I dig my nails into the flesh of my thumb pads. I slept with him. I'm interested in his people and his cause, but I still need to do the right thing. Wake up, Zandy! I take a long look at him. In the hardness of his eyes, I see the seduction was a setup, a ruse to distract me.

More than ever, I need to be clearheaded. I harden my own eyes to show he's not denting me with his assault.

As I stride towards the glass doors, the heat along the length of my spine tells me his stare is on my back. The electric doors glide open. I emerge into the sunlight. The gravel crunches underfoot as I point myself towards my little white Peugot.

Place one foot in front of the other. Just do it.

I'm committed to changing the world by revealing important truths. I can't live with myself if I pretend I never saw that contract.

This man romanced me so he could control me. He used me, sexually. This is the story he's been trying to keep me away from all this time.

I reach into my bag for the remote, find the unlock button, and depress it. *Clunk.* The doors unlock.

French man seduces idiot journalist who has been drugged

with the pleasures of the South of France. Just as Yves Severin duped Rodrigo Pereira into believing his friend would return his business to him after the war.

I've known Stewart six years. I've known this man for eight weeks.

I jump in my car and hurtle out through the gates, down the mountain pass through Tourrettes sur Loup. Just before Vence, I pull off on a deserted track. I need somewhere safe and quiet, where Dominique Severin won't find me.

I inhale a long, slow breath and tap open the photo app on my phone. I select the six photos I took of the Pereira contract and ping them to Stewart.

I'm going to tell both sides of the Severin story.

It's 5:30 a.m. in NYC. He calls me right back.

"I think Yves Severin committed a great crime." I burble the details into the phone, my hands shaking.

He listens.

I hear mumbling and rustling in the background followed by his voice, "Go back to sleep, honey. . . Go on, Zandy," he says. And then, "Just what we wanted."

"How do I verify the document is real?"

"I'll call you right back," he says.

My shoulders tingle with nerves as I sit in this lay-by, in a craggy overhang of rock and sand dotted with tendrils of green growth.

Ten minutes later, he's back on the line. "I've emailed you the contact details for our lawyer in Nice, Philippe Kergeuno at 26 Avenue Jean Médecin. Get the contract down there right away. Have him put it in his safe."

"Roger that." I jiggle my foot with nerves.

"He'll have it authenticated. Zandy, get back on your shooting schedule and don't let Severin mess with you. Do your work, then get out of France."

I end the call so shaky I could faint.

Through the window I look at the rockface to the side of this lay-by, puckered with black hollows and deep cracks. Millions of years ago, to form these mountains, pieces of the Earth's crust smashed against each other in a head-on collision. Just like that January 18 of my eighth grade. That day of slush, ice, and freezing rain when the headmaster Mr. Woolton made the announcement at the morning meeting. "I have very sad news to share with you today. Rita Papadopoulos died yesterday afternoon. The family asks for privacy at this very difficult time. We will keep you posted about services."

Rita had thrown herself in front of the 4:32 p.m. to NYC at Walnut Street Station.

"You shouldn't go to the service. You're too young. It will be too upsetting for you," said Mum.

"The family's a mess. The whole thing is a mess," said Dad.

I ignored Mum's advice and sat leaden in the back of the school bus, while my classmates giggled and shoved each other on the way to and from the service.

I'd lost Rita four weeks earlier when she'd spat at me that it was my dad's fault that her dad had gone down.

When they lowered her casket into the stony earth at the Holy Trinity Greek Orthodox Church, a piece of me died–together with any last trace of respect I had for my scumbag father.

That day, any flickering hope I'd had that things were the way my dad said they were died too.

And I knew for certain that I should have gone to the police and told them that Rita and her dad *had* been at our house that Sunday and that my dad had leaned on me to lie about it. Her death was partly my fault.

A black crater still smokes inside me from that day.

My family loaded up and moved from New Jersey to Bridgehampton. For the rest of that year I was numb, surly, and spaced out, barely noticing who or what was around me.

In high school I figured out he'd shopped Rita's father, used him as the fall guy in some money-making scheme, one of the many that came fast, one after the other. And that he was despicable. The day I graduated from Bridgehampton High School I left home. I haven't been anywhere near my mum and dad since.

Now in this lay-by, inches from the rockface, I scroll through my photos and find the image of Rita that I had digitized. I tap through my iPhone settings and set it as my wallpaper.

Now I'll see it every time I pick up my phone. At any moment of weakness, I'll see what's at stake here–TRUTH MATTERS.

Chapter Twenty-Three

DOMINIQUE

I call an immediate crisis meeting. One hour later, five of us are gathered in Grandpapa's office with Maman seated at his desk. I sit across from her while Camille paces up and down behind me. First I need to know exactly what Maman said to Zandy—whatever she said is surely the cause of all the trouble. Then we decide how to prove to Zandy that she's wrong.

Louis Fournier, senior partner from our outside counsel, and Paul Martin, our inhouse lawyer, are perched on the window seat, facing Maman at a right angle. Jacqueline observes from the corner.

Ashamed and shocked by Zandy's accusation, I lost my cool. I have regained control of myself now. I want Maman relaxed, so I take the chair on the opposite side of the desk, as though we are having a business meeting.

"What did you say to Zandy Watson?" I ask Maman. She alternates between two states of mind these days—vague and distracted or lucid and clever—giving a window into the CEO that she once was. These states roll in one after the other with no hint or warning of the change to come.

"What were you doing when you met her?" I ask Maman.

"I was working." She opens the leather photograph album sitting on the desk and leafs through glossy photos of Les Voiles de Saint-Tropez, the classic yacht race she sponsored back in the eighties.

"See those?" She nods, pointing at a cluster of sleek wooden yachts circling a buoy, the word SEVERIN marked out in bold white letters on their spinnakers.

"What on earth were you doing here?" I say to Maman.

"It's lonely in the house," she says.

"What did you talk about?" I ask.

"We talked about the yacht races. Those beautiful boats with our name emblazoned on their sails. And the spinnakers all lavender. I insisted on lavender." As she smiles, a series of lines furrow the powdery skin around her mouth and jaw.

"And you didn't talk about the Pereira business at all?"

"Of course not," she says. " . . . or maybe we did."

Camille appears through the double doors, holding an archive box. She's beetroot red in the face and shaking her head. "You nearly destroyed the business with your drinking."

"What's all the fuss?" says Maman. She opens the top right drawer, retrieves a copy of *Vogue Italia* and thumps it, heavy as a brick on the desk in front of her.

"Now you're making up stories to this filmmaker?" Camille storms off again through the double doorway. Camille is right, but she isn't helping.

Maman flicks through the glossy pages. "*Oui,*" she says, looking intently at a page displaying a tweed cape and matching hat.

Fournier observes in silence, his hands steepled. Sixtyish, an expert on EEC law in member nations, he leans towards her. "Madame Catherine, it's very important you recall exactly what you said to the documentary maker." He has been loyal to us, a kind of parent we never had. He helped me tremendously when I was wresting power from Maman and represents the continuity of the business to me. "Madame Catherine, what did you say to her about the purchase of Pereira et Fils?"

"Pereira was a long time ago." Maman turns her head and gazes out of the window. "I don't remember."

I clench my fists in exasperation. "We'll not get anywhere with this line of pursuit," I say.

"Why don't I talk to Zandy?" says Jacqueline. "She'll open up to me and I can find out what's going on with her."

I nod and address the lawyers, "Can you give me a moment?" I'm drawn to the library by the sounds of cupboard doors opening and heavy file boxes being plonked on surfaces. Camille must be taking the place apart. I open the doors and find her sitting crosslegged on the floor surrounded by paper.

Camille looks up at me. "If it's true, then what kind of man was Grandpapa?"

I stand over her as dread flows through me. "A vain, self-seeking, dishonest man taking advantage of his friend at his most vulnerable moment. It would be heinous. There would be no words to describe him."

"And Maman?"

Through the open door, I see Maman gazing out of the window. I can just hear her singing to herself, "*Tous les garçons et les filles.*"

"If she knew and didn't tell us, we've been living a lie our whole lives," says Camille.

The very thing I've been thinking, only I wish she hadn't said it. I don't want to think about it. I can't think it.

She breaks eye contact and looks down at the floor. "I blame myself." Camille hangs her head. "If I hadn't pushed you into this, we wouldn't be in this mess."

I could be furious at Camille for persuading me to make this movie. But I bury away the spurt of anger inside me. There's no time for that now. I squat and stroke her shoulder. "It's okay, *chouchou.* We will resolve this. But we need to take action, not get lost in what-ifs."

"It's not true. It just can't be!" she blurts.

"We will find the documents." I slam my fist against the wall. "We'll find the evidence, and we'll show the world Grandpapa bought Pereira et Fils like Maman told us he did." Do I believe this? I have to because the alternative is too wicked to imagine. I go to the double doors and ask Fournier and Martin to join us.

The lawyers face us, standing between the open doors.

"Can she use this lie in her film?" Camille asks Martin.

He holds up a sheaf of paper. "The contract prohibits her from revealing intellectual property." Over two meters tall, he's constantly bending his neck like a swan. "That's perfume formulas, financial details, customer or employee contracts, and correspondence such as executive communications."

"These contracts can only ring-fence what belongs to the business and its area of operation," says Fournier.

Dread sluices through my veins. "Meaning?"

"Meaning sourcing material, producing, marketing, and selling perfume," he says.

"If that cow tells lies about us on screen, I'll skin her alive," says Camille.

"Surely the mention of Pereira is covered by 'sourcing'?" I have my back to the window and face them straight on.

Fournier shakes his head. "That wouldn't hold up in court."

The word thwacks me in the solar plexus. "Court?' I haven't even imagined this.

"It's common to start out one way with a documentary and then find there's another story."

Just what I most dreaded. I must keep calm.

"The point is, Dominique, the onus is on you to prove the Pereira purchase was bona fide," says Fournier.

I should never have allowed this documentary. I squeeze the edge of the sofa to steady myself.

"Find the records," I say. "Ransack everything."

He nods. "We'll assemble a team," he addresses Martin, "and go through every piece of paper with a fine-tooth comb. Check the trade registry, the tax authority, and the Ministry of Public Accounts."

Fournier holds his chin in his hand and strokes it. "The challenge is that no one filed records in June of 1940. The Jews scribbled agreements on notepaper, the back of envelopes, and took off in the night–their lives were at stake. Every moment counted."

I feel sick at the thought. "Contact the notary," I say. "I need to disprove this. The bank will have a record of the payment." It's stifling in here, and Camille is spraying paper all around her on the floor. She's not working systematically, she's just making a mess.

Fournier shakes his head. "Money in the bank would have been no good to the Pereiras. They needed gold, jewelry, or cash to get across the border to safety." He draws himself up and takes a long inhale through his nostrils.

Something about his gravitas scares me.

He steps towards me. "Dominique, you must prepare yourself. We may find no record." He places a hand on my shoulder. "And if we find nothing, we have no way of establishing whether this tale is true or not."

I've known this all through this meeting, but hearing it from Fournier, who is solid and knowledgeable and who never exaggerates, is a shock.

My feet are weighted to the floor. Do I close this documentary down? I squeeze my hands at my sides. Of course I do. Our good name is all we have. We must protect it. I owe it to my hardworking ancestors and all those who have toiled for Severin Frères.

But I can't cancel it now. I pace up and down the length of the sofa. We're too far in with the new scent. It's terrific. And without the publicity from this movie, we'll have to close the business anyway. A thickness in my chest. I've committed to production in Taiwan and I've promised the moon to Noor Haddad. It's too late now to turn back. I need to calm myself. We'll search for the contract and find it. I know Grandpapa is innocent, even if it will be challenging to prove it. Right is on our side, and maybe Jacqueline can persuade Zandy not to go on with this madness.

Fournier has his back to us and is making calls to his office. Martin is scribbling pencil notes on the documentary contract.

I walk to the fireplace where I see the brass paperweight Grandpapa used to roll in his hand when I was a boy. I reach for it. It is something wonderful to hold, a beautiful piece of art from the twenties, with twirling shapes like swirl of soft ice cream, yet solid at the same time. When I was a boy, I'd come in from the garden with my butterfly net hanging over my shoulder. I'd enter Grandpapa's office, where he would bounce me on his knee and tell me stories of how I would one day run this business. He'd hand me this paperweight, and I would play with its smooth heft and hand it back to him. A private game we played.

Now the weight of this moment is heavy like this paperweight. I'm canceling this documentary. I must act to save our name, our honor. Even if the business goes down, our good name is something we can hold on to. That Zandy will not destroy our reputation with her fabrications, her lies.

There's something broken about Zandy. I knew it as soon as I met her. I stride to Fournier. He turns to face me. "I'm coming to the office with you. I'll go through every piece of paper myself." I thrust my head towards the door. "Come. We'll call her boss from the car, this Stewart Stevens. And we're going to shut that woman down. Close the film. And get me a private detective. Let's have that Zandy investigated."

Chapter Twenty-Four

ZANDY

Right after I lodge the contract with our lawyer in Nice, I leave the Severin apartment in Tourrettes sur Loup and move into the tacky Hotel Virginie, in mini-roundabout land by Sophia Antipolis.

I pace around my little box of a room, trying to ignore the guffaws and banging from the room next door. I wait for Dominique to come with a document proving the legitimate sale of Pereira to Severin. I want him to prove right is on his side, to be the person I thought he was.

There's no contact from him. In the silence, in the void in which he doesn't visit, righteous indignation enflames me like a bush fire.

At midnight, Stewart calls. I get the pep talk, "Keep going, Zandy. You can do this." Then comes the less heartening, "Hurry. We can't keep Severin at bay forever. He's trying to block you."

A tall redhead about my age sits outside the hotel all night in a silver Skoda with the right wing bashed in. Clearly Dominique has set a detective on me.

I still need footage of the Severin family home, so three days later, I meet my crew outside the entrance. There are a good hundred bodies around us, excited to watch the filming. The detective sits in the lane watching. It's creepy, and I've got Stewart's "Hurry up" warning on my brain.

At the entrance, elegant stone pillars flank an elaborate wrought iron gate. From here we see the driveway overhung with foliage and the promise of a gorgeous house at the end. I stand with my back to the gates. Jacques faces me a few feet away with his Sony PXW-FS7 draped like a baboon over his shoulder. To his left, our sound tech Paul, with his oversized boom mic and pole, trails cables. To his right, our lighting tech Jules, who looks about fourteen with that mop of blond hair.

I look into the soul of the camera to create an intimate connection with my audience. "This luxurious country estate," I say, "family home of the Severins, is the former Monastère de Saint-Maximin." I watch myself in the iPad Interrotron under Jacques's lens, to be sure I'm looking natural. "The collection of buildings that make up the estate were built by Valbonne monks in 1697. It has a rich cultural history as well as working olive groves and vineyards."

In summer, the light is incandescent by midday and gives only washed-out colors. So we always film early to get contrast, to capture bright prismatic hues and subtle color changes. "This estate truly has it all," I continue. "The Severin family can play tennis surrounded by lavender bushes or enjoy a swim in the large pool which enjoys spectacular views of the surrounding area."

From the corner of my eye, I spy Jacqueline at the front of the crowd, elegant in a crisp shirtwaister and red court shoes.

Stay calm, do your work, I tell myself.

All night she's been texting me, asking to meet. I blocked her number in order to wall off the affection I feel for her and the anger which tells me Dominique told her to contact me. I just about gasp seeing Camille at her side. Foot soldiers together.

I want to yell out, "I'm sorry. I'm doing my job." And "I wish I didn't have to hurt you," but that's foolish. This is the tension in documentary making, between the relationships you build and the truths you need to tell. I'm going to upset people. I won't always see the story the way they see it.

"But behind the glamorous facade you see today nestles a corrosive secret, which I reveal for the first time." OMG, there's the baker and Alain, the janitor. Pursuing this Pereira storyline is going to hurt Camille, Jacqueline, and all these locals who depend on the business. I remind myself of Rita. She's in my pocket as the wallpaper on my phone, looking at me with those huge mournful eyes and that cheeky smile that lit up my first years in New Jersey. Rita reminds me to worry about the truth (and justice) for the Pereiras, not go soft.

I hear rustling and scuffling behind me. I keep my eyes locked on the lens and continue my voice-over. "Yves Severin, grandfather to the current heir and CEO, acquired a small perfume house called Pereira et Fils." I relate the details. "He promised to return the business and the secret formula after the war, reneged on his bond to his friend, and made his fame and fortune from that ignominy."

Dominique steps forward and stands between me and the camera.

"Stop filming," he commands.

I swipe my hand to the left, gesturing for him to move aside. I've got three days of filming left. I need to be steely. I've got right on my side, and I can't afford for him to interfere.

Two suits scuttle up carrying slender French briefcases, the kind they slide under their arms like thermometers. They flank him like an armed guard.

"I don't know the details of what happened with my grandfather and Pereira. I'm doing everything in my power to find out," says Dominique.

Jacques is less than a foot away from him. I catch his eye to indicate he should capture this on film.

"For heaven's sake, man, turn that off," Dominique says to him.

"We have the permit to film here," I say.

Voices from the crowd intensify. We hear the scuffling of feet as people push to get closer.

Jules circles us, gesturing to them with the palm of his hand to keep back behind the tape and electrical cable cordoning us off.

"Keep rolling," I shout above Dominique's head. I lock eyes with him. "I've given you all the time you need to prove that your grandfather bought Pereira legitimately."

"We've filed for permissions to access the public archives." He looks right and left, making eye contact with the two men at his side. He nods at them. "You're not giving me a chance to tell the truth and to act justly," he spits at me.

"Behind your glamour story, there's a terrible secret you never told me. A secret the world needs to know about you."

He stamps his foot. "You're defaming my family. You're the criminal, not me." He swivels to face Jacques. "Stop shooting now or you are in contempt of court."

The older sidekick, sixtyish, tall, and lean as a racehorse, steps towards me. Smooth skin, a kindly face. "Mademoiselle, are you Zandy Watson of CNM Documentaries?"

"I am . . ."

"I hereby serve you with this order to cease and desist any and all filming relating to the business Severin Frères, or the family Severin," he says.

It's a body blow. I open the sheaf of papers. At the head is the banner of *Le Tribunal de Grande Instance.*

My hand shakes as I read:

Mademoiselle Watson et CNM Documentaries, il s'agit d'une décision de justice rendue par Le Tribunal de Grande Instance qui ordonne . . . elle entre en vigueur à compter de ce moment-là pour cesser de filmer tout ce qui appartient à Severin & Frères.

Followed by the English translation:

> *Mademoiselle Watson and CNM Documentaries, this is a court order issued by Le Tribunal de Grande Instance ordering you . . . it goes into effect from this moment onwards to cease and desist from filming anything which belongs to or pertains to Severin Frères.*

This is an act of war.

"This property belongs to the Severin Family and is thus beyond your limits," says the other suit.

Do I ignore the lawyers and keep going or make a run for it? The longer I stick around, the more Dominique gets to me—personally. And the more likely he can access my existing footage. Can he? I don't know. And I'm not taking that risk.

But we've got three more days of work. I can't leave now. I've got big holes in my film.

The crowd seems to be closing in on us. The truth matters. And so does justice. "Run," I say to Jacques.

We belt through the crowd to the white van parked on the side of the lane, leaving cables spooled on the ground.

"You broadcast this, and your career will be in ruins," Dominique says as he pursues me.

Jacques lugs the camera on his shoulder. I yank open the door and leap into the front seat. He stows the camera and jumps into the driver's seat. He slams his door. Tires screeching, the van gyrates and rolls as he accelerates into a spurt.

We tear down the road, hurtling around mini-roundabouts, passing Vence and Saint-Paul de Vence on our way to the coast. Two black cars chase us from behind. Keeping silent, I focus on my commitment to the truth.

I need to get today's footage out of here, before Dominique gets his hands on it. One week ago, we made love on a mountainside. Now I'm getting as far away as possible from Dominique

Severin and pronto. The Severins didn't send their Jewish friends to the gas chambers, but they stole their assets and their future livelihoods, when that family was at their most vulnerable.

Bye-bye South of France. I'm jumping on the first flight back to New York. When I board that jet, I'll be telling him this is war. So be it. War it is.

Chapter Twenty-Five

Wednesday, August 25, New York

Eight weeks later, I'm buried in the editing room, staring down banks of controls and the array of screens blinking at me. Upstairs, the office is eerily quiet with many of the long desks abandoned. People go to the beach for the weekend and return late on Monday morning in flip-flops, trailing sand from their duffels. Not me. I'm plunged in darkness down here. The second half of doc making is about getting the piece broadcast, which is as complex a task as writing and shooting. Success depends on my doing a first-rate editing job.

I'm in a mad rush to complete my final edits. All I can manage is work all day then dash to the gym at 9:00 p.m. Edit, box, sleep. Day in, day out. We air *The Perfumer's Secret* in eleven days.

Beautiful drawings of medieval alembics move across the screen in front of me. "The apparatus first used by ancient Persians to create perfume," says Jacqueline. "The liquid in one flask is boiled. Then the vapor rises into the alembic hood, where it cools by contact with the walls and condenses, running down the spout into a receiving flask. Today we also use the word 'alembic' metaphorically for anything that refines or transmutes. Like the phrase, 'philosophy filtered through the alembic of Plato's mind.'"

I will myself to focus on the job at hand, not at how uncomfortable I feel about seeing Jacqueline on screen and wondering what she thinks of me now. I need to shape the narrative in such a way that my audience, who has never been to Grasse or encountered Severin, will feel the story. Movies are only as good as they make us feel. I would have liked to include a storyline about the carbon footprint of the business. But there was no room. We are stuffed with storylines.

There's a quick knock and the door opens. In comes Stewart together with a blast of air conditioning.

I hit my mouse to pause the screen. "Al and I have been texting." I say. "We're going to the zoo when I'm through with this."

"Thanks, Zandy. You make a difference in his life." He stands with one hand on the door jamb. "Climate is getting traction upstairs," he says.

My heart thumps.

"Tom Lee's daughter is at Smith. She's been lobbying him about climate change. Suddenly he's all over the crisis. Your lucky day." He smiles and quirks his eyebrows. "That's not why I'm here. We're wanted upstairs," he says.

"What is it?" I say.

"The lawyers . . . c'mon, we'll talk on the way up."

Side by side, we navigate the basement corridors where the editing suites are housed. "It's legal pushback from the Severins," he says.

Everything tenses. I clench my laptop into my body. We've come this far. We can't lose the project now. But the legal stuff is out of my control.

"I want you to do most of the talking," he says.

I lean my back against the cold steel wall of the elevator. "You know I'm not exactly versed in the law . . ."

"You know the details better than I do. It will be good experience for you."

My quads clench.

The ding announces that we've arrived at the twelfth floor, and the doors part. He strides ahead, and I follow a few paces behind. Green light, green light, green light, I chant to myself. We are going to broadcast this documentary, whatever lies on the other side of this door.

I stand tall as we enter the boardroom. I'm going in strong until I realize I'm wearing ripped white dungarees and a skimpy tank. I slip my arms into the ratty old sweatshirt draped over my shoulders.

Three men in dark suits sit along one long side of the oval conference table. They stand as we enter. The room is wood paneled, airless, corporate. The table is shiny wood, not white Formica like ours downstairs.

Stewart handles the introductions. He and I sit opposite Danny Cohen, the senior guy, and his two cohorts.

"I'd just like to confirm the date of broadcast," says Cohen.

"Sunday September 5," says Stewart.

Cohen checks his watch. Cartier. "Eleven days out?"

"You got it." Stewart beams, unfazed.

Cohen twiddles with his shirt cuff. "We've received notice of intent to sue by the Severin company."

Heat rises up the back of my neck. "They can't do that." I lean forward. "I offered Dominique the opportunity to refute the story on film. He refused." I swivel towards Stewart on my right. "Most important, we received notice just two days ago from the US Holocaust Memorial Museum in DC that the document I found is authentic."

I make eye contact with Stewart, who gives me a little nod.

"And we've got the letter from the authentication service setting out their analysis of the paper, the handwriting, the phrasing. They're sure it's real. They signed off on it. So how can there be a problem?"

The three of them exchange glances. Cohen tugs on his lapels. "Slow down here, Ms. Watson. The litigation concerns breach of contract."

"In what way did we breach contract?" asks Stewart.

There follows a twenty minute argy-bargy about the definitions of "sourcing" and "areas of operation" per the contract. A vein throbs in my temple. Focus on your breath and your "footwork." Handle this. Cool it, I tell myself. Under the table I'm twirling the metal button which fastens my dungarees at my hip, round and around.

"We're happy for you to proceed with the documentary about the Severin Frères perfume business," says Cohen. "We recommend you delete any mention of the Pereira transaction."

That pulse in my temple is thundering. I'm tensed on the edge of my seat.

Stewart leans forwards. "No way." Right now the pudge around his middle speaks less of poor habits and more of experience, confidence, and a fatherly style I'm grateful for.

A ripple of warmth spreads through me. Thank goodness. "I absolutely agree," I manage to say in a soft voice.

Stewart shifts to face Cohen square on. "Guys, we appreciate your calling us in. We understand everything you're saying. Go ahead and put your advice in writing and send it to the Head of Editorial."

"You can be sure I'll do that."

"I'll take it from here," says Stewart. "I need to discuss this with Zandy."

"Stewart, we strongly advise that you do not proceed without removing the offensive material," says Cohen. He tidies up his papers and slides them into a manila folder.

Stewart nods. "Thank you again. I'll square this away upstairs myself."

Cohen sighs, tilts his head, and gives a nod to his cohorts. They stand and leave.

I look at Stewart sideways, straining to read any signal his face might show.

All I get back is an implacable stare from behind those *Mad Men* glasses. "This is your call, Zandy. I wanted them out of here because I want you to decide."

"Aren't you always telling me to keep my nose out of CNM's business?"

"Zandy, it was you on the ground. It's your judgment call as to whether you think Severin cheated Pereira out of that business."

"And the lawyers?"

"Leave the pen pushers to me," he says.

"Really? We've got eleven days until we screen. Do you want to go ahead or pull the movie?"

Stewart drums his fingers on the table and swivels to face me. "You've lived this for four months, so you decide . . ."

"I decide if this is ethical?"

He nods.

I push my leather swivel chair back from the table and stand. I pace the length of the boardroom table, my work boots making tire marks on the beige and green patterned carpet. Do I give the green light to screen, or do I pull this doc now?

My film MFA focused on subjects like cinematography and digital animation. It offered no module in ethics and decision making. Take a breath, Zandy. Of course we're going to screen. The Pereiras deserve justice. What about the ethics of not revealing this truth about the Pereira crime? Are they thinking of that?

I stand with my back to Stewart and look out of the window. Now my gut is twisted as I think of all the locals who surrounded our last shoot. I don't want this doc to affect them negatively. I don't want this to affect Noor Haddad and her WomenUP foundation.

I have to choose. Twelve floors down, white light bounces off concrete pavements. I watch the bustle of New Yorkers hurrying to their tasks. Why should I wobble because the lawyers are nervous? It's their job to be nervous and mine to be bold. I didn't choose this profession because it's easy. My job is to tell the truth, not to sort out the lives of businesspeople across the world. CNM has employed authentication services to confirm the contract I found is real. Nothing bold happens in life without stepping through fear. Truth matters. I am on the side of right.

I pivot round and stride back to Stewart. He's standing, his papers under his arm.

"It tells the truth. It gets to the bottom of the story. We go ahead."

He beams and throws me a high five. "Send it to the lab for a negative of the final cut," he says.

My heart lurches.

"I'll call Euan Robertson and tell him right away we've received notice of Severin's intention to sue. We'll spill this all over the internet, and we'll get a healthy uptick in viewing numbers," he says. "This is a great day, Zandy."

My lips tremble. I shove my hand into my pocket and the denim is soft on the pads of my fingers. There's a weight pressing on my chest. Is that because of what I'm doing to Dominique or because of what he did to me by concealing this? I pinch my flesh through the fabric.

In eleven days, I'll see "Zandy Watson, Director/Producer" roll across the screen, my first solo credit. I've been busting a gut for eight years to get here. I should be thrilled and excited. Instead, I feel like I'm locked into the seat of a massive rollercoaster. And there's no getting off now.

Chapter Twenty-Six

DOMINIQUE

Sunday, September 5

We've given The Fifth department stores the exclusive contract to sell Lindissima across North America for a year, so I'm in New York for the launch of our new perfume tomorrow.

For the sixty-nine days since we shut down CNM filming, all I've done is try to find out whether Zandy's version of events regarding the Pereira purchase could possibly be true.

We never found any document. Our New York legal counsel discovered that CNM was in possession of a written record, some kind of contract between Grandpapa and Rodrigo Pereira, stating he would return their business to them after the war–devastating.

The next blow came when handwriting experts authenticated said document. I don't have words to describe the torment I've been going through. In fact my mind cannot grasp this new reality and square it against believing for my whole life that Grandpapa purchased Pereira et Fils.

Right up until two days ago we thought we could block *The Perfumer's Secret* from broadcasting, but the legal machinery has failed.

Tonight at 6:00 p.m., the documentary airs across North America. I hope with all my heart that it will not be as bad as I fear. I hope that by clenching every muscle against this outcome, I might somehow ward it off.

At 5:55 p.m., I talk my way into the Dolby Screening Room on Sixth Avenue and East Fifty-Fifth Street, where CNM is showcasing the documentary to advertisers and marketing executives.

I'm not going to hide out in my hotel room and watch this on cable. I need to be present at this first screening, to see this disgraceful defamation, to feel the full force of how these people experience it.

As the lights go down, I pray with all my heart it won't be as bad as I fear. Zandy won't do that to me, will she? Last time, outside our gates, tempers were running high. Surely she's had time to reflect on her actions and what they might mean to us all.

I station myself at the back of the small room with its plush carpeting and fabric-covered walls. It's as claustrophobic as a submarine. There's no way I could sink into one of those plush leather recliner seats, instead I stand alert, all my senses primed.

The titles come up. In huge letters inhabiting a third of the screen, the title itself: THE PERFUMER'S SECRET. I've got the chills and it isn't just the intensity of the air conditioning.

Vivaldi's *Four Seasons* saturates the room with its bright horns as we pan in across the foothills of the Alpes Maritimes to the grassy slope where our office and factory stand.

I watch a kaleidoscope of interviews to camera, interwoven with stills and moving shots of the landscape and the interior of our facility. Zandy includes photographs from our archive as she describes the key events in our three-hundred-year history. The heart of the story is about the creativity in developing the new scent and our connection with Noor Haddad and her foundation.

My heart swells to see our story spill across the huge screen. The story is beautiful and elegant. The work is skillful, modulated, thoughtful. She understands craftsmanship; the painstaking daily work and the slow building of layers. Maybe my fears are unfounded. I hope against hope that this is *The Perfumer's Secret* of the title. She shows how Severin blends artisanship with science, how over the decades the Severin craft has evolved into a true art. This was the promise of the documentary.

The audio and visual quality are perfect–the hues and shades of my homeland are displayed in clear, clean colors. In front of me, a grid of heads watching, absorbing the details of my family's story. I count eight rows across and ten rows back from the screen. Eighty viewers.

Here is a beautiful photograph of Maman at the height of her powers, one of those stylish 1980s photoshoots, portraying her as feminine but also the CEO, a perfect blend of the masculine and the feminine.

I soften because she's my mother and something inside me will always reach for her. But I grit my teeth thinking that Maman told Zandy that story about Grandpapa.

My mother lived a lie her whole life. And then by omission, lied to her own children.

Why didn't she tell us? Oh, the rows we've had over these past days about this, until Camille said, "Don't you see? She was ashamed of her father, so she couldn't tell us. And now she's shamed us with her own lack of control."

How can I breathe in here? I'm bathed in the odor of 4-phenylcyclohexene from the carpet backing. There's not enough ventilation to pull it out of the room.

If only Maman had told me, I could have made reparations to the Pereiras. I haven't a *sou* to give back, but I could at the least have made a public apology on behalf of the family.

I fear I may be permanently estranged from Maman–the destruction she caused the business was hard enough and now this betrayal.

Now comes a somber drumroll. My limbs shake. A thickness clogs the back of my throat, as my gut tells me Zandy has been scaling this gorgeous mountain only to–hurl us off the rock face at the summit.

On screen I read, "The Corrosive Secret Behind the Glamorous Facade." I grip the back of the seat in front of me, the nylon fabric repulsively tinny and slimy on my finger pads. This wretched documentary states that I knew about it and covered it up. I almost collapse from shame and despair.

Eighty people in front of me, watching this. I pull and tug at my shirt cuffs. I turn my face away from the screen. And on cable TV, 1.5 million viewers sitting side by side in their living room or glancing up at the screen while they slide a frozen pizza into the kitchen microwave. Weak at the knees, I let out an uncontrolled moan. I expected it to be bad, but seeing it in front of me now, it's worse, far worse than I could have imagined.

I feel the emotion in the room, how each of them is held by the story. I'm naked, exposed, powerless. As though I'm standing on a platform at the Gare du Nord watching the whistle blow, the steam rising from the stack, and a chain of carriages rumbling and pulling out of the station. I press my palm to my lips to suppress a cry. I have seen my family heading to doom–our whole story gone, destroyed.

One and a half million cable viewers have watched that story tonight. They think I knew that Grandpapa cheated the Pereiras and that I deceived everyone. There's not a single thing I can do about that. A great perfume leaves its trace in the air. For us, the trail we leave behind is our good name and our honor. Zandy has destroyed ours.

The last credits roll. I feel I might vomit. I clutch my throat and rush out.

I stand alone in the midnight-blue lobby. I've lost control. Surely it's time to give up the fight.

A waiter approaches bearing champagne on a circular silver tray. I stare at it dumbfounded. No, I must alert The Fifth as to the contents of the documentary. The one last thing I can do is to shore up that account.

But the thought of facing The Fifth's Chairman makes me want to keel over. I cannot face another moment in the public eye. The shame and disgrace is too much to bear. I want to hide out of view. I could go to the airport, fly to Japan and wander incognito, work in a pottery studio as I've always wanted.

The crowd spills out into the lobby, talking and gesticulating. A tower of Babel. Anger spurts through me as I remember I'm a Severin. It's my absolute duty to do what I can. I will never give up.

Zandy emerges, her chestnut mane coiffed and gleaming. She raises an arm and an array of slender bracelets falls to her elbow.

A group of paunchy men form a circle around her as she shakes their hands and laughs, tossing her head backwards like some glamorous, but wicked, goddess of the silver screen.

A burning sensation builds hot and acrid in my esophagus. I can't let her get off scot-free.

I must call The Fifth, but before I do that, she will hear me out. I move towards the group around Zandy. I inch my way into the center, clenching my fists to stop myself from lashing out at her.

I step forwards and stand face to face with her. "You betrayed me."

She startles.

"You betrayed all of us. And I know your secrets."

She blanches.

"Your father betrayed Mike Papadopoulos by turning State's evidence on him. And you used the trust I placed in you to betray me, so you're as bad as your rotten father."

She narrows her eyes. "This has nothing to do with my father."

I shake my head. "You knifed me, just like your father knifed his friend and employee."

"Stop it," she says.

"To think I actually had empathy for you . . . for what you went through."

Stewart Stevens steps forward. "Mr. Severin?"

I glare at him.

He thumps his hand on my shoulder. "Please stop harassing my employee. And now kindly leave the premises."

"I'll see you in court," I say through clenched teeth. There's no more to say or do here–these bastards couldn't care less.

I stride towards the exit to salvage our beautiful new perfume.

The following morning I arrive at 7:00 a.m. at the flagship store of The Fifth on Fifth Avenue. I'm determined to keep this exclusive deal afloat–in spite of that slanderous documentary.

Entering the Beauty on Two floor, I'm heartened to see that The Fifth has given all 32,000 square feet of its futuristic white space to Lindissima.

Beside each of the open-plan counters stands a lifesized hardboard display of Noor. But as we walk across the space, my leg muscles tighten. My shoulders go stiff. Some thirty men and women, clad like ants, top-to-toe in black, are dismantling the displays, breaking them apart. Here's one yanking out the iPad from the middle of the exhibit.

My legs go weak at the knees. These iPads are placed there so buyers can hop online and learn how Noor's foundation helps the poorest women in the world start their own businesses. They can see that five dollars from their purchase will go towards helping women gain the skills and dignity to clamber out of poverty.

Banging and clanking reverberate across the floor as these workers lay the hardboard cutouts of Noor onto large utility carts and dollies. The floor hums with activity as they pack the iPads into boxes and wheel them out towards the back of the room.

Noor. What will I do about Noor? I sprint to the elevator and ride up to the tenth floor where Woolman Chase III, the Chairman of The Fifth, awaits us in his personal office.

At seventy, he wears pebblethick glasses that make his warm round eyes the most prominent feature on his face.

I shake his hand. "What's going on?" I pant.

"We saw the documentary and called a Board meeting last night. We're removing all the inventory." He indicates a seat on the far side of his leather top desk.

"What do you mean?" I say.

He pushes a pile of papers aside. "Please, take a seat."

I sink into the gilt bamboo chair across from him.

The door opens and Noor enters, pale but stately. "This is an out and out disaster." She takes a seat beside me. "That documentary . . ."

I survey the Chinese porcelain ginger jars standing on either side of the fireplace, taking in a breath to calm my nerves.

"Kindly explain what's going on," Noor says to Woolman.

"We cannot sell Lindissima!" He locks together his bony, suntanned hands on which the veins stand out and the nails are manicured to a sheen.

My mouth falls open. He has the exclusive contract for Lindissima. "I don't understand."

"I regret to say we're pulling out of our contract." He tugs on the lapels of his impeccable charcoal suit.

"Surely not." Tremors pulsate through my body. Tossing and turning all night, I'd expected a severe telling off. But I could never have envisaged this.

"Again, I'm sorry, Dominique. But we've decided."

"The Fifth has been doing business with Severin Frères for

seventy years." My heart pounds in my chest at what seems like double speed.

I swivel my eyes towards Noor. A red stain has torched up her neck and across her cheeks. She inhales a long breath through her nostrils and leans in towards the desk. "Woolman, you must reverse this decision."

The second hand moves in ticks around the face of the ormolu clock on the mantelpiece.

He shakes his head. "I cannot."

I grip the bony arm of the little gilt chair. "I didn't know about the Pereiras. I promise you, I had no idea about any of this. We're working hard to make sure the public knows this."

"I believe you, son," says Woolman. "But we will not sell Lindissima. Nor in fact, any perfume produced by Severin Frères," he says.

I stare down at my feet. Eight floors down, The Fifth's merchandising staff will have removed each of our display stands by now. Lindissima dismantled and discarded.

Noor flicks her gaze back and forth between Woolman and me. "If you pull out, it will be a disaster for my reputation. It's akin to your blacklisting me." She stands upright as a gazelle.

Surely Noor can persuade him. She's powerful and his business depends on the intricate relationship between celebrity and retail.

She paces around the office. "You can't do this. It's my face on the bottle, my face all over the marketing materials. Lindissima is linked to my wedding via the press I've been doing this past month."

Woolman steeples his hands. "Had I been acting alone, I might well have made a different decision. I regret, it's out of my control."

Noor is a major international brand, glamour to the moon, all the consumer pull a retailer could ask for, and he's still saying no. "There's nothing we can do to persuade you?" I say.

He shakes his head.

"This scandal will also drag Prince Karam into the mud. Can you imagine what political capital his opponents will make of this?"

I lock eyes with Woolman. "Surely our relationship counts for something here." I wring my hands, which are drenched in sweat. It's as though a horsedrawn cart is dragging my beloved Severin through the streets and setting it on the guillotine at La Bastide. "Please, I beg you to reconsider."

"I can't. Two of our more prominent board members are Jewish. At the meeting last night they were adamant about withdrawing Lindissima. The Board approved this decision. The press releases went out at midnight last night," he says.

Noor taps her long red nails on her phone, madly texting.

My own phone has been buzzing with calls and texts since I woke. I ignore it.

Noor swipes a finger pad across her screen and narrows her eyes. "The media is having a field day. 'Wartime profiteering,' they're calling it," she says. "Apparently, I'm to blame for it too."

She, too, is in disgrace now.

She holds her phone to her ear and swipes to answer a call. She speaks quickly in Arabic. I don't know what she's saying. Whatever it is, is not good. "I'm coming right away," she says in English and ends the call.

She steps towards me, her eyes brilliant and glowering.

I stand.

"That was my CFO. He's fielding calls from our financial supporters," says Noor.

I shudder.

"Our donors are withdrawing their money. They no longer want to be associated with me."

I grind my teeth. Here's a superb woman who's suffering from associating with me.

"Thanks to you, thousands of women and their families will go hungry. They will stay mired in poverty and ignorance. You have let me down in the worst possible way."

Woolman stands, head bowed. He does not interfere.

She glares at me. "I never wanted to get involved in this. You persuaded me with your empty promises."

I accept the blows. What else can I do?

She snatches her bag from the desk. "I wish I'd never heard of Severin Frères," she says.

"I offer my sincere apologies." I bow. I raise my head, and she's looking right through me with those big black eyes, which smolder with rage and a hatred that seems to come from across the generations. As implacable as the stone ruins of Petra.

She sweeps out, slamming the door behind her.

What in God's name have I done? I could never have imagined harming others in this way.

"I have sympathy for your position," says Woolman.

"Position?" I shake my head in disbelief. Black and white framed photos adorn the leaf-green walls to my right and left. Photos of Woolman welcoming Madonna, Michael Jackson, Carolyn Bessette Kennedy, David Bowie, Princess Diana, and Michelle Obama to The Fifth. He is surrounded by his story. Whereas mine, the Severin story, is over. "There is no way back from this."

"Business is about hard work. But it's also about luck. Getting in at the right time, like your grandfather did. And bad luck, like yours today."

My phone vibrates. There it goes again, whirring in my pocket. *Brrr, brrr, brrr . . .*

I have to stop the damned thing. "Excuse me." I pull my phone out of my pocket.

```
To: dominique

From: camille

Call me urgently

Call me urgently

Call me urgently

Story gone viral. Check your news feed.

Story gone viral. Check your news feed.

Story gone viral. Check your news feed.
```

My chest is tight as I flick open my news aggregator. What now?

The New York Times:
SUCCESS STOLEN FROM JEWISH FAMILY

My throat clutches. Oh my God, the race card!

International Herald Tribune:
PREYING ON WEAKEST: SEVERIN DISGRACE

"No," I moan.

Woolman comes around the desk and looks over my shoulder.

Wall Street Journal:
NEW PERFUME DISASTER:
THE FIFTH ON FIFTH PULLS OUT

He nods his head. "I'm so sorry, son."

This is a wildfire out of control. I'm dizzy now. I clench my thighs and my fists to pump the blood around my body.

I scroll through photos showing protesters massing outside our shop on the Avenue Montaigne and in Grasse. They carry placards:

DOWN WITH SEVERIN.

JEW HATER.

THIEF.

SCOUNDREL SEVERIN.

WAR PROFITEER SEVERIN.

TIME FOR JUSTICE.

There's nothing more to be done here. Woolman is immovable. And the press have set their dogs on us. Not only is our name destroyed, but also the business is utterly finished. We cannot survive.

We stand.

Woolman doesn't hurry me out. I'm grateful for that. He opens his arms and pulls me in for a hug.

I'm a child, limp in the embrace of his warm, bony shoulders, where I stay for a long time.

I pull away and take in a long breath. "I should have known about the Pereira theft. I'm chief executive. As you say in the States, 'the buck stops with me.' I made a disastrous decision in agreeing to this documentary. I have only myself to blame."

Chapter Twenty-Seven

ZANDY

The morning after the screening, Stewart hauls me into the office at 7:30 a.m.

"Take a seat, Zandy." He points to the two armchairs nestled around a coffee table.

I perch on the edge of one of them, eager to put *The Perfumer's Secret* behind me and press ahead with *Climate*.

Headlines flicker across the bottom of the TV monitor in the corner, announcing voter suppression, police brutality, and unionization at Amazon.

He flips open a cardboard box of Dunkin' Donuts.

I shake my head. "Can we talk about *Climate*?"

"Relax." He plucks out a tan sphere with gloopy pink stuff slathered all over the top. "Donuts for your first Director/Producer credit. We have to celebrate."

Celebrate? Dominique's taunt, "You're as bad as your father," echoes in my ears. I slide myself into the hollow of the armchair and drop my head.

"I've pissed off plenty of people on my way to the forum." He shoots me a soft smile. "And the upstairs execs are thrilled with *The Perfumer's Secret*."

"How can I parlay that into getting *Climate* on the schedule?"

"By doing press on *The Perfumer's Secret*."

I tighten my hands into fists. I want to get as far away from *The Perfumer's Secret* as I can. "Surely I've done enough."

Stewart's phone jiggers on the table between us. He reaches forward, answers the call, and blurts, "Oh my gosh."

Turning sideways, he lurches for his desk and picks up the TV remote. Flicking through channels, he turns up the volume.

The news anchor, Savannah Gilbo, says, "News just out. The Fifth on Fifth refuses to sell Lindissima, the new perfume from esteemed French perfume house, Severin Frères." Above her runs the headline: PERFUME HOUSE DISGRACED.

My insides fall away. Like a fire has ravaged my body and cleaned it all out.

"What does this mean for the three-hundred-year-old perfume house, loved by celebrities Meghan Markle and Oprah Winfrey?" she asks. "And what does it mean for Noor Haddad? The scent was commissioned for her wedding on September 22, the fall equinox."

I close the Dunkin' Donuts box and slide it under the table. I think I'm going to be sick.

"Euan, I've got Zandy right here. I'll put you on speaker."

"We need to capitalize on this," says creepy Euan. "Let's start a Twitter blitz.

I shake my head. "No," I say.

"The Fifth on Fifth killing Lindissima! We can extend distribution and reruns. The numbers could be stratospheric," says Euan. "Imagine how many viewers . . ."

"You'll assemble the team?" says Stewart. "We'll come right up."

Stewart raises his eyebrows as he ends the call and stands. He leans towards me. "You okay, Zandy?" he says. "You've gone very pale."

I feel like a louse. "Severin is crashing and burning and we're jumping for joy? I wasn't in this to destroy a business–"

"Remember you're telling *both* sides of the story." Stewart closes his laptop and slips it under one arm. He makes for the door. "You don't choose filmmaking to have an easy life."

I can't breathe in here.

"We need to get upstairs, see how we can build on this. Let's go."

My knees are weak as I stand. "I'll be right up. Meet you up there?"

He heads out, leaving his door open behind him.

I need air. I stumble across the office. Out in the hallway, I hit the elevator button. They want to spin *The Perfumer's Secret*, make it worse than it already is. My body takes me downstairs, through the foyer, and out onto the street.

Outside on the pavement, New Yorkers hurry along in droves–some stride purposefully, others are bent over phones. I'm dizzy with the storm of electrical activity in my head.

They need me upstairs to do press. Stewart won't take no for an answer, and I can't duck out of a meeting with the executive team. The line for Starbucks snakes right to the door of our building. I'll get a coffee and go right upstairs. The Fifth isn't going to listen to me. I'm a storyteller. I have no power over what a 150-year-old retail chain does or doesn't do.

I shouldn't get coffee. Starbucks dispenses eight thousand paper cups a minute, more than four billion a year. One and a half million trees. As I take a few breaths, I sense someone standing over me. "You in line?" he says.

The Irish accent comes with twinkly blue eyes and black hair.

My insides melt, like he's pouring his wholesomeness right into me. I need to stop this disaster at The Fifth, right now. I'm involved and I can't pretend I'm not.

I move aside for the Irish hunk to join the line. "Thanks." I swivel on my foot. "You've done your good deed for the day."

"What's that?" he says.

Bugger Stewart, I think, and bugger, bugger, bugger creepy Euan. I sprint crosstown to The Fifth.

Chapter Twenty-Eight

The Fifth has refused to sell Lindissima and I have to stop this from happening. This was never my intention. Arriving at Forty-Ninth Street, I see the windows of The Fifth are all decked in Lindissima. Every window is a field of alluring eggplant, a sensual color that speaks of depth and creativity.

Looking closer, I see a giant bottle of Lindissima hangs above an Ionian column in the middle of the window. Etched on the bottle is an impression of Noor's face, neck, and shoulders, a white line drawing on an eggplant background, simple and deft as a late Matisse. It represents a woman in her strength, sensuality and essence.

It's okay after all. Excitement spurts through me–my approach to Noor put this outline of her face in every window of The Fifth.

I head towards the main doors and see young men and women in stockinged feet removing the columns and bottles, packing them in cardboard boxes, dismantling the displays. Round here, the windows are an ungainly mess.

I sprint around the whole block from Forty-Ninth to Fiftieth Street. In every window, two or three employees are hacking at the eggplant backdrop with hammers, wrenching out screws with power tools, or lugging huge blocks of eggplant board out through the doorway at the back into the store.

I stand open-mouthed as this image of destruction repeats

itself over and over, as Lindissima tumbles down before my eyes. I'm a small-time filmmaker, battling to make movies that will have an impact. And now–this? I resist the riptide of dread telling me this disaster is of my doing.

I've got to persuade The Fifth to change their mind about this. I sprint back to the main entrance. The store doesn't open until 10:00 a.m., and the double doors are locked. I push and pull at the handles.

They must reassemble the displays and sell Lindissima as planned. I wanted justice and reparation for the Pereira family. It was never my intent to cause harm like this to Dominique and his business.

I bang my fists on the doors, desperate for someone to open up. An imposing figure in a mustard-yellow dress and matching cape strides towards the double doors from the inside.

A slender arm flies out of the cape and pulls open the door. Noor's eyes widen. "You!"

I feel tiny against her imposing presence. She's regal like a panther, her skin pale like alabaster, making her black eyes all the more powerful.

She marches out onto the pavement. I met her woman-to-woman in a basement loo at the Colombe d'Or. Here in NYC, her presence is huge and her celebrity looms–with her black Celine handbag and matching stilettos.

"I'm going to tell The Fifth to stop this," I say.

"You've destroyed my reputation. Twitter says that I, Noor Haddad, am cheating Jews out of their livelihoods."

"That's not true," I say.

"You may have destroyed WomenUP too."

Tourists gather around us, snapping pictures with their iPhones. "That's Noor Haddad!"

Bodyguards step forward, making a ring around us with their arms.

"Fix this with another movie," she hisses. "Say you got it wrong."

"But Dominique's grandfather stole the Pereira business. It's the truth."

"You're destroying the lives of the poorest of the poor. You chose to destroy the good we're doing today, because of a crime committed by a man seventy years ago. Are you enjoying this truth?" She storms past me, raising her hand to her driver.

"I haven't the money or distribution. I'm not the network–"

A bodyguard opens the passenger door.

"You said you were powerful. Show me your power."

She glides in.

The bodyguard ducks into the front seat.

The car pulls away.

I need to find the CEO of The Fifth on Fifth and persuade him to change his mind. I talk my way into the store and push my way into the perfume hall. The enormous space is decked with Lindissima, but the place is a mess. Staff are loading the custom Lindissima displays onto dollies.

From the left-hand corner, Dominique walks towards me.

My insides tighten. "You're as bad as your rotten father," he spat at me last night.

He sees me and cocks his head towards the older man at his side and whispers into his ear.

I shuffle towards him.

We stop, all three of us.

I shudder.

Dominique looks at me, his eyes hard and broken.

"I'm Woolman Chase III, Chairman and CEO of this great company," says the older man.

"You must stop this." I gesture towards the perfume hall.

"It's too late for that, young lady. I gather you're responsible for this disaster. I'm losing untold business, thanks to you. In more than one hundred years, The Fifth on Fifth has never had empty window displays. Not to mention the distress and destruction you are wreaking on my good friend here."

He wraps an arm around Dominique's shoulder. "Safe journey, my friend. I regret deeply that it has come to this."

He turns to me. "You're a disgrace to your profession." With a stoop in his back, he hobbles back to the elevator.

I swallow hard and do what I can to deflect the blow.

Ignoring me, Dominique darts onto the floor in pursuit of the trolleys laden with Lindissima boxes.

Should I go after him? I need him to know it was my moral duty to reveal the truth. But my phone has been buzzing in the pocket of my cargo pants ever since I left the office. I can't stay here a moment longer. Stewart's going to be furious that I'm not up there now, and creepy Euan will have my head on a platter.

"Where are you taking that?" Dominique calls out, chasing the middleaged uniformed man. "That's my company's perfume."

The employee half turns towards Dominique. "Orders, sir. I'm to get it off the floor and shipped back to where it came from."

For goodness' sake, he needs to know that in spite of this devastation, I was acting honorably. He has to believe me. I tear after them as they disappear through the doors at the back of the store.

Back in the air-conditioned warehouse, I walk towards Dominique. I've got to explain why I had to expose the true story. I want to reach out, put my hand on his shoulder.

I can't. There's too much pain between us. I stuff my hands into my pockets.

He points towards the door. "Just leave."

No. He's got to understand that what's happening here isn't

my fault. "I showed the truth about Severin. All that is beautiful and excellent."

"You think you're so clever telling the 'truth' about my grandfather, but you didn't tell the 'truth' about me."

"Dominique, I never wanted this to happen."

He stamps his foot. "I despise you."

"I *had* to tell both sides of the story." My legs are glued to the concrete floor, trembling.

The Fifth employees load cartons of Lindissima onto metal shelving around us. I'd feel safer in the office, fielding the press, brainstorming *Climate*. Anything but this. There's no color in his face. His skin is gray, as though he hasn't slept since I left France. He looks gaunt and fragile in spite of the neat navy suit.

"I didn't know about Grandpapa. Or about that contract and that he cheated them."

A weight clenches around my heart.

"You lied about me," he says.

Something isn't right. Instead of the fire of righteousness, a blanket of black doubt enfolds me–wet and heavy.

"You didn't know your grandfather stole the Pereira business?" My voice is tremulous.

He stares at me.

"Tell me honestly."

Dark circles hang beneath his bloodshot eyes. "I did not know." He maintains eye contact with me. The sadness and pain in his face show me he's not angry. He's resigned. His chest is open, not hunched. His arms hang limp at his sides. He is facing me square on, heart to heart. He's telling the truth.

Clanks and bangs echo through the cavernous space as employees hump their loads of display materials onto the shelves. "Your mother knew of your grandfather's crime. Why didn't she do something? Why didn't she tell you?"

There's a gap between his shirt collar and his neck. He's lost several pounds since I last saw him.

"She was too ashamed and she fought constantly with him about it." A cold sore encrusts his bottom lip. "After he died, she hid it, because she knew it would destroy the business. She says that's why she never told me and Camille."

Dom didn't know. I shift onto my left leg and cross my right over it, clenching my ankles and thighs together. I'm perspiring in my armpits.

I believed I was acting with integrity by revealing the truth, that this would make my life matter. I was wrong. Even though the Pereiras deserve justice, I did the wrong thing. What's happening here is my fault.

I sink my head into my hands. "I've made a terrible mistake." I haven't shown the real truth. I've added to the world's massive collection of lies.

A lithe woman, phone clutched between her ear and one shoulder, barrels her cart laden with Lindissima cartons in front of us.

He raises his arms and throws open his palms in her direction. "This is the end of Severin Frères. I want to repay our debt to the Pereiras. But you've destroyed their chance of getting anything."

My boot leather creaks as I rock from one foot to the other.

"Tell CNM to stop spreading these lies about me."

"I don't have that power," I say.

"Issue a retraction." The heat of his breath reaches my skin.

"CNM won't–"

"Just do it. I trusted you. You've destroyed everything dear to me."

My arms fall limp at my sides. "I can't fight CNM, the press, social media, and The Fifth on Fifth." I push out a long sigh.

Dominique faces me, arms akimbo. "I'm flying home to tell

our employees we're closing the business, that in exchange for their loyalty over several generations, I've got nothing to give them." He bangs a clenched fist against his thigh. "If they want to feed their families, they'd better reach under the mattress and look for cash there." His eyebrows pinch tight and his pupils constrict. Perspiration beads at his hairline.

Those brown eyes hold my gaze.

Anguish corkscrews through my flesh. I've hurt this man–and thousands of innocent others–a man who was patient and decent with me.

My eyelids are hot and gummy. I make out dark shapes moving around me. I see only a fuzzy outline of Dominique as he turns on his heels and trudges out.

My head flops down towards my chest. It's as much as I can do to stay standing.

I'm not the person I thought I was. What I've done is despicable and there's no turning back. From my scalp all the way to my toes, my body trembles. I've as good as run through these aisles kicking down all the metal shelves, until every glass bottle lies smashed on the floor, and Severin's perfume from the last three hundred years runs like a river down Fifth Avenue.

Chapter Twenty-Nine

I stumble out of the store and sprint.

I want my lungs to inflate, my heart to pound so it hurts, so it overwhelms my despair. I run harder, crossing Fiftieth Street. I hurl myself up the shallow steps of St. Patrick's Cathedral.

My phone vibrates with incoming texts.

I ignore it. This disaster is my fault. What in God's name do I do now?

Buzz, buzz, buzz. Like I've got a bee in my pocket.

I snatch a breath and answer the call because I need to keep my job and Stewart won't put up with my absence any longer. "Zandy Watson." My voice wobbles.

"You said you'd be right up."

I grasp the brass handrail by my hip. "I'm so sorry, Stewart."

"Check your feed, #ThePerfumersSecret is exploding," he says.

Bugger the feed. I squat. I feel sick and dizzy thinking about what I've done.

"We're all waiting for you. What the heck's going on? We've lined up interviews with *USA Today*, the *Times*, the *Washington Post*, *Newsday*, and *Documentary*."

My body shakes. No way I'm fanning the flames even more.

"Zandy, you're letting me down. D'you want to make *Climate,* or shall I assign it to Kalsang?"

"Kalsang?" Do I belt back there to save *Climate*? I need to decide. Right now. I bite the inside of my cheek. I need to do something to make amends to Dominique and Noor. I can't do that in the PR circus back at the office. But I can't take on social media and the whole world. And the film is out there. People have seen it.

"Where are you?" he says.

My throat burns. It's never too late to do the right thing. "I'm sick as a dog," I lie.

"Oh, for God's sake."

"I've got–stomach flu." Lying is never the answer. "I thought I could tough it out, but I need the day off."

"For God's sake, Zandy. Get your butt in here first thing tomorrow. We need you to blog too." He ends the call.

Placing one foot in front of the other, I get myself into the marble-clad cathedral.

Slender marble pillars rise up one hundred feet. Cross-ribbed vaults span the nave. An immense lofty space, cool and soothing.

I take in a breath. Then out. In . . . out. Silence. Only feet shuffling, voices whispering.

The muscles around my ears soften.

I enter a pew at the back and slide into a smooth wooden seat. Underfoot, worn stone.

"Blog," said Stewart. He wants me to blog . . .

I pull my phone out of my side pocket. It's musty here. My breath is tight with the sticky particulate of incense.

I open the video app on my phone, hold it in front of my face, and hit RECORD. "I'm Zandy Watson, Director of *The Perfumer's Secret* documentary. I made a mistake."

I sense heads turning. They must be staring at me.

I take in a long, slow breath as though I'm pulling it up through a straw. Warmth spreads across my chest and I smile. "I believe that Dominique Severin didn't know anything about his grandfather's crime." I focus on the camera lens located at the top of my screen. "I made a big mistake."

More onlookers shuffle into a group watching me. Good. I want everyone to hear this. "There are more truths to tell. This story has many strands of truth."

I nod, keeping eye contact with the lens. "I made a mistake. I apologize." I hit the large red circle to end the recording.

My palms are clammy so I wipe them across my cotton pants.

I turn and look towards the rose window. Its jewel tones red, blue, and yellow reach towards me. I squeeze my fists tight and upload my vlog to Instagram and YouTube. I hit the "public" button.

I roll my head to the left and the right, loosening my shoulders. I did what I needed to do. I feel calmer.

I forward the link to Dominique, Camille, Jacqueline, Ruth, the PR Director, and Noor Haddad. "With sincere apologies," I add.

A couple of minutes pass. I open my eyes and flick open YouTube.

No hits.

My chest tightens.

I check Instagram.

I have two likes, from my roommates.

My abdomen hardens.

Out there on the World Wide Web, I'm a speck of dust.

I recheck my phone. Response from Dominique, et al.?

Nothing.

Under my ribs, I feel a gaping hollow. I want to make an impact. I want the universe to respond. But *nada*.

Thirty thousand hours of new content is uploaded to YouTube every hour. My vlog is a dot of phytoplankton in an ocean of moving images out there. It won't change anything.

I sink my head into my hands. With all the drama about the

doc, I thought I'd get attention by challenging this story because everyone loves a fight. But I'm just a thirty-year-old documentary maker. I'm not creepy Euan with an army of PR bots obeying my code.

I stuff my phone back into my thigh pocket and make my way through the onlookers out to Fifth Avenue. Do I try and dream up some other way of making reparations to Dominique?

I sit on the church steps. The hard stone presses against my sit bones.

I've given it my best shot, and I'm out of ideas. The traffic on the Avenue is picking up–cars and pedestrians. The noise and heat and pollution are building. Tomorrow I get back to the office, salvage my job, and pursue *Climate*, which affects a whole lot more people than a French perfume business. Tourists hurrying up the steps jostle me. My ears ring with the honking of car horns.

I look across the Avenue to the sculpture in front of Rockefeller Center–a massive bronze figure of Atlas holding the sphere of the heavens above him. "Exert yourself!" it seems to scream at me. Do something.

The problem is I'm no celebrity. I twiddle the zipper on the side pocket of my combat pants, the slider smooth and hard in my fingers–open, shut, open, shut. A jolt of energy spurts through me and my hands tingle. I stand bolt upright.

I'm no celebrity, but I know a big one.

Her conference room smells of cardamom, cloves, and coffee. Noor flings open the door and sails in, flanked by a suave man in a pale gray suit. "You talked your way in here?" She glares at me, her face as unyielding as the orange bucket chairs around her white marble conference table. "You need to leave." Her skinny arms would make her look fragile but for the vigor of her eyes, nose, lips, and the scent of power she gives off.

"I'll get her out of here," says the man with dark, mournful eyes. "I'm Zaid Haddad, legal counsel for WomenUP and Noor's brother." He's pudgy, kempt, and alluring.

"Let me explain–please." I try to feel as upbeat as her WomenUP offices with their brightly colored sofas and pale wood floors.

I step towards her. "I'm here to make a movie about *you*." The floor-to-ceiling glass wall behind her shows silver skyscrapers stretching to the heavens. I've got to be as purposeful as those standing stones out there.

"I'm going to fix this," I continue. I place my army-green messenger bag on the conference table. "You told me to make another movie. That's what I'll do." I clasp my hands behind my back, opening my chest.

Zaid stands next to Noor across the conference table from me clasping a leather attaché case under one arm. He raises his hand, pointing to the door. "Go do it."

Trembling, I explain that I've told the world I made a mistake and that no one has picked it up. "So I need to shoot you–"

"How would that help?" says Noor.

"You're Noor Haddad. You'll get a zillion hits."

"We don't have time for this," says Zaid. "There are protesters downstairs blocking our doorway." He flares his nostrils. "I want you out of here."

My cheeks burn. Downstairs on Madison Avenue, lines of protesters carrying placards are chanting, chanting,

"JEW HATER,"
"FASCIST,"
"ARABS GET OUT."

"You've brought the Middle Eastern war to my doorstep," says Noor.

"Let's start a movement," I say.

"What kind of movement?"

"The #IMadeAMistake movement," which I dreamt up hot-footing it over here from St. Patrick's.

"Explain what you mean. How does this connect to *The Perfumer's Secret*?"

"We take advantage of the drama around the documentary. Let's ride their wave, play CNM at their own game," I say.

Zaid sits. "Why are you wasting your time with her," he says to Noor. "This is crazy."

"Ask the world to give you a second chance," I say.

She picks up a pencil from the center of the table and twiddles with it.

"I shoot you speaking straight to camera. 'I made a mistake,'" you say.

She taps her vermillion nails on the gleaming table.

"CNM will never let you do that," says Zaid.

"Bugger CNM." Perspiration bubbles at my neckline.

"She betrayed you. You'd be mad to trust her again," he says.

She nods. "You're right," she says to her brother. "No, Ms. Watson. You've done enough damage. Please leave."

Damn, damn and damn. I scoop up my bag and head for the door passing a wall of portraits. Women's faces look at me, women of every hue in all kinds of headdress. My hand is on the silver doorknob and Zaid is one step behind me. In my mind's eye, I see those portraits, the fire in those eyes.

Should I leave as she asks or can I find something to persuade her?

I swivel and, skirting Zaid, take several steps back into the room.

"The people who will suffer most if Lindissima doesn't sell are these women."

I'm lightheaded, pointing to the portraits covering every inch of the wall to my left. Bright faces smile out, individuals and groups in patterned headscarves and flowing robes. Sunlight, earth, fields, and mud huts from Egypt, North Africa, Turkey, and beyond.

She drops her shoulders.

I read out the captions beneath them. "Pinar bought a dairy cow and sells milk to send her children to school." My body tingles. "Joud saved up for a secondhand taxi she rents out. Anisah took out a loan to start brewing local beer."

I step up to the conference table, put my hands on it, and lean towards Noor. "These are visionary women. They had the courage to take the first step and that's what I'm asking of you. Are the people you help climb out of poverty tied forever to their past? Or are they sparks of what they might become in the future?" I'm floating an inch off the floor. "Story is the most powerful weapon we have for change," I say.

She shoots a sideways look at her brother.

None of us moves. The moment hangs in the air.

My belly flutters. "Use the story weapon. Make this movie with me," I command.

She leans over to her brother. Their heads nearly touch as they exchange animated phrases in Arabic–which I don't understand.

She seems to soften.

My chin trembles.

He thumps the table with the side of his hand.

She raises her head. "You betrayed me. I won't work with you again."

He stands. "I'll see you out, Ms. Watson."

I trudge out through the open-plan office, through rows of twenty-somethings staring into laptops.

I keep a couple of paces ahead of him. I want him gone.

"I'll see myself out," I say over my shoulder.

"I'll see you off the premises," he repeats.

I thought I had a chance to put this right, but there's nothing for it now. I'm out of options. At the elevator doors, I stand apart from him, staring up at the LED display. The red numbers indicate that the elevator is going up to floor 6 . . . 7 . . . 8.

My palms are clammy. This elevator is taking forever.

I open the flap of my bag, feel my way in, and remove my phone. I check social media. No further likes. No further comments. *Nada.* I cram my phone into the bottom of my bag and close the flap.

Finally the doors open. I step inside the steel box.

Zaid follows me in and presses the L button. His scent of sandalwood and patchouli, mingled with perspiration, hangs in the air.

I stare at the marble floor. The elevator descends, and with it, my heart slides down through my chest and settles in the lower regions of my stomach.

At the ground floor, the doors open. I step into the huge foyer, with its soaring ceilings. Sunlight pours in and a din of voices echoes off the glass walls as office workers cross the floor.

I need to get out, get away from this.

A throng is huddled on the street, stretching across the whole front of the building.

The glass doors are guarded from the inside by three beefy uniformed security guards facing the crowd on the outside, like policemen warding off a riot.

We approach the doors. "Ms. Watson is leaving." Zaid nods to one of the six-foot-five giants.

The man turns a key in the door and opens it for me.

I slide through.

He yanks it shut behind me.

A crowd of about one hundred is massed in a semicircle a few feet in front of me, holding aloft placards proclaiming:

JEW HATER

NAZI PIG NAZI PIG

OUT WITH HADDAD

My chest tightens. To my right, a burly woman with scarlet-dyed hair bellows through a megaphone, leading the group's call and response:

"OUT WITH HADDAD!"

"OUT WITH HADDAD!"

They bang the wooden poles of their placards onto the pavement and stamp, matching the rhythm of their chant.

The aggression, the noise. Again, I can't breathe. Bowing my head, shrinking into myself, I step towards the human barricade in front of me. It's like entering a swarm of bees.

Imagining I'm in a beekeeping suit, with helmet and veil, I push forward.

As one, the crowd pushes back against me.

Headfirst, I thrust myself onward.

They swarm and repel me.

A bearded man bears his teeth and yells, "Jew hater!"

They think I work for WomenUP. They don't know it's worse than that–I caused this.

The beard and his neighbor, a pale-faced beanpole, shove at my shoulders. One thrust snaps my right elbow backwards. A sharp twang of pain shoots through my shoulder as I hit the ground. "Hey!" I yell.

Staying low, I half crawl through the darkness of the throng–like a child clambering between her parents' legs. The chanting has them in a frenzy. They're almost dancing.

In the daylight behind the crowd, I stand up. My shoulder throbs. I clasp my bag to my side and run, my boots thudding on the hot concrete slabs. I run and run.

At Park and Fifty-Third, I stop and bend at the waist. Cars roar and honk around me. My heart pounds as I catch my breath. I stand and find myself staring through the glass storefront of a Chipotle Mexican Grill. The customers inside form a line. They make their selections and proceed with steady rhythm, with purpose and orderliness, like a giant caterpillar on the move.

But I'm on the outside, with my nose to the window, and I'm lost.

At the till, the young man in a black net skullcap stacks their foil food containers in brown paper bags. The customers slide their credit cards into the electronic reader and retrieve their food. I don't want Stewart to give *Climate* to Kalsang. If he does that, my efforts will have been for nought. What do I do?

The customers know what to do. They turn towards the street, holding their paper lunch bags at their sides. They exit the store, talking on phones through AirPods or chatting to each other in groups of twos and threes.

I shot the Greta footage on a CNM camera. It sits on the CNM server. Do I own it? Or do they?

I stumble into the subway at Lex and Fifty-First. I don't know. I don't know. I don't know anything.

I come up into daylight at Lafayette Street and plod home to my flat share. Midtown to Bed Stuy, Brooklyn, is my daily commute. I do it on autopilot.

At 437 Greene Street, I traipse up the stairs of the brownstone. Three floors up, I insert the key in the lock and open the door. The hair on the back of my neck prickles. I'm never home in the middle of a weekday and it's eerily quiet as I step into the hallway.

I edge towards the sitting room, like a trespasser–like there's some gas cloud permeating the place into which I must not enter.

I'm going to do what everyone else does. I'm going to numb out and get lost.

I lie on the sofa, propping my head against some cushions. In my first year of grad school, I used to skateboard at a park near Brooklyn College. I attempted a kickturn and crashed. They inserted six screws and a metal plate to fix my tibia. Finally, they sent me home with pain meds. Once they wore off, a gargantuan headache, nausea, and biting pain rolled over me like waves onto the shore.

That's me now. I see Stewart's office with the ticker tape, I see Dom's eyes at The Fifth, and I see how atrociously I've handled this.

I pull my laptop from my bag and fire up Netflix. The odor of rotting garbage wafts in from the kitchen and half-empty mugs and glasses are strewn about from last night. A miasma of sadness inhabits the room.

I need to be numb. *Scandal* will do it for me. I'm going to lose myself as Kerry Washington struts her stuff in impossible black stilettos and her white belted coat, as she orders her staff about then slips into the White House and seduces President Fitzgerald Grant III in all manner of ways and places. And I will struggle through the twisty plot to figure out who the bad guy is.

I toggle through the episode outlines. Am I on season five or six? It's too long since I watched it. I flip through "what's trending." *Bridgerton*–no thank you. Nothing appeals.

Over the rim of my laptop, I spy a plate with leftovers of something Mexican on the coffee table. I extend my left leg and shunt it out of view with the toe of my boot.

There's a shuffle. Max, my roommate's screenwriter boyfriend, stands in the doorway.

"Hey." He lumbers in. Shaggy blonde hair and clean, even features.

"Hey back."

I close my laptop and slide it onto the floor.

A slim reefer lies in his right hand.

He proffers it.

"Sure." I flip my legs to the side, making room for him on the sofa.

The sofa springs groan as he slams the weight of his six-foot-three body onto it.

I take a drag of the joint. It hits my bloodstream. Everything relaxes. I stare at the orange lampshade, intrigued by the depth of color.

The room blurs.

I giggle. He laughs and slaps my leg.

Sometime later, I've got the munchies and we're in the kitchen, yanking open cabinet doors, searching for something sweet, no something crunchy . . . no something . . .

I wake fully dressed on top of my bed, feeling grimy. My mouth is dry and caked. I'm sweaty in my groin and my armpits.

I sit bolt upright. How did I get here? I don't remember–I release the hair plastered to the back of my neck. My fingers are doused in perspiration.

Kerpow. I went to France so as not to turn into Max. Now, I've turned into Max. I leap off the bed and grab my towel and shower caddy from the inside of my cupboard. Legs trembling, I stumble down the passageway to the bathroom.

I step inside and close the door behind me. White tiles and crumbling grout stare back at me. The long mirror above the basin has a large chip on the right side. The space feels like it's closing in on me.

I dump my caddy on the wooden stool, open the shower door, and run the water.

Peeling off my clothes, I drop them on the floor.

I retrieve my bar of soap and step inside the glass-doored shower cubicle.

I turn the dial to hot. My skin crawls. I want out of this body. I stand with my hair directly under the shower. Steaming water cascades around my head and down my whole body. I soap my armpits, my groin, my feet, my hands.

First, long and hot. Then two-minute bursts of cold water. Hot, then cold. I repeat this over and over. I need to wash everything away, to emerge clearheaded and sharp.

My skin is soft and raw when I step out onto the bathmat, squeaky clean. I wrap my body in my towel, pick up my gear, and pad barefooted back to my room.

I slip on a clean set of clothes and slide my phone into my bag.

I've got to get out of here. I want oblivion, but not this. I will not be Max.

My bag swings against my hip as I tramp down the street. I need to move my body. I hop onto the subway and hang off the strap in the middle of the car. Maybe I can lose myself in boxing. Next to me, a scrawny man in a black shirt leans towards the woman next to him. "Let's go in. Let's solve it. Send me a list of what you need to do to fix it."

I swivel away.

Twenty minutes later, I emerge into the warm breeze in Queens. I pick up a coffee at Dunkin'. Up high, lookouts patrol flat roofs. Dealers hang in doorways chanting "smoke," "charlie," "junk" at me. Fastfood wrappers and half-eaten chicken legs carpet the pavements. I keep my eyes down.

In the changing room, I strip down and look at myself in the mirror. My reflection is ghostly, green, skinny. I turn towards the lockers and it hits me–dammit–I didn't bring my workout gear. I pick up my pants from the floor and hurl them at the locker.

I yank my clothes back on and head into the gym. I slump onto the long bench at the side, lightheaded from hunger. My tongue tastes bitter and metallic. The new coach, Muhajir, is working a white geezer in the ring. No one I recognize because I only come after work or on weekends. Three Black teens are warming up to my left. I watch the old guy at the far end skipping, trying to lose myself in the *clip, clip, clip* of his rope hitting the deck.

After a few minutes, Lamar comes over, his step springy.

He slides in next to me. "What you doing on the bench?"

I gaze off at the peeling paint on the far wall. I came to move my body. But I can't.

"Why ain't you boxing?"

I shrug.

The rest bell peals into the air.

"I've got a kid for you. See Jayleen?"

"What did you say?"

He nudges me in the rib. "I'm talking to you, girl." He points at the skinny kid with a patch over one eye and knobbly knees.

I look over.

Taut, lean, wired, he's thwacking the Everlast heavy bag. "He knows more boxing than I'll ever know," I say.

"You take him for a soda."

"What's with his eye?"

"He lost it in a gang fight last year. I want you to mentor him," says Lamar.

No way. Not now. "What do I do?"

"You ask about his life. You listen. You build trust."

I look down and grind my boot into the brown stain on the floor. Build trust. That's the last thing I'm ready to do. Round and around I grind my boot. "I'm not fit for it. He deserves someone better than me."

"What the hell's going on with you?" he asks.

Jiggliness fizzes through me. I've got a sparkler inside me that I can't extinguish. I pace over to the cubbies.

Lamar, motionless, eyes me.

I tidy the gloves, organizing them in pairs, matching left to right.

Lamar's gaze bores through me.

I return and pace in front of the bench where he sits. Six paces up. Six paces back.

"Speak."

I tell him everything. I pour it out–the whole sorry story. "Should I do the damn PR on my perfume doc so I get to make *Climate*?" It's the only thing over which I have control.

If Lamar says something, I don't hear it. I thrust my hands into my pockets. "I've got to help Dominique." My voice is small and dry as I look down at his face.

Lamar stands and places a hand on my shoulder. "You'll figure out doing the right thing by this guy."

God dammit. "I just told you. I tried everything. There's nothing more I can do."

He shakes his head. "Pull yourself together, Zandy. You've got a life. Jayleen don't have nothing. Hey, Jayleen!" he calls out and moves off towards the boy hammering the fig bag.

On the way towards the exit door, I stumble on a jump rope. My ankle twists. Pain spurts through me like a comet. "Dammit," I wail. My hand flies out to cushion my fall. I land hard on my wrist. It hurts like hell. "Damn, damn, damn," I holler. At myself, at Lamar, at the room, at the world.

Lamar made it worse, not better. Stumbling out of the gym, I don't even have the wherewithal to slam the door behind me.

Not long after, I ring Luke's bell.

He opens up.

Now, I'm standing in his kitchen. I don't know why. We've had no contact since I threw his keys in the skip four months ago. But I can't go home, and I can't be alone.

He's on the other side of the countertop, tidying the detritus, making piles of the papers that cover the wood surface, flipping shut his two laptops and stacking one atop the other.

Last time I was here, Samantha was flying around in her thong. The memory burns through me and I deserve it. I'd like to pick up a bottle of vinegar and chug it back, feel it corrode my esophagus.

Also, I need to eat. I pull out a barstool at his kitchen counter and slide my backside onto it. "Mind if I eat?"

"Be my guest." He grabs the open packet of smoky tempeh, the vape stick, and the vodka bottle, and shoves them next to the kitchen sink behind him.

"You never returned my key."

"Yeah. Sorry."

"I've missed you."

"Thanks," I mumble. I reach into my bag and fumble for the great, fat burrito I bought at the corner bodega. I unfold the silver wrapper and set it on the counter. Warm, tangy smells of the whole-wheat wrap reach my nostrils from inside the greaseproof shell.

"Congrats, babe. I watched your doc last night."

Was it just last night?

"*The Perfumer's Secret* is blowing up on social media."

"I just want to eat." I raise the burrito to my mouth and chomp down on shredded lettuce, red cabbage, and black beans in spicy salsa. It's moist, soft, and comforting.

"You made waves. Proud of you."

I stare at him.

He prattles on.

I chew and swallow. As the food reaches my tummy, warmth spreads through my torso. My brain is now connected to the rest of my body.

I scrunch up the wrappers and the brown paper bag, enjoying the sound it makes and the feeling of finality it gives me. I slide off the stool, walk around the counter, and open the kitchen cabinet behind Luke. I stuff the wrapping into the recycling bin under the sink.

"Let's not talk about *The Perfumer's Secret*." I swivel and face his back. "Not now." I lean in and rest my chin on the soft warmth of his Henley T-shirt.

Clean, comforting soap smell. Something with honey and rosemary. I press my chest against his back and run my hands around his hips, pressing into the denim of his jeans.

Laying my head on his shoulder, my fingers probe and fumble until I find the metal clasp with one hand, the leather strap with the other. I unbuckle the belt. "Babe," he groans.

My palm feels his manhood pushing through his jeans. A thrill runs through me, and now we definitely don't have to talk about *The Perfumer's Secret*.

The edge of the counter presses into the small of my back as we have sex, my legs wrapped around his buttocks.

He pushes the papers onto the floor, lays me on top of the counter. We do it again there. We're in that space of no thinking. Just bodies moving together. He finishes me off in front of the fireplace that is full of old movie reels.

Upstairs, between the sheets of his bed, we're curled around each other. I'm cocooned in the sticky smell of incense he burns up here. I stare at the honeycolored timbers in the ceiling. Outside a siren wails. Time stops. We snooze in the afternoon sunlight.

We wake. He rolls onto his right side, facing me, shrouding me with the warmth of his body pressing along the length of mine. "They must be all over you at CNM. I bet they'll promote you."

In the haze and glow after sex, my limbs are loose. I'm floaty. Some catch in me has released. "They want me to do press on *The Perfumer's Secret*, to blow it up even bigger," I say now that my defenses are down.

He runs his index finger round and around in a circle around my belly button. "Proud of you, babe."

I roll away and swing my legs over the side of the bed. "No." I stand and trudge down the black metal spiral staircase to the bathroom. I sluice my face with water, wash my underarms, my feet, my genitals. He's got it all wrong. An ancient graying towel hangs from a hook on the wall. I dry myself with it. The stiff fibers invigorate and prickle my skin, cooling and composing me.

I return and sit on the side of the bed, my back to him. I pull on my safari shirt and combat pants. "I need to put things right for the damage I've caused."

He's got his back to me on the other side of the bed. He pulls on his underpants and jeans.

"And there's no way for me to do that." I cinch the belt tight, so it constricts me. I squeeze the metal end of my canvas belt, hard between my fingers. I lean over and grab my combat boots. I thrust my feet into them. I yank on the laces, pulling them taut against my skin. I want to rein myself in or hurt myself. I don't know which.

He stands and comes around the bed. He takes my hand and pulls me up and into his arms. His flesh warm and salty. The tang of sweat from his armpits. "Forget the fallout. You told the truth."

Recoiling at the animal smell coming off Luke, I release

myself from his embrace and step backwards. "You don't understand. It's not the truth. It's only a sliver of the truth."

He takes my hand and squeezes it. "Stay on your side of the camera."

I stare at the thicket of dense hair in his armpit and my insides hollow out.

"Don't try to change the world," he says.

"Oh my God, Luke." Are you that empty? I push him away.

"Let it go."

I grab my messenger bag and clump down the iron staircase. I can't let it go. I stride across the main level of the loft, his uneven floorboards squeaking underfoot. His walls are alive with his oversized, brightly colored posters publicizing *The Abattoir*, *Berlin*, and *After Porn*–all the films he's made.

Is that what you did, Luke? You hacked out those stories and left a human pileup behind you? What about integrity, Luke? What about truth?

My groin throbs. I'm opened up but emptied out by the sex. Spent, like a bullet fired into the abyss. I used him for sex, like he used me for so long. I slam the loft door behind me. I'm never coming back here.

The gym didn't work.

Sex didn't work.

Nothing works.

Chapter Thirty

DOMINIQUE

Paris

At JFK yesterday, after that disastrous meeting with Woolman, I was tempted to board a flight to Tokyo, to run away to Seto, and work with my hands, making pots–let that be my balm. Instead, I took the first flight to Paris. Now driving towards our party, the joint celebration of our three hundredth anniversary and the new perfume launch–I see mini-bottles of Lindissima hanging from tiny parachutes, dropping out of the skies over Paris. A wonderful idea of Camille's. Yet I'm in no mood to celebrate.

A heaviness presses on my chest as I see police barricades blocking off the Avenue Montaigne, which is the location of our flagship shop. More trouble. Even tonight. We pull through the throng of protesters carrying placards denouncing us as "JEW HATERS," and "NAZI PIGS," and demanding "BURN SEVERIN."

Inside the barricade, Camille has decorated the whole of the Avenue Montaigne. Posters of Lindissima emblazoned with the simple line drawing of Noor's face hang from every lamp post.

Tall and short, disabled and able-bodied, curvy and skinny,

Black and white models prowl the avenue handing out Lindissima samples to the guests. Models of every type, to represent everywoman, the spirit of Lindissima.

Look at this! Look at what Camille has pulled off. My sister is a rock star. But we are now reviled from every corner. And our North American inventory lies in some dockyard in New Jersey waiting to be shipped back to us.

The driver drops me at the entrance to the main tent. Jacqueline comes toward me in a purple taffeta dress, the full skirt cinched at the waist. I embrace her. "Did you see the protesters?" I ask.

"I hope we make it through the night without a major incident," she says. "Desmarais is waiting for you in one of the side tents."

Sébastien Desmarais is the Chairman and CEO of the luxury goods conglomerate, SVBD. They've been badgering me all summer to sell the business.

I place my hand on Jacqueline's shoulder. "I'm so sorry it's turned out like this."

"Our fathers were both shits. *Et voilà*!"

Thanks to me, she has this new version of her father to deal with–as well as the tragedy of her daughter. She sucks on the cigarette she holds in her right hand. She makes an O with her lips as she blows out the smoke. She walks me through a flap in the side of the reception tent.

My shoulders are tight as can be. Desmarais will love humiliating me, but I must sell to raise what little money I can for the employees, my family, and the Pereiras. I can survive this, I tell myself. It's my duty to meet him. I must grit my teeth and put a brave face on it.

Just as I'm about to enter the side tent, I see Alain dressed in waiter's uniform; cream evening jacket, white shirt, black tie.

I embrace him.

"I worry about my grandson, what will happen to his job." He bites the inside of his cheek. "You'll do what's right, boss. You'll know what to do."

If only . . .

Inside the tent, I find Desmarais unchanged, tiny and stooped at sixty-eight, with wiry salt-and-pepper hair. We exchange greetings and take our seats opposite one another in this makeshift meeting room with its painter's table and two folding chairs.

"Why isn't Noor Haddad here tonight?" He's steely, a product of the industrial Northeast.

My nostrils flare. He's trying to get me on my back foot. "Unfortunately, she had to cancel because of the proximity of her wedding date." I lock eyes with him.

A pair of granite pebbles stare back at me. "Or she's doing her utmost to distance herself from Severin Frères?"

He's brutal. My mouth parches as I hand him a sheet outlining our sales projections–prior to *The Perfumer's Secret.* "We're seeing strong demand from the Chinese consumer. And we haven't begun to tap the millennialization of the sector."

He reviews the figures.

I scroll through Sun Tzu's aphorisms on my iPhone. I search for the wisdom I need to handle this battle.

"No miscalculations mean the victories are certain," says Sun Tzu again and again in different ways. There is no discussion on how to cope with failure in *The Art of War* because it is a given one does not fail if the principles are truly followed. Where does that leave me? Lying like Maman half-unconscious, in a pool of urine and vomit–the alcoholic at rock bottom.

"Our best offer is equipment value and inventory per your balance sheet . . ."

I scowl. "Asset value?"

He tugs at his impeccable shirt cuff, flashing his ultrathin gold wedding band. "We're wary of associating ourselves with Severin because of the documentary." He turns his left wrist to check his watch as if to say, "I'm on my way somewhere much more important." Desmarais left home at fifteen penniless, so nothing dazzles him. He places his faith only in himself, and on his rightness.

He nods and stands.

Everything in here is white, stiff, and starched. "Nothing for our brand?"

"Your brand died with that documentary."

I push back my chair and stand. I cross my arms tight. "I've apologized to the Pereira family–publicly and unreservedly. I will do everything in my power to make restitution to them." I bite down on my bottom lip, determined to stay in control.

Silence from him.

"You offer nothing for our revenue streams?"

"You had revenues before the documentary aired. Asset value is my best offer."

My gut tightens. He's saying we're worth no more than our physical plant. Not a *sou* for our brand–which in perfume accounts for 80 percent of value. "You'll commit to the workers, at least." I grip the back of my chair. "To continue their jobs for at least 180 days?"

"No conditions."

My stomach somersaults as I escort him out to the avenue.

I've always dreaded selling the business, breaking the chain of three hundred years in the Severin family, but I must raise what I can for my employees and their families, for Camille, Amélie, and for Maman. On the other side, this is outrageous; we still have our intellectual property, the knowhow of our perfumes, our employees, our best practices.

"Take it or leave it." He slides into his limo, which awaits him purring on the avenue.

Nausea rises in me. "No deal."

The car pulls away.

There's a hint of cool in the air now that night has fallen. I want to slip away, take a long walk in the cloak of darkness until this headache has dissolved and my limbs give out. I'll return to my club, a small place I use when on business in Paris. It's clean, simple, and without fuss.

I imagine myself spent, climbing between the beautifully ironed club sheets. I want to escape into oblivion where I don't have to cogitate and review, don't have to regret and chastise myself.

But I must tell Camille about Desmarais's insulting offer, tell her I've turned it down. And it would be disgraceful to leave Camille carrying the responsibility for this evening.

Grace Jones's *"Pull up to the Bumper"* pulsates from inside the oversized party tent which stretches the width of the Avenue Montaigne. I head inside and make my way through the six hundred handpicked guests in search of Camille.

This is the last place I want to be, but I force myself to put on a brave face as I shake hands, make small talk, thank the waitstaff handing out Cristal champagne and canapés from silver trays.

Models prowl the catwalk which Camille has installed down the center of the tent. As each one pauses before the crowd, she releases a miniature bottle of Lindissima. It hangs suspended by its own parachute until it plops into a river of water and is carried out to crowds on the street.

I wave to Jacqueline, who is talking to *Le Monde's* lifestyle editor. Ruth too works the crowd, talking up the brilliance of our new perfume.

The creative director of Dior and the PR honcho of Louis Vuitton encircle Maman, seated as if on a throne, opposite the end of the catwalk. They bend down to talk with her.

Ah, there's Camille in an apple-green silk jumpsuit, her hair arranged in a huge pile on the top of her head. She's holding little Amélie's hand.

My chin trembles, and I curl my hands into fists. I've destroyed their heritage. I sidle up to them and caress Amélie's shoulder.

"It's a disaster." I whisper the facts of my meeting with Desmarais in Camille's ear. "He's offering asset value. Can you believe it?"

Camille purses her lips and nods. "We should take it anyway. It's cash in hand."

"No," I say to Camille. "We're not some bit of rubbish lying on the carpet. We're not going to let him bend down and pocket us. He's arrogant and insulting."

"Yes he is," says Camille. "But a bird in the hand . . ."

Amélie skips into the center of the crowd. She prances and twirls amongst the guests, proud of herself in pristine white dress and shoes.

We watch her, mesmerized by our little jewel. I squeeze Camille's shoulder.

Alain approaches her, a tray of champagne balanced on his right hand.

Amélie tugs on his jacket sleeve.

He beams down at her.

"Desmarais won't even commit to the staff. What about the staff, Camille?"

"You've done everything you could to save the business . . ."

"I should have sold back in May, like you told me to."

"It's not your fault, Dom. Life is messy. We do our best and it doesn't always work out."

I relax my shoulders. The headache dissipates some. I'm

grateful to Camille for her compassion, for standing with me, not against me.

The models dance amongst the guests now. The Grace Jones lookalike takes Amélie's hand and twirls her round and around. Amélie shows off the fullness of her skirt. She shakes her curls, laughing. She backs into Alain.

He collapses sideways, knocked off his feet. His tray of flutes springs into the air, spraying champagne in every direction before smashing into smithereens on the black and white checkered floor.

Camille rushes forwards, crying out, "*Non*, Amélie . . ." She grabs her daughter.

I leap towards them. Amélie with her blonde curls and big round eyes. She's beautiful and joyful and full of innocence. I place my hand on Camille's arm. "It's okay," I say. "It wasn't her fault."

Nor was it Alain's. And nor has this catastrophe been my fault. In spite of the outcome, I've done my best.

I stroke Amélie's shoulder. I hug Camille, who relaxes in my arms. She turns her face to me. Her eyes are clear and bright. Smiling, she shakes her head. "*Oh, là là*!"

Has the time come for me to accept that we too are in smithereens, that I don't have to be perfect? I can be whole and honorable just as I am.

I hold onto Camille's warmth and relax my body. Severin Frères is like that set of flutes now, smashed into ungainly pieces. I've struggled to save this business through Maman's overspending, a changing industry environment, and the uncovering of this awful secret.

Is there something more I can do? I think not.

My temples relax. Peace washes over me, even in this mêlée. Blaming myself, always feeling responsible, doesn't help.

I don't strain to pick up the broken glass all around. Others can do that now. I bend my knees and reach down to my left for a small warm hand. Head erect and spine straight, I lead darling Amélie out of the shattered glass and onto the center of the checkered floor. Smiling, I bow from the waist.

Looking up into my eyes, she curtsies.

I twirl her and lift her to the glam disco, electro funk of "Dancing in the Rain." I clasp her to my chest, enjoying in my heart my talented sister and her beautiful daughter.

I've acted with integrity, which is all that any of us can do.

After, we leave the floor and I go to Camille. "You always said an independent house can't survive in the twenty-first century," I say in her ear. "Time to let go. I'm calling Desmarais to accept his offer."

Chapter Thirty-One

ZANDY

I'm doomed. I can't solve this–and I was dumb to think anyone else could solve it for me. So the next morning I head back to the office having made a "miraculous recovery" from stomach flu. I'll do as little press for *The Perfumer's Secret* as I can get away with. And it's on to *Climate*, which is the only good I can do here, the only way I can make some meaning from this disaster. *Climate* is a truth the world needs to hear. It's the only thing over which I have any control.

Back at the shop I'm flavor of the month. Of course I am. Everyone is riding high on the success of *The Perfumer's Secret.* I have leverage. I have agency. I'm not happy. Six months ago, this was all I wanted–a Director/Producer credit and enough buzz about my work that I'd join the ranks of real doc makers.

Two days later, I arrive at 10 Rockefeller Plaza. I'm here to promote *The Perfumer's Secret.* I don't want to, but I have to. I feel like a broadsheet newspaper someone's torn into shreds. I'm about to be interviewed by Savannah Gilbo of the *What's Hot Now?* show. CNM has arranged an exclusive with her about *The Perfumer's Secret.* That's the sensation it has become in the news cycle.

I head through the main doors and present my ID to the paunchy security guard who checks my name on his list. He rifles through my bag then motions me through the metal detector. Once upon a time this kind of exposure was my dream. But I'm a failure. I tried my little movie. I tried pitching Noor. I told the world that I made a mistake. But no one is listening.

On the far side, I'm met by a young man in dress shirt and pants. "Zandy, it's so great to meet you," he enthuses, opening the entry to the studio complex with his key card.

I nod. I just need to do the goddamned interview. Tonight I'll get to the gym and box it out of my system. Tomorrow is a new day. Tomorrow I start on *Climate.*

First stop, hair and makeup. Then the greenroom, which is like an airport lounge–with coffee and creamer, packaged snacks, sofas, and TV monitor. I've got this dull ache. There's nothing I can do but accept and move on. I will focus on craft, beauty, and artisanship. I will talk up Severin and I'll promote Lindissima as best I can.

As I wait my turn in the greenroom, I wonder if I'll remember my lines. To distract myself, I watch the TV screen, which is showing a clip on homelessness.

Lean towards the camera, I remind myself. That will help with presence and intimacy.

And look at her directly. Don't look around or you'll appear shifty and untrustworthy.

". . . our special report on rising rates of homelessness in our major cities," says Savannah onscreen in her husky voice.

The camera zooms in on a homeless guy not yet forty. Shaggy and wild looking, he is swathed in granite-colored layers. Poor bugger. May his luck improve today. Plastic bags shroud his feet protruding from the end of a stained old sleeping bag. McDonalds coffee cups and Big Mac wrappers form a semicircle around him. As a New Yorker, I know this sight too well. I can almost pick up the stench of baked-in hopelessness and filth.

Clear gray eyes stare into the camera. He looks into the distance and shouts, "Tackata, tackata, tooo."

The camera backs away, revealing a cardboard sign perched on his lap proclaiming,

> "YOU WILL KNOW THE TRUTH, AND THE TRUTH WILL SET YOU FREE." (JOHN 8:32)

I rock back onto my heels and clasp my arms around my torso. Those words are directed at me.

I thought the truth would set me free, but maybe there is no single truth. Maybe everyone has their story and the truth is a blend of all those stories.

"Time to go, ma'am." The young man shepherds me out of the greenroom.

I know now that exposing the truth isn't always the right thing to do. The truth and integrity aren't always the same thing.

I'm caked in makeup and wearing a corporate-style charcoal-gray pantsuit (yuk). I follow him along the passageway towards the studio. The walls are lined with framed photos of world leaders, superstars, and legends who walked down this corridor to appear on the *What's Hot Now?* show.

Perspiration spumes on the back of my neck as I sit in a leather armchair across from Savannah, also encased in makeup and poured into a royal blue sheath dress.

She introduces "the documentary making waves across North America and Europe with the shocking revelation about the glamorous house of Severin Frères," flashing her coral silicone manicure with deft hand movements.

She beams at me. Someone's overdone her hair highlights, and this former Department of State reporter now looks like a shaggy rug from the 1960s. "So you were making a documentary about a world-famous perfume house when you found this 'corrosive secret' behind the glamorous façade?"

I return her big smile. "That's right, Savannah, and I was

fascinated by the way Severin blends artisanship with science." I duck her question because this is about clicks and money–and it will drive Dominique, the Severins, and WomenUP deeper into the ground.

"Your documentary has gone viral. Everyone's talking about it."

I made Dominique into a puppet for me. Now the *What's Hot Now?* show is using me as their puppet–but only if I let them. My heart thunders. I'm on prime-time TV. Do I use this to do the right thing for the Severins and WomenUP?

I thought perfume was beneath me. But it's me who needs to get off my high horse. I can't trample over Dominique in pursuit of my own agenda.

Then again my work in the world is to make *Climate*. I've been building my way towards a doc like this for eight years and four months. I'm closing my hand around it. I do this press and it's mine.

"How does it feel to be in the eye of the storm?" asks Savannah.

"Severin's craft has grown over centuries into a true art." My media training taught me to reply with my own soundbites, regardless of the question.

"I don't suppose you imagined making the *What's Hot Now?* show and the front page of all the newspapers?"

Savannah is in the same club as CNM–sensationalism brings more viewers and advertisers. The cameras are on me. My heart races. It's not studio nerves. If I keep mum here, I'm as spineless as my father. I'll be building my career out of the Severin family's downfall. I need to act with integrity towards my documentary subjects. This is my chance.

I look directly at the camera. No TV novice should do this, but I'm a pro. I'm taking control of this conversation. "Dominique Severin knew nothing of his grandfather's crime. I should have known that."

Savannah jerks backwards in her chair. "Really, Zandy?" Her

hands fly open, palms upwards. "You're asking the public to–"

"I made a massive mistake." I hold up my phone. "Check out #IMadeAMistake."

I'm looking into the eye of the camera to the millions of viewers out there and broadcasting my vlog.

Is Savannah signaling security? Am I about to be booted offstage? "I've told the Severin story and the Pereira story. But what about Dominique, and Noor, and the many thousands of innocent families who are connected with the business? There are so many more truths here that I haven't told."

The lights are hot. The cameras are swooping in to get angles of my face. I've only got seconds . . . "Please, support #IMadeAMistake." I stand. "I invite you to join our movement. Go out and buy Lindissima. Do your bit. Support women entrepreneurs in the developing world–"

Savannah makes eye contact with me. There's a flash of . . . excitement there. "New controversy this morning," says Savannah, "as Zandy Watson, Director/Producer of the film that's making waves, says she made a huge mistake."

Savannah Gilbo repeats it for me! Way to go, people.

A jingle plays. It's a wrap.

Back in the greenroom, picking up my messenger bag, I shake like a dog. I hand over my security pass, and in a blur, I'm escorted out of the building.

Out on the street, I ignore the texts and calls spamming my phone. I welcome the cool breeze, overheated as I am in this ridiculous suit. I've let Stewart down. Now I need to look him in the eye. I walk back to the office.

I shan't apologize. I did what's right for me. But I want to give him a chance to fulminate and fire me–obviously. He's been good to me over the years. I want to acknowledge that. I want to do the right thing.

All eyes are on me as I walk across the floor with makeup

running down my neck and making sticky pools in my clavicle. I wonder whether creepy Euan might delight in this twist, saying the controversy I've created on the Savannah Gilbo show will help CNM and *The Perfumer's Secret* by fanning the flames even more. To hell with creepy Euan.

I knock and go straight in.

"You didn't stick to the script." Stewart stands behind his desk. "You betrayed us."

I keep eye contact. He's right. And I'm right. And that's okay.

"You've given the spotlight to Severin. Now he's got the mic."

I nod.

"I'm *not* happy about it."

"You've been very good to me. I want you to know that."

"That doesn't change anything, Zandy. You're out." He points to the door. "You'll never work in this town again."

"I know," I say. "I thought a film like *Climate* would make my life matter. I was wrong. I matter. I'm happy when I do the right thing, when I act with integrity–even if the story is perfume."

"I've worked hard to get *Climate* on the schedule for you. That's over for you now."

"I know, Stew. You're doing the right thing. So am I."

"I'm calling HR. I want you off the premises."

"Yep." I swallow. "What about Al. Can I still see him?"

"I don't know, Zandy. This is a mess."

"Right, yeah–but I'd like to."

"Noted. Now–*get out.*"

I don't know if my #IMadeAMistake pitch on *What's Hot Now?* will change anything. But I'm doing my best.

I hope Dominique knows that. Noor too.

I'm sad and proud, finding that it's possible to be both of those things in the same instant.

Chapter Thirty-Two

I leave the office with my cardboard box of belongings. Noor barrages me with texts. She joins my #IMadeAMistake campaign, bringing her social media team on board to boost our efforts.

Over three days, we brainstorm celebrities who need help with their image. I pitch them #IMadeAMistake. For every "yes," I cowrite the script and executive produce the shoot with local teams in London, Los Angeles, Bombay, and beyond. I live on late-night pizza. The work is so hard I perspire. Within days, it's gone viral.

"I drank way too much. I made a mistake," says Bongo James.

Jenn Fields and Aniston Delilah throw a series of cream pies in his face.

Laughing as he wipes away the mess, he says, "I'm in therapy. Now I'm a better man and a better father," he says.

"Drinking and driving was a terrible mistake," says Lohan Winehouse before receiving her round of face pies. "Give me a second chance."

"Drink made me say stupid, offensive things," says Gibson Maloney. "I made mistakes." Jodie John and Robert Jameson Jr. throw twenty pies right in his face. "That was my past. I'm asking for another chance," says Maloney, emerging from the cream tsunami.

Publicists call from the world over asking to add their own #IMadeAMistake pie-fest vlogs to our channel. The talk everywhere is #IMadeAMistake and #PieParty.

Two weeks after I leave CNM, it's Noor's turn. It's Wednesday, 1:00 p.m. She sits at a round table in the oasis of calm that is Le Bernardout on West Fifty-First Street. Around the restaurant, gastronauts sit in black leather chairs facing white tablecloths.

I'm in white jeans and a white opennecked shirt, Annie Liebowitz style, while I shoot her vlog.

My Sony PXW rests on a tripod. I pan from a wide angle onto the sea image covering the wall at the far end of the room, then onto the white orchids standing to attention out of tall glass vases.

Next, I zoom in on Noor. A shallow bowl of poached halibut, radish medley, and daikon-ginger dash lies untouched in front of her.

To her left sits her pal, Mayor Lee Wang, the first person she called after we'd put our script together. *Vogue* editor Jordan Jerome sits to her right in a brightly patterned shortsleeved dress.

I hope I've scripted this right, the words she'll say, and the venue. I nod at Noor, indicating that we're ready to film.

She won't give me a signal. She's "on," with her commanding, glacial beauty. She's out of my league. But she's here and I'm recording her.

"Have you ever made a mistake?" she says straight to camera. "I made a big one."

To her right, Jordan Jerome nods.

"A lot of people are angry with me," says Noor. "Because I associated myself with Severin Frères. I should have known about the disgraceful theft by Dominique's grandfather, Yves Severin. I made a mistake."

Around the room, the clang of silver on china fades. Heads turn towards us. Voices hush and a blanket of silence descends on the restaurant. "I made a mistake." Her voice is rich and confident.

Moments later, Chef Balmain comes to the table. "You ordered Peruvian chocolate fondant? I prepared something especially for you." He lifts the silver dish cover, revealing a puffy cream pie on a paper plate. "You made a mistake." Beaming, he leans towards her and slams it into her face.

A roar goes up as she's covered in gloopy whipped cream.

Chef Balmain tosses his head back and laughs.

Noor, face scrunched, wipes a layer of gloop from her eyes and nostrils. Heavy dollops of cream are smeared through her long black tresses and over the shoulders of her purple sheath dress.

A waiter glides in, pushing a trolley piled high with plates and their silver covers.

The chef hands a pie to Mayor Wang.

"You sure messed up." Wang slams it into her face and leans back, laughing.

Jordan Jerome slams another pie into Noor's face. There's a stir as LeBron Marks drops by and picks up a pie and throws it at her.

Noor takes her oversized white napkin and wipes her face. "I made a mistake and I'm asking for a second chance. I'll take cream pie after cream pie, if you'll forgive my mistake and buy a bottle of Lindissima." She wipes the gloop off her face and drops it onto the plate in front of her. "Ten percent of the profit goes to WomenUP. Each bottle you buy helps a disadvantaged woman start her own business. Each bottle helps lift a family out of poverty."

Chef Balmain walks to the other tables, followed by the waiter wheeling his trolley. He offers around the cream pies.

The hubbub picks up. One by one, diners accept a pie and stand in line in front of Noor's table. Some give her a wave of acknowledgment or a pat on the shoulder. Each slams another cream pie in her face.

"It's a wrap," I say.

Noor pulled it off. It was pitch perfect. And as for all those other diners I captured on film–fabulous, the icing on the cake.

I sense movement to my left at ten o'clock. I glance over. Holy cow. My heart accelerates into a gallop.

Fifteen feet away from me, just to the side of the hostess table, stands Dominique.

He hangs back, watching us.

Perspiration wells behind my knees, inside my elbow joints and armpits. I swivel to my right and plunge my head into my viewfinder. Jeez Louise, what's he doing here? I focus my attention on Jordan Jerome. Take a breath, Zandy. Focus on your work. I zoom in. Can Jordan's thick mane of hair be real at her age? Is it anorexia keeping her so skinny?

I want to stay on Jordan. My mind yanks me back to Dominique standing close by, all put together in a light wool jacket, emanating that propriety he has. He's reserved, not supercilious as I first thought.

Breathe, Zandy.

Noor leans over and whispers in Jordan's ear. She rises and slithers off the banquette.

Noor shimmies out and stands to her five feet, ten inches of height. All eyes are on her, her head high, spine erect as she crosses the floor to the restroom, soaking up the attention.

Dammit, Noor. Now I've got no reason to peer through my viewfinder.

Noor deposited a change of clothes in there–she'll be a while now.

I step back from the camera. I want and don't want contact with Dominique. Is he watching me or is he here for something else? I turn to my grip, who is dismantling his lighting umbrella.

"You'll pack up pronto?" Talking to him keeps me from the force field around Dominique that tugs at me, drawing me towards him. Oh, for goodness' sake, I can't stand here like an idiot with my back to the room. I turn towards Dominique.

He steps towards me. Like we're playing Red Light, Green Light.

"Hi." I twiddle a USB cable while something hot and searing rides up and down my insides like an elevator.

"Hi."

No hint of what kind of "hi." I've had no contact with him since that day at The Fifth two weeks ago.

Now what? Should I apologize for the devastation I caused, or is it so huge it's beyond an apology?

Maybe I don't apologize. I've worked my butt off with this #IMadeAMistake gig–this is my version of making amends, my walking the Camino de Santiago as penance.

He tugs at his shirt cuffs. He's nervous.

My shoulders relax a tad.

A wave of his vetiver scent wafts around my face. The color is back in his cheeks.

I take the camera off the stand and house it in its black ballistic nylon case. I should apologize. I'm humbled but it's never too late to do the right thing. Just do it. Now or never.

"I'm done filming . . . shall we take a stroll?"

"Okay." He nods.

What's he thinking?

It doesn't matter. I just apologize and move on. I collapse the stand and hand the gear to my sound engineer. "I'll be back shortly. Can you watch the gear?" I ask him.

Dominique and I head out into the sunlight.

My face, neck, and ears are burning hot. "It's still so hot," I say.

"Yes," he says.

"Is it hot–in France?" My voice is scratchy.

"It's pleasant."

We cross Sixth Avenue, leaving Radio City Music Hall to our right and St. Patrick's Cathedral to our left. The Fifth on Fifth is one block over. My breath is tight, thinking we might have walked past it.

Heat flares off the pavement. I clasp my messenger bag with my right hand.

He could say something, could help me out. He doesn't.

We head towards the park. I turn left onto Madison, thinking the storefronts will provide a distraction–luxury goods are right up his street. We're walking in sync with each other and I drop my attention into that rhythm to soothe myself. "Dom–" I can't stand the silence a moment longer.

"Don't call me that."

If it goes on like this, I'll say a quick goodbye at Sixtieth Street. I'll dive over to the East River. The streets will be packed, I can lose myself in the crowds before returning to Le Bernardout. I'd better just get this over with, say what I need to and go.

At the Tourneau store, he stops and looks at the rows of luxury watches laid out on burgundy velvet cushions.

I trace patterns on the glass with my finger. I make a heart out of reflex. I cringe and rub it out.

"I want to apologize." The back of my throat is dry. I feel like retching. "It doesn't change what's happened, but I'm so, so sorry."

"What do you want me to say?"

"Nothing. I just need to say it. I know you can't forgive me." I shove my hands into my pockets.

"You wish you hadn't told the Pereira story?"

"I regret the slander on your name, and the destruction I caused. I never told your story, never said you're innocent, that you didn't know. And ditto Noor." I relax my hands. My arms hang long at my sides. I've said it. The air is sweet with summer, but there's a note of fall too, something crisp, astringent. Fall clothes deck the shop windows in russet, khaki, and gray. The new school year feels like a fresh beginning.

Now I can leave him.

"Who gave you Grandpapa's contract?"

He wants to keep rubbing my nose in it? "It was in a file box in your library. I found it taped inside."

He shakes his head. "I invited you into my private archive, and you stole my property?"

"I'm sorry, Dominique. I needed the authentication. I'll get it back for you."

We walk. At the northwest corner of Sixtieth and Madison, he sizes up oversized cream raincoats on mannequins in Celine.

I'm done with this. I'm not bloody window shopping with him.

"Are we going to the park?" he asks.

Enshrouded by tall buildings here, the throngs in the street, the busyness of the window displays, I feel a smidgen of safety. I don't want to be in an open space with him. "I need to get back. If someone swipes my rental gear, I'll have thousands of dollars to pay."

"I want to thank you," says Dominique.

"Thank me?"

He takes my elbow, guiding me westward.

He touched me. I let him touch me. Breathe, Zandy.

"It's a couple of blocks to the park," he says.

We walk over. Traffic barrels down Fifth, dispersing grit and dust into the atmosphere. The entry to the park is a zoo–as usual. The sidewalk is splattered with old chewing gum and pigeon droppings. We skirt around tourists lining up to buy pretzels, hot dogs, and phone cases from street vendors.

"Here." I indicate the pathway to our right. I pick up my pace to get out of the mêlée.

Shrubs sprout on each side of this pathway, overhung by

horse chestnut and plane trees. There's a hardedged quality to this foliage, unlike the lush, delicate blooms of the Alpes Maritimes around Grasse.

"I was ready to kill you," he says.

I sigh.

"Now the business has never been stronger. With all the publicity around #IMadeAMistake, we've got long lines outside the Paris shop. We're mobbed with twenty-five-year-olds buying Lindissima."

"Holy cow." I've been working all hours on the #IMadeAMistake vlog, pitching celebrities and producing shoots. This is a shock.

"The price of Severin has gone through the roof. There's job security for our workers on the table."

My heart flips. "That makes me happy." It's a mere two weeks from that dark day at The Fifth.

From across the bushes, children's voices tinkle across the air, tinged with the sweet brown smell of autumn. The ground rises and falls underfoot in the park, a welcome change from the flat and hard pavements in the city. A big-bellied guy lumbers past us puffing and jogging.

"Lindissima has taken off. The business will sell a for good price."

I'd like to take credit for making this happen, only I'm conscious of the catastrophe I also caused. I squeeze my hands tight. "That's great, Dominique."

A huddle of Indian women pass us, their heads covered in brightly colored saris, handbags swinging at their hips. Sunlight catches on their bangles and nose rings as they laugh and gesticulate.

"I also made mistakes," he says.

"No."

"I was nervous around my poor mother, afraid of you revealing her sad state and how shameful that is for our family."

I hang my head. "Tough situation."

We arrive at the entrance to the Children's Zoo. Stone pillars and curlicue ironwork topped by a boy gamboling with wolves. Maybe we should look at the seals–take a break from this intensity. "You want to go in?"

He checks the watch on his left wrist, a vintage thing on a battered leather strap. "Sure."

"Camille will join the new owners. She's excited to be part of a bigger group. Maybe she'll meet someone nice. Someone to share her life with."

"And Jacqueline?"

"She's going traveling. She needs to mend her heart. She says she'll never work for Desmarais. But I can see her changing her mind down the line."

I'd love to see her again, but I don't say so. This is all so raw, so new.

"With the sale of the business, I can make reparations to the Pereira family," he says.

I skip along the path. This is what I wanted, and now it's here. I flip around. Facing him, I walk backwards along the path to the pool. "What will you do now?" I ask.

He shrugs. "Don't know exactly."

I laugh. "You've known exactly what you're doing every minute of your life from age six onward."

"That's been a privilege and also a burden. Feels strange not knowing, but exciting too. A weight lifted from my shoulders."

Two orthodox Jews, large-hatted, wearing white shirts, black pants, and black lace-up shoes, walk beside us. I love how multicultural New York is.

"I'll be a consultant to whoever buys Severin. And I've got other ideas–"

"Like what?"

"I told you. I want to study ceramics with the Nakazatos in Karatsu, Japan."

We approach the oval pool. We hang over the railing, gazing into the dark-brown water. "Sounds like the subject of a great documentary," I say.

"Absolutely not!" He laughs. "What are your plans?"

"I'm going to mentor a kid at my boxing gym. I'm going to get super fit."

"And documentaries?"

"I'm going to skip town and find a new career–"

"As bad as that?"

"CNM fired me. Two days later, they decided they loved the brouhaha about *The Perfumer's Secret* and called me to come back."

"What did you say?"

"I'm going to finish up work on the #IMadeAMistake movement. After that, I'll make up my mind."

"You'll figure it out," he says.

"If it weren't for *Climate*, I'd leave right now, but I do want to make that movie."

He takes a step backwards and sideways. He stands right behind me, his warm breath whispering across the back of my neck.

My spine tingles.

He presses comforting palms on my shoulders, drives his thumbs into the muscles, and draws circles inside my shoulder blades.

Warmth spreads across my back and down the backs of my thighs. I receive the tender, protective message it sends. I lean into this moment, the first time I've let go of the tension in my body for–weeks? "Maybe I'll just stand here and have you rub my back," I say.

I flip around to face him and pick up lavender and bergamot in his scent. "Maybe you can come through New York on your way home from Japan, update me on your progress?"

"Maybe I will. Maybe you'll come back to France? We have so much more to explore."

"Like what?"

"Like French wine–" He lifts an eyebrow.

"*The Vineyarder's Secret*?"

"*Parfait!* And a documentary about French cheese?" he says.

"What about French fashion and French mistresses?"

"You must visit me often." He takes my hands in his and squeezes. "Friends for the long-term?" he says.

I tilt up onto my toes and plant a kiss on his forehead, inhaling that top note of lemon. "*Absolument.*" I pluck at his lapel, lightweight and a cashmere blend. "But for now I'd like to ruin this very good jacket of yours with a large cream pie."

"*Non*!"

"*Oui*! I'll film you announcing your gift to the Pereiras."

Water splashes from behind. I half turn to see a shiny black seal surging through the surface of the water. Ripples spread in concentric circles as it curves into the air playful and joyous–like a gymnast clearing the high bar.

"C'mon, Dom. I can't wait to do this."

"Okey dokey."

"*Allez-y*." I grab his arm. "Let's go."

Book Club Questions

1. Zandy's goal is to make a documentary about climate change, but her boss sends her to work on a perfume documentary in the South of France. If you were in the same situation, would you pursue your passion for climate or follow instructions and switch to perfume?

2. Dominique is faced with a difficult decision about the future of his family's perfume business. How does his character evolve throughout the story, and what factors influence his choices?

3. Zandy's relationship with Dominique develops over the course of the novel. How does their relationship affect the choices they make and the direction of the story? What do you think of their dynamic as a couple?

4. Noor Haddad plays a significant role in the plot, inspiring Zandy to take a different approach to her documentary. How does her character contribute to the themes of the story, and what do you think of her impact on the characters' decisions?

5. Zandy faces a moral dilemma in deciding whether to expose the truth about Severin's history. Do you think

she makes the right choice? What would you have done in her place?

6. The power of social media is evident in this story, particularly in Zandy's efforts to right her wrongs. How does this narrative illustrate the influence of social media in our lives today, both positively and negatively?

7. Discuss the role of redemption and forgiveness in this novel. How do the characters grapple with their past mistakes, and what lessons can be drawn from their journeys?

8. This book has a strong sense of place, with the South of France and the world of perfume as significant settings. How does the setting contribute to the atmosphere and themes of the story?

9. Zandy's decision to publicly admit her mistake leads to the #IMadeaMistake movement. What does this say about the power of admitting to our mistakes and trying to right them? How does it reflect the themes of personal growth and redemption?

10. What do you imagine might happen to Zandy and Dominique after this story ends? How do you think their experiences will shape their futures?

11. This novel explores the themes of truth, morality, and the consequences of one's actions. How do these themes resonate with you, and what message or lesson do you think the author intended to convey?

Acknowledgments

Most especially, I thank Linda Grosse. Darling Linda, your unfailing love and wisdom inspire me to become the writer and mother I hope to be. Linda, 1958–2023, most beloved friend, witness, and confidante. May her memory be a blessing.

And thank you of course, to Dorothy Berwin, Kendall King, Fionnuala Ni Aolain, India Lacey, Violetta Lacey, Fay Ballard, Sandra Lawson, Sonia Cairns, Nicholas Berwin, Charlotte Friedman, Edward Barbour-Lacey, and Nya Barbour-Lacey.

There is a special place in heaven for writer friends and critique partners. I couldn't begin, or end a book without you. Thank you, Leanne Farella, how lucky I was to find you. Ditto Andrew Solomon, Anne Holliday, Jule Kucera, Kristina Bak, Sujata Massey, Laura Zam, Laura Scalzo, Barbara Longley, Anne Hinnenkamp, Nancy Evertz, Louisa Treger, A.M. Homes, Mary Kay Zuravleff, and Kathryn Ster. Profound thanks to my superstar team: Savannah Gilbo, Sue Campbell, and Caroline Gilman. Thank you to my beta readers Maria Reeves, Mia Rutledge, Densie Webb, and Sarah Beaudette. Thank you Brooke Warner, Shannon Green, Lauren Wise, and my gorgeous fellow writers at She Writes Press. Thank you Alexandra Wong, Dana Pittman, Drema Drudge, Robert Dallas, Leslie Miller, Anne Durette, Helena Drysdale, Zara Daisy Drummond, Victor Lopez Castro, Andrea Orejarena, Alicia Lawson, Tracey Rose, Eloise Lawson, and Lisa Hofer. And at every hour of every day, Roger Lacey. My cup runneth over.

Here's how:

Or go to
https://nerolilacey.com/sign-up

If you enjoyed this book, please leave a review on your preferred site. And spread the word in whatever way feels good to you. Books like *The Perfumer's Secret* can only thrive with your support.

I'd love to visit your BOOK CLUB.
Please email me: **neroli@nerolilacey.com**

About the Author

Neroli Lacey has been training to write delicious fiction for clever women her whole life. As a journalist, she wrote for all the great British newspapers—*The Times*, *The Daily Telegraph*, *The Independent*, *The Sunday Times*, *The Guardian*, and *The Evening Standard*—as well as for *Vogue*, *Tatler*, and *The New Statesman*. She's also been an investment banker and commodity futures trader. She's traveled all through Asia, Africa, Europe, and the Americas. She's the proud mother of two wildly spirited daughters and an adventurous stepson. She and her husband divide their time between New York City and a medieval village in the South of France.